Paul Doherty was born in Midd[...] at Liverpool and Oxford Univer[...] for his thesis on Edward II and [...] headmaster of a school in north-east London, and has been awarded an OBE for his services to education. He lives with his family in Essex. Paul's first novel, *The Death Of A King*, was published in 1985. Since then he has gone on to write over one hundred books, covering a wealth of historical periods from Ancient Egypt to the Middle Ages and beyond.

To find out more, visit www.paulcdoherty.com.

Praise for Paul Doherty's historical novels:

'Teems with colour, energy and spills'          *Time Out*

'Deliciously suspenseful, gorgeously written and atmospheric'
*Historical Novels Review*

'Supremely evocative, scrupulously researched'
*Publishers Weekly*

'An opulent banquet to satisfy the most murderous appetite'
*Northern Echo*

'Extensive and penetrating research coupled with a strong plot and bold characterisation. Loads of adventure and a dazzling evocation of the past'          *Herald Sun*, Melbourne

'A well-written historical novel with a fast-paced, action-driven plot. Highly recommended'
www.historicalnovelsociety.org

# MOTHER MIDNIGHT

## PAUL DOHERTY

HEADLINE

First published in 2021 by
HEADLINE PUBLISHING GROUP

First published in paperback in 2021 by
HEADLINE PUBLISHING GROUP

4

Cataloguing in Publication Data is available from the British Library

ISBN 978 1 4722 8478 5

Typeset in Sabon LT Std 11.25/14.5 pt by
Palimpsest Book Production Limited, Falkirk, Stirlingshire

Printed and bound in Great Britain by Clays Ltd, Elcograf S.p.A.

HEADLINE PUBLISHING GROUP
An Hachette UK Company
Carmelite House
50 Victoria Embankment
London EC4Y 0DZ

www.headline.co.uk
www.hachette.co.uk

*In memory of the beloved parents of
Linda Gerrish (née Stack),
John and Hannah Stack,
of Cork and Kerry in Ireland*

# CHARACTER LIST

**The Court of England**

| | |
|---|---|
| Edward I | King of England 1272–1307 |
| Edward II | Son and heir of the above, King of England 1307–1327 |
| Peter Gaveston | Edward II's Gascon favourite, created Earl of Cornwall |
| Thomas, Earl of Lancaster | Cousin to Edward II and his most inveterate opponent |

**The Royal Clerks**

| | |
|---|---|
| Sir Hugh Corbett | Keeper of the King's Secret Seal |
| Ranulf-atte-Newgate | Principal Clerk in the Chancery of the Green Wax, Corbett's henchman |
| Chanson | Corbett's Clerk of the Stables |
| Ralph Manning | Senior clerk in the Secret Chancery |
| Luke Faldon | Royal clerk, Manning's henchman |
| Faucomburg | Leading clerk in the household of Thomas, Earl of Lancaster |
| Catesby | Faucomburg's henchman |
| John Daventry | Clerk |
| Simon Mepham | Chief Scrivener in the Secret Chancery |

| John Benstead | Master of the Keys in the Secret Chancery |

**The Convent of St Sulpice**

| Eleanor | Lady Abbess |
| Margaret | Lady Prioress |

Sister Marie
Sister Fidelis
Sister Perpetua
Sister Callista
Sister Constantia
Sister Agatha (Isolda Manning)
Isabelia Seymour (Megotta the moon girl)

| Katherine Ingoldsby | Ralph Manning's great love |
| Agnes Sorrell | Former novice at St Sulpice |
| Mathilda Blackbourne | Former novice at St Sulpice |
| Stigand | Leader of the convent labourers |

**The Queen of the Night**

| Mother Midnight | Taverner |
| Janine | One of Mother Midnight's leading ladies |
| Sherwin | Captain of *The Picardy* |
| Brasby | Sherwin's henchman |

**Others**

| Brother Philippe | Corbett's physician friend, a member of St Bartholomew's Priory in Smithfield |
| Thomas Turbeville | English spy for the French court, executed 1295 |
| Raul Briscoe | Harrower of the Dead, officer of the city council |
| Lady Maeve | Corbett's wife |
| Edward and Eleanor | Corbett's children |
| Sir John Kyrie | King's Admiral |
| Ap Ythel | Corbett's friend, Captain of the Tower |

# HISTORICAL NOTE

In the early spring of 1312, England teetered on the verge of civil war. King Edward II was determined to protect and promote his Gascon royal favourite, Peter Gaveston, whom he had created Earl of Cornwall. Edward's barons, led by the turbulent Thomas, Earl of Lancaster, opposed the king, fiercely determined on Gaveston's removal and death. The king hurried north, depriving the royal precincts at Westminster of good governance. The deepening crisis soon made itself felt both at Westminster and in the rest of the city. Lancaster's bully boys swaggered the streets, whilst other more sinister figures flexed their muscles too, determined to profit from the deepening crisis. Murder was no stranger to Westminster, nor was it a respecter of so-called holy places, be it convent or church. Royal clerks such as Hugh Corbett tried to remain firm in allegiance and loyalty to both king and Crown. Nevertheless, these were murderous times . . .

Please note: the extracts used before each part are from 'The treason of Sir Thomas de Turbeville', in *Chronicles of the Mayors and Sheriffs of London 1188–1274*, ed. H. T. Riley (London, 1863), pp. 293–5.

# PROLOGUE

Turbeville who had been taken prisoner by the
French . . .

Newgate was the devil's own manor. A pit of darkness and even deeper despair, especially on a Thursday, the eve of the great hanging days, proclaimed for the morrow at Smithfield, Tyburn Stream or just outside Newgate's iron doors. These formidable barriers fronted that house of hell, that domain of demons. The great gates overlooked the fleshers' market with its broad sloping stalls where slabs of meat, fresh and bloodied, were spiked for customers to see and even touch.

Inside the prison, Murder's Eve, as it was popularly called, truly was a godforsaken occasion. Prisoners who had received notice of hanging, read out by the chief turnkey, prepared for death in many different ways. Some queued to kneel at the shriving pew and confess their sins to a Friar of the Sack, who sat on the makeshift mercy stool to hear litany after macabre litany of the penitents' sins in all their squalid detail. Murder, infanticide, torture, wounding, theft, adultery, sodomy, fornication, drunkenness . . . the list was endless, reflecting the hunger and violence of the human heart. A few prisoners roistered and became hopelessly drunk on the heavy Newgate ale, hoping this would render them unconscious until they were turned off the ladder to dance in the air at the end of a rope. A good number of the condemned just sat slumped against the filthy, mildewed prison wall, staring at the cesspit that surrounded them like some malignant marsh. The prison floors were in truth a bed of lice and vermin, which scuttled in and out impervious to the great cobwebs, rich with the flies they'd caught, spanning every corner and crevice.

Megotta the moon girl – the child of the sun, as the mummers' master described her – closed her eyes in desperation. She tried to recall that journey so many months ago, when spring had turned into a glorious summer then a majestically vibrant autumn. She had been with her troupe, their gaily decorated carts festooned with eye-catching ribbons that snapped and fluttered in the welcoming warm breeze. Last year had been a good one. They had enjoyed the nights when they sat in the clearings of Epping Forest, the massive ancient oaks grouped around them, the sky a dark velvet canopy above, the stars hanging low like so many fairy lanterns; a joyful, peaceful time. Megotta loved the world of the mummers. She couldn't remember her early days, except that she was an orphan, a beggar child, whom the mummers had taken in to become one of their company. They claimed she had a talent, a God-given gift for acting, mummery, mimicking, singing and all the tricks of the masque.

She had lived a happy, contented life until earlier in the autumn, when the mummers had stopped at the White Horse, close to the village of Woodeforde on the road into London. A cold, hard night. They'd camped out as usual in the forest and Megotta had been dispatched to buy fresh milk from the tavern, a common enough occurrence when they were following that route. She had walked into the taproom and, as usual, tried to act the merry maid. Two men, however, changed the lines of that harmless act. They had followed her out into the yard, where she was waiting for the tap boy to ladle milk from the churn. Both men were mawmsy, deep in their cups. One tried to seize her, but Megotta was skilled in using the thin dagger she kept concealed on her belt. She drew this and struck once, a killing blow beneath the ribs and up towards the heart. She had practised such a thrust, being taught it by soldiers her troupe had entertained. Men of war who realised that such a good-looking wench might have to defend her honour. The second assailant was so surprised, he just stood gaping as his comrade staggered back, blood bubbling from nose and mouth. Only when his comrade collapsed to the ground did he draw his own dagger. He lurched forward and almost ran onto Megotta's knife, a deep, slicing cut that opened his fat belly from end to end.

Megotta had fled, but the two dead men had been the retainers of a local lord, and she was put to the horn, proclaimed to be utlegatum, an outlaw, a wolfshead to be killed on sight. The comitatus of the shire had been raised. Megotta's description and crime were loudly proclaimed. The swift-moving comitatus caught up with the moon people's long line of carts just as they passed Bow church, going towards Mile End. They had brought the tap boy with them. He immediately recognised Megotta, and her fate was sealed when the comitatus ransacked her chest and found her smock still streaked with her victims' blood.

The sheriff's men had been summoned and Megotta had been taken into a tavern close to the Tower, where three justices of oyer et terminer had been sitting in session, dealing out summary justice to a queue of chained defendants. She had tried to plead self-defence, but this proved futile: her angry-faced judges were determined on her death. They donned their black skullcaps and condemned her to hang till dead on the common gallows above Tyburn Stream. Megotta had kept a brave face. She was determined that she would not plead, though she was intrigued when a young blonde-haired man, dressed in the costly garb of a high-ranking clerk, pushed his way between the justices once sentence had been passed. He stood whispering hoarsely with them, now and again glancing towards Megotta. The justices were evidently in awe of him. They listened to what he said, then the principal justice replied swiftly in Norman French. Satisfied, the clerk stepped away and returned to where he had been standing close to the taproom door.

'God knows,' Megotta whispered to the darkness. 'God knows what that was all about.' She tried to compose herself, fighting to control the terror seething through her. She attempted to sleep, only to start awake as the chief turnkey slipped, silent as a snake, into the condemned cell. He knelt beside her, unlocking the manacles around her wrists and ankles, heavy irons that rattled ominously. His flushed, brutal face betrayed no emotion. When Megotta asked what was happening, he simply shook his head, pulled her to her feet and pushed her towards the two gaolers standing by the open door. Catcalls and jeers from the other prisoners followed her into the dank, freezing, dimly lit passageway, its slime-drenched walls and hard-stoned flooring covered with insects that crackled under her bruised bare feet.

'Where am I going?' She paused, only to be roughly pushed up a stone staircase onto a gallery that did not reek so strongly as the stench below. A door was opened and she was thrust into a cell bereft of all furniture except for a table, with a shuttered lanternhorn creating a glow of light around it. She was ordered to stand quietly. The lantern hid the shadowy figure sitting on the other side of the table. The two gaolers pushed her a little closer, then the door was slammed shut. Glancing swiftly over her shoulder, Megotta realised she was alone with a stranger whom she suspected was the same high-ranking clerk she had glimpsed at the judgement table.

'You are Megotta, yes?' The voice was harsh and

carrying. 'A mummer in the Guild of the Holy Spirit. A troupe of moon people who wander this kingdom and go wherever they wish. You are a member of that cohort. Yes or no?'

'I am.'

'Megotta, take off your clothes.'

'I . . .'

'I will not harm you, I swear that. I am here to save you from hanging. Trust me, I mean you well. You can help me and I can help you. So divest, I need to see your body. Better that,' the voice added, 'than swinging by your neck from a Newgate noose.'

Megotta lifted her torn, soiled gown, followed by the stained undergarment. She stood naked, hands hanging by her sides.

'Turn,' the voice ordered. 'Turn slowly so that I can see all of you.'

She reluctantly did so.

'Very good,' the voice murmured. 'Now, Megotta, dress.'

She did so as swiftly as she could, feeling a surge of excitement. She was not to hang, she was sure of that.

'You perform in the mummers' plays, yes?'

'Oh yes, I do.'

'And you've learnt all the roles?'

'I have.'

'You have played in *The Annunciation*,' the voice continued, 'so show me, Megotta, play the Virgin Mary. How would she stand or kneel?'

Megotta just blinked.

8

'Come,' the voice urged. 'Act the part. You are a prisoner, but you can shake yourself free. I need an actress,
Megotta. I watched you in the court. You know that.'

'Who are you, sir?'

'I am Ralph Manning, senior clerk in the Secret
Chancery. I carry the king's authority. I have the power
to enquire and to make judgement. I answer to no one
but the king and His Grace's representative, Sir Hugh
Corbett, Keeper of the Secret Seal. Mistress, I deal with
issues of life and death. I am not here to abuse you but
to judge if you can help my cause.'

'What do you want me to do?'

'On second thoughts, Megotta, act the nun. Come,
woman, break free of your fear. How does a nun act?'

Megotta stood for a while, eyes closed, then walked
to the door and back, slowly, piously, like the nuns she'd
seen process into church to sing hymns through their
noses. Manning clapped his hands and laughed softly as
this young woman transformed herself from a condemned
prisoner to an ever-so-devout woman of God.

'Good, good,' he breathed. 'And now I want you to
act as Pilate's wife in the mummer's masque *The Death
of Pilate*. You remember the speeches, yes? So give me
one.'

She did as he asked. Eyes closed, fists clenched against
her chest, she played the role of Pilate's wife as she begged
her husband to spare Christ. Manning studied her carefully. He recognised a young lady of great talent who
could act the part and play the role. She could deceive
and yet she was intelligent enough to remember what

she saw and to report everything needed. He stared at this gifted young woman and thought of the good sisters out in their convent of St Sulpice. He was determined to discover the truth of that place. He owed it to his beloved Katherine. She had raised the spectres and he was determined to resolve the mystery. Just as important, his sister, Isolda, was now a member of that community. True, they had taken a solemn vow not to communicate with each other this side of heaven, yet he had a sacred duty to ensure she remained safe in her life of atonement.

'Master.' Megotta had now squatted down before the table. 'Master, I have done what you asked. I am tired, I can do no more.'

'You have done very well, Megotta, but now you must change. You are no longer Megotta, but Isabella Seymour, from a village in the West Country. You are a novice in the Benedictine order, a member of the community of St Sulpice out on the heathland to the north of London. You are about to enter a place of prayer, of fragrant incense and melodious plainchant. You must learn how to walk, smile, turn and be ever so gracious. Can you do that? I am sure you can,' he added drily. 'It's better than hanging in the air above Newgate yard.'

'And what is the purpose of this?'

'Oh, the purpose is very clear. I need to discover what is happening out at that convent. So enclosed, so secretive, so pious, so holy, and yet I believe a place where mortal sin has been committed.'

'And why should I do this, master? What do I gain?'

'Oh, Megotta, a rich reward indeed. A royal pardon, full and complete. A purse of coins and the Crown's protection and patronage wherever you go. Do you accept?'

'Of course.'

'Good. So let's begin this mummers' play.'

Sister Fidelis of the Convent of St Sulpice rubbed her eyes in disbelief. She had come from one of the granges to inspect the carp pond, which stood at the far end of the grounds. The pond – or lake, as Lady Abbess Eleanor liked to call it – had been cleverly constructed many years ago to house the fat carp that could then be caught, gutted and prepared for the convent table. The weather this morning was bitterly cold, the lake almost turned to ice, so Sister Fidelis was amazed when she saw the squat bum boat bobbing in the middle of the water, its oars out, when it should really be tied up against the very jetty she was standing on, close to the sluice gate.

The mist rolling across the water parted abruptly in ghostly wisps. Sister Fidelis, who openly proclaimed that her sight was not as sharp as it should be, peered again. Despite her protests, her eyes were still good enough to pick out a cowled figure, garbed in the earth-coloured robes of the order, bending ever so slightly over the oars. Nevertheless, the boat was not moving. The figure was not rowing, just sitting impervious to the ice-ridden water and a breeze as sharp as any cutting knife.

'Who are you?' Sister Fidelis called out, her voice echoing eerily across the water. The only answer to her question was the persistent harsh cawing of the crows in the thick copse of trees that bounded the lake. Fidelis, hands clasped in prayer, gazed up at the sky, but the lowering iron-grey clouds provided neither answer nor comfort. Frustrated, she walked along the jetty and stared down at the second bum boat, chained securely with a heavy, rusty chain and an equally stout padlock. The second boat had no oars, these being kept in a nearby boathouse. The three benches of the second boat were still covered by canvas sheets, stretched tightly and securely nailed. The boat was totally dry, inside. It was obvious it had not been used for months. Curious about what she had seen, Fidelis was tempted to prepare the boat and row out herself. 'No, no,' she whispered. 'Not on a day like this, it's freezing and it would take me too long.' She turned and hastened off the jetty, following the path between the trees.

Breathless and flustered, Fidelis reached the main convent buildings, which bounded the great cloisters. She hurried round the garth, then abruptly paused. She had glimpsed something down at the jetty, something amiss, but she couldn't place it. What was it? She tapped the side of her head. Sometimes her memory failed her, but she'd remember soon enough. She hastened on, asking the good sisters for the whereabouts of Lady Margaret.

Eventually she found the prioress busy in the refectory. She was supervising the movement of the lectern for the novice who would read from the *Lives of the Saints* whilst the community ate their meal. Lady Margaret, sharp faced and of even sharper eye, told Fidelis in no uncertain manner to sit, calm herself, then explain the cause of all the commotion. When she did so, the prioress also became alarmed. She ordered labourers to be brought in from the granges, stables, fields and gardens to join her at the jetty. Then, with Fidelis accompanying her, she hurried out across the convent grounds, almost running down the woodland path to the edge of the lake and onto the jetty.

'See, Lady Prioress, it's not moved.' Fidelis pointed across to the sinister-looking figure sitting rock still in the boat, hands on the oars.

'What's happened here?' the prioress murmured. 'What is it? Where are they going? What are they doing?'

'Perhaps whoever it is was going out to the carp nets.' Sister Marie pushed herself between the prioress and Fidelis. Elegant and calm, Marie was Lady of the Halls, responsible for the care and upkeep of the convent buildings. Her soft, sweet face was puckered in concern, but even in the brown garb of the order with its snow-white coif, she looked as poised as any court lady, and the prioress was comforted by her presence. Marie was serene and orderly, unlike Fidelis, who could become agitated at the sight of a mouse.

'It's possible,' the prioress agreed. 'Yet at this hour of the day, and in such terrible weather?'

They heard their names called and all three nuns stood aside, bowing as Abbess Eleanor swept onto the jetty, pausing to grasp a post to steady herself as she stared out across the lake. The good sisters of the convent often whispered amongst themselves about how their lady abbess had all the tenacity and harshness of a hunting falcon. This was certainly mirrored in her long, pallid face with deep furrows either side of her bloodless, thin-lipped mouth, slightly hooked nose and small, darting black eyes.

'For heaven's sake and that of St Sulpice, bring the boat in,' she declared.

As if in answer to her prayer, Stigand, leader of the convent labourers, brought his comitatus out of the treeline and onto the jetty. Big, burly men, surprised by what was happening, they pushed and shoved each other until the abbess's lashing tongue imposed order. Stigand and three of his companions prepared the second boat, hastening to the boathouse to bring the key to the rusting padlock, as well as a set of heavy-bladed oars. Eventually everything was ready. They undid the mooring ropes, then clambered into the boat. The nuns had to help them push away, for there was no current. The men brought the boat under control, and two of the labourers bent over the oars, moving slowly towards the bank of rolling mist that still obscured a clear view. Eventually they reached the first boat.

Sister Fidelis, who had walked as far as she dared along the jetty, watched the labourers move from one boat to the other, then her heart chilled at the shouts and cries that floated across the water. At last both

boats turned and made their way back, coming alongside the jetty. Fidelis glanced at what the first boat
contained and wailed like a child, then turned and stared
in horror at her abbess.

'It's Sister Constantia! She's, she's . . .'

'Dead!' Stigand declared, climbing onto the jetty.
'Sister Constantia has been murdered.' He stepped aside
to allow two of his men to lift the corpse out of the
boat.

Ignoring the abbess's orders, Sister Fidelis crouched
beside it. She stared in horror at the frozen dried blood
that almost masked the dead nun's snow-white face,
then glanced at the cause of it all: a bone-handled
stiletto, its long, pointed blade driven deep into the
woman's heart. She could hear the cries and exclamations of the rest; nevertheless, all she could think of
was what was hidden away in her secret cache at the
top of Devil's Tower. She wished she was there now.
She wanted to sit, reflect and recall what she had seen
this morning, which was so amiss, so out of place. But
what? If she could only have the comfort of a deep-
bowled cup of the best Bordeaux . . .

'How?' The lady abbess's harsh voice made Fidelis
flinch. 'How,' she repeated, 'could this happen? Did
someone swim out to the boat? Yet the water is freezing.
Moreover, such a swimmer would have immediately
alarmed Constantia.'

'Was she killed, then placed in the boat?' Sister
Marie's words trailed away at the prioress's abrupt
sarcastic laugh. 'I know, I know,' she conceded. 'A dead

woman cannot row. So how did the boat reach the middle of the lake? There is no current, whilst it is obvious that the second boat was not used, the heavy chain, the rusting padlock, the canvas sheets have not been removed and the boat is bone dry within.'

'And yet . . .' Sister Fidelis murmured.

'And yet what?' Sister Marie demanded.

'I saw something this morning, but I cannot remember what.'

'Do so,' Lady Margaret snapped, 'and do so swiftly. Anything that could resolve this blasphemous murder. Stigand, remove the fishing tackle from the boat and take the corpse to the death house. Sister Marie, you are Lady of the Halls; see that it is dressed properly for burial . . .'

Ralph Manning, senior clerk in the Chancery of the Secret Seal, sat back in his chair. He stared around the bleak chamber, a room specially reserved for clerks of the Secret Chancery, where they could work without any interruption, well protected against spies or eavesdroppers. A truly stark chamber, its bare walls were plastered white. No decoration, no paintings or gaily coloured cloth to distract, just a crucifix on the far wall. No window, no other entrance, whilst the heavy iron-barred door was, according to custom, firmly locked and bolted.

Ralph gripped his quill pen as he stared down at the notes he had made. He half smiled to himself as he wondered how Megotta, the mummers' girl, was faring.

He truly believed he had chosen the best. Despite the charges levelled against her, she was a good soul, caught up in the swirl of life. She had just been unfortunate. If she'd been able to hire a lawyer from the Inns of Court, she could have successfully pleaded self-defence. She was a born actress with an almost cruel ability to mimic, be it a tavern slattern, a mincing court lady or, most importantly, a devout novice in a nunnery with the ability to sing through her nose, keep her eyes down and adopt the most cringing pose of devotion. She could walk, talk and sing any role he had assigned her. A highly attractive young woman, she had convinced him she would keep her word.

He tapped the scroll on the desk before him that granted her a full royal pardon for all or any crimes she may have committed. Once her task was over, she would be given this as well as a purse of coins and letters of reference sealed and signed by himself. Of course, she might well choose to return to the moon people, but she showed promise and could be assigned other duties. Manning rubbed a finger round his lips. He could have asked for the help of his sister, also a nun at St Sulpice, but to all intents and purposes she too had disappeared, though that was not the full truth. Isolda was a bitter scourge of a memory – of deceit, deception and death. He had killed Daventry, once a bosom comrade, at her insistence, only to discover that the allegations and accusations were false. No, he reasoned, Isolda was best left alone; brother and sister had taken a solemn vow to keep it so.

He picked up his quill pen, nibbling at its end as he recalled the instructions given to the moon girl almost two months ago. Suitably dressed, she had entered the Convent of St Sulpice. She was supposed to watch and listen, and so she had. Every so often, at the appointed time, she would meet Manning in the stairwell of Devil's Tower, close to the convent wall, and in hushed whispers would tell him all the gossip of the convent, yet she had not reported anything seriously amiss. On one vital issue she could only provide sparse information. Yes, would-be novices presented themselves at the convent; at the same time, others left, though not many – three or four at the very most since she had arrived there.

Manning closed his eyes, rubbing his mouth again. What he had planned for St Sulpice was not really royal business, though he intended to inform his master, Sir Hugh Corbett, Keeper of the King's Secret Seal, as soon as his superior returned to Westminster. He truly believed there was something very rotten in that convent. He murmured a prayer as he recalled meeting Katherine, the love of his life, in that same stairwell close to the convent wall. Matters had moved swiftly in their affair. Katherine, an orphan, had lived with her ancient aunt in her mansion along Paternoster Row, beneath the shadow of St Paul's. Manning had met her after mass on the feast of St John the Baptist last. He was no troubadour or minstrel, yet he and Katherine believed theirs was love at first sight. Secret meetings and hidden trysts soon followed. He had hired this chamber or that chamber in the taverns along Cheapside. Katherine had become pregnant, but lost the child before it was born. Her aunt soon found out. No mercy was given, no compassion shown. Katherine was bundled off to join the good sisters of St Sulpice, and Manning had dutifully followed her there.

They met in secret and discussed the future. Weeks passed, and Katherine began to hint that things were not as they should be in the convent. She talked of young women leaving, but she could not precisely describe what was wrong, and then, most abruptly, she herself disappeared. Manning had returned to the convent time and again, waiting in the usual place, yet Katherine never came. Eventually he approached Lady Abbess Eleanor and said he was concerned about what had happened to her. The abbess simply pulled a face, pointing out that St Sulpice was not a prison. Some young women elected to come and others chose to leave. She informed him that Katherine's cell had been found in complete order but stripped of all personal possessions. She had shrugged elegantly and said she had no idea what might have happened except that Katherine had left.

Of course Manning had protested. Surely a young woman like Katherine would inform the abbess of her imminent departure? But that hawk-faced, arrogant woman had simply shaken her head. 'It is quite common that if these young women wish to leave, they do so quietly, mysteriously.'

'Did anyone see her go?' Manning queried. 'She must

have made friends. Someone would have known what she intended.'

'Have you visited her relatives in the city?'

'She has none: her aged aunt died recently – I believe she gave this convent a most generous bequest. Surely,' he persisted, 'you have a care for Katherine Ingoldsby. I mean, she left so swiftly, so quietly.'

'Master Manning, if a young woman intends to flee, to leave us, then of course she would shroud it in silence, wouldn't she?'

Manning put the quill pen down, closed his eyes and quietly intoned the Veni Creator Spiritus. He did not know what to do. This was not chancery work and yet he would have to account for what he did and where he went. He had searched high and low. He had talked to his informants, the street spies, the cunning men and their ilk. He had even visited Mother Midnight at her tavern, the Queen of the Night, a place where, according to those who informed him, young women who had escaped from here or there might find refuge. It was all to no avail.

Suddenly he felt a deep discomfort in his belly. He crouched forward, clasping his side as his mind wrestled with this nagging problem. He recalled his conversations with Katherine. He now believed that something hideous had happened to her, and that the root of all this was the Convent of St Sulpice and the tavern. He fully intended to go back to question both the lady abbess and the taverner to discover what was really happening.

He had not informed anyone else about what he was

involved in, except for his loyal henchman Luke Faldon. 'Yet even there,' he whispered to himself, 'matters have turned sour.' He was growing deeply concerned about Faldon: he knew he was visiting that pleasure house the Queen of the Night, and strongly suspected he was becoming increasingly infatuated with one of the young French ladies there. He did not really mind this if Faldon could learn more about the place. Manning himself had revisited the tavern and knew there was something very wrong with it, yet he could not articulate what it was, except that Mother Midnight was too glib, too easy in her answers.

He moved to clear the discomfort in his belly and glimpsed the parchment with the name Turbeville scrawled prominently, beneath it a roughly etched three-stemmed fleur-de-lis. Katherine had glimpsed the same at St Sulpice and promised to bring him a drawing, but then she'd disappeared. He groaned. All of this was taking so much time. He kept reminding himself that it was not chancery business, certainly not a Crown secret. It rose out of his great love for Katherine and his determination to discover what had happened to her. Perhaps when Sir Hugh Corbett returned from the West Country, he could formally ask for his help and assistance.

He paused in his reflections. He did not feel at all well. The pain in his belly had spread to his chest, and he was finding it difficult to swallow, even to breathe. He got to his feet, but the pain had become so intense he had to crouch down beside the chancery desk. He fought for a while, trying to control his breathing, hoping that the pain would pass. He wondered if he could get help, yet the door seemed so far away. It was locked and bolted. He lurched forward, only to fall back and slip into the encroaching darkness.

# PART ONE

Turbeville was induced to act as a spy for the French.

S ir Hugh Corbett, Keeper of the King's Secret Seal, Chief Clerk of the Secret Chancery, arrived back at Westminster like God's own messenger. Corbett was respected, deeply feared. He was a king's officer who took no bribes, who could not, would not, be overawed by any great lord or powerful prelate. A family man, he kept his wife the Lady Maeve and their two children, Edward and Eleanor, safely away from the byzantine, murderous politics seething through Westminster and the royal court. He had created his own sanctuary of peace at his spacious fortified manor of Leighton in Essex.

Sir Hugh had recently returned from the West Country, where he had enforced royal justice with fire and sword, sentencing criminals to hang on the gallows or be committed to the sea. He had burnt the strongholds of the wicked and dispensed justice in a manner the people of that region would never forget. Now he was back, summoned by murder at the very heart of royal justice and in no mood for petty distractions.

Garbed in a dark leather jerkin, woollen leggings pushed into high-heeled riding boots, the spurs still attached clinking like bells, he strode along the corridors and galleries of the majestic mansions that housed all the important offices of state, those departments of the Crown: the Exchequer, Chancery, Wardrobe and King's Bench. He had thrown his military cloak over his shoulder but had kept his war belt fastened, being one of the few royal officials to be allowed to appear armed in these royal precincts. Clerks, servitors, couriers and other officials hastily stepped aside. Corbett was no bully, far from it, but his usually serene olive-skinned face betrayed the anger seething within him, his deep-set hooded eyes scrutinising those he passed. That was important. He would remember what he had seen, take note of what he should do and be sharp and vigilant over what he was about to scrutinise. Now and again he would stop to stare at something that caught his attention. He'd stand chewing the corner of his lip, his gauntleted hand shifting a drop of sweat from his forehead or touching his raven-black hair streaked here and there with faint silver, tied in a queue at the back of his head. He wanted to sense the mood of the place, of the galleries he was striding through.

Behind him came Ranulf-atte-Newgate, Principal Clerk in the Chancery of the Green Wax, Corbett's loyal henchman. Ranulf, a true child of the slums around Whitefriars, was Sir Hugh's constant shadow. He was well known around the royal precincts, with his cropped red hair, pale face and slanted green eyes, ever watchful, ever vigilant. Secretly he referred to Corbett as 'Master Longface' but, despite this gentle teasing, his loyalty to Sir Hugh was unwavering, steadfast, especially now, when dealing with murder in the chancery chambers of Westminster.

Ranulf, like his master, was under no illusions. Power meant struggle, struggle meant bloodshed. In turn, this gave rise to grievance, grudge and revenge. Hands were ready to fall to sword hilt or dagger. The blood feud could be swiftly invoked and the threat of violence was ever present. The royal precincts at Westminster seethed with murderous intrigue, especially now that King Edward II had moved to bloody confrontation with his barons over the matter of his Gascon favourite, Peter Gaveston. Edward had created Gaveston Earl of Cornwall in the teeth of fierce opposition from his magnates. The kingdom now teetered on civil war, and Westminster had become a veritable hive of intrigue and conspiracy.

All the clerks to the powerful lords had assembled here. Some were representatives, others couriers, and the rest were spies or brawlers for their masters. Now murder had occurred. A high-ranking clerk in the Secret Chancery had, earlier that day, been found poisoned in a fortified chamber deep in the royal enclosure. Was it part of some blood feud? Some clash between the various court factions? Ranulf realised they were about to enter a bear pit and be invited to sip from a poisoned chalice. Corbett had been very blunt with him. He had ordered him to be vigilant but to remain quiet. Ranulf recalled this instruction, his hand on the dagger kept hidden on his war belt, then turned and raised a hand towards Chanson, Corbett's Clerk of the Stables. A round-faced young man with all the characteristics of a simple plough boy, Chanson, as usual, was finding it difficult to keep up with Corbett's long stride.

'Keep close,' Ranulf taunted. 'And don't sing or touch anything sharp.'

Chanson simply glared back. He knew he was notorious for having the worst singing voice in Westminster, whilst his handling of any weapon made him more of a danger to himself than anyone else. Nevertheless, as Corbett had declared on more than one occasion, no one knew horses like Chanson did.

At last they entered the Secret Chancery enclave, guarded by men-at-arms and archers wearing the royal livery. They were allowed through and reached the Hall of Secrets, a place where the king was advised of all the chatter and gossip from the various shires. The serjeant on duty ushered them quickly inside. The hall was long and bleak, its lime-washed walls bereft of any ornament except two royal standards either side of a crucifix. A fire burned in the hearth built into an outside wall, whilst wheeled braziers, firmly capped, provided more warmth. Cresset torches flamed in their sconces in a brave attempt to drive away the shadows.

Two men sitting at the head of a table placed beneath the window rose to greet Corbett, both officials dressed in dull clerkly robes. They clasped hands with Corbett and Ranulf, then ushered them to chairs placed around the table. Corbett, making himself comfortable, exchanged pleasantries with Simon Mepham, Chief Scrivener in the Secret Chancery, and John Benstead, Master of the Keys. A third man came out of the shadows, where he'd been helping himself from the buttery table. Corbett peered through the murk and smiled at Luke Faldon, Manning's henchman, a clerk in the Chancery of the Red Wax. Faldon was a narrow-faced young man, his head and cheeks completely shaven. He was garbed in funereal black, with Ave beads wrapped around his right wrist. Corbett had met him on a number of occasions. He and Ranulf exchanged pleasantries and condolences with Faldon as well as the other two officials.

Conversation was desultory, comments about the weather and how difficult the roads were. Corbett let himself relax. Ranulf now sat on his right, while Chanson stood on guard by the door. Faldon offered refreshments. Corbett accepted for Ranulf and Chanson: goblets of mulled wine and slices of cheese toasted on bread. The servants in charge of the buttery table served them and left.

Corbett, who had refused any food or drink himself, sat up straight. He'd taken off his war belt and cloak and thrown them over the back of an empty chair. Now he stared at them, lost in thought. Benstead coughed noisily, but stopped when Ranulf lifted a warning hand for silence. Corbett continued to stare at his war belt, then turned, placing both hands on the chancery satchel Ranulf had set before him. He closed his eyes momentarily and recited the Requiem. Ralph Manning, Clerk of the Secret Chancery, had been a good colleague and a firm friend, a truly loyal royal clerk who could not be corrupted. A man who would never sell his soul whatever the price, a warrior, a mailed clerk who had seen military service both along the Narrow Seas and in Gascony. He had served with Corbett in Scotland, where they'd stood shoulder to shoulder in the shield ring against this enemy and that. True, there was the business of Daventry, but that had been a most tragic mistake caused by Manning's sister Isolda. Manning, as always, had tried to act chivalrously. Now he lay poisoned in a chamber not far from where they were sitting.

Corbett fully recognised the dangers of being a royal clerk. Murder in all its forms and guises lurked constantly in the half-light, prowling backwards and forwards, peering deep into the darkness of men's hearts. Over the years he had crossed swords with the sons and daughters of Cain. Time and again he had followed them into the nightmare, seized them and dispatched them for judgement by both God and the king. Manning's murder, however, was a grim reminder that whatever his status, whatever his power, whatever protection the new king might offer, the meadows of murder around Westminster sheltered killers and assassins. They lurked like fierce beasts, ready to strike out with the dagger, the garrotte or, in Manning's case, a phial of deadly poison. Would that one day happen to Corbett himself? he wondered.

If he proved careless, or didn't duck fast enough? Would it happen here as he began the hunt for his comrade's killers? He had arrived in London the previous evening, taking lodgings with Brother Philippe, his physician friend at St Bartholomew's Hospital in Smithfield. Ranulf had immediately taken messages to the Chancellor, and that morning, just before the Jesus bell, the Chancellor's courier had arrived at the hospital with news of Manning's murder, so Corbett had hastened here when he should be riding to join the king.

'Sir Hugh?'

He glanced up and smiled his apology. 'I am so sorry,' he declared. 'The news is very sad and I am so tired. Tell me now, what was Manning so busy with?'

The Master of the Keys took a deep breath. 'As you know, Sir Hugh, Manning acted as the receiver in the Secret Chancery. He collected and sifted all the information flowing in from sheriffs, harbourmasters, port reeves and royal bailiffs, but I also know, as we all do, that he was working on something else, something secret to himself.'

'Something,' Faldon interrupted, 'to do with . . .' He held up a hand as he searched for words, and Corbett noticed the ink stains on his fingers, the sign of a very busy clerk. He stared at Manning's henchman.

'For God's sake, man, what is it?'

'I am sorry, Sir Hugh, but I suspect that Master Ralph was deeply involved in matters of the heart. That's all I can say. He became very withdrawn. He would spend hours locked in that fortified chamber. He was recording something, making notes. Once I stole a glance at these, but . . .' He shrugged.

'Written in a cipher?'

'Yes, Sir Hugh.'

Corbett turned to Benstead. 'The murder chamber has been sealed?'

'The door has been rehung; everything inside is now marked with the seal of the Secret Chancery.'

'And his personal chamber? Where did he live?'

'Above the sign of the Golden Aureole,' Benstead replied. 'A tavern in Ave Maria Lane. I journeyed there myself. I never went inside, the landlord will bear witness to that, but I did seal both door and lock.'

'And Manning's corpse?'

'Still where we found it. You wish to view it?'

Corbett said he did. He told Chanson to stay on guard whilst he and Ranulf followed Benstead and the other two through a side entrance and down a dimly lit passageway with cells on either side, each sealed by a fortified door. They reached Manning's chamber, and Benstead took a key out of his pocket.

'As you know, Sir Hugh, there is only one key to each chamber. The lock on each room is unique.'

Corbett scrutinised the door; both it and the lintel were badly scarred where it had been forced, but as Benstead explained, it had since been mended with new bolts, lock and hinges.

'And when the door was forced this morning?'

'Sir Hugh, the key was in the inside lock and the bolts at both top and bottom were drawn across.'

Benstead pushed open the door, fracturing the chancery seals imposed along its edge. Corbett asked his companions, Ranulf included, to stay outside in the passageway, then he himself cautiously made his way in, closing the door behind him. He leaned against it and stared around the box-like chamber, at its unadorned walls and black-raftered low ceiling. Nothing, be it Turkey rugs or supple green rushes, covered the paved stone floor. All the chamber could boast was a chancery chair, a table, a stool and a small coffer. There were no jakes pots, no lavarium, these being available in a separate room at the end of the passageway outside.

He gazed down at the chancery table, littered with documents. Each of these had been sealed to the table, whilst Manning's chancery satchel had also been made secure. Corbett wiped the sweat from his face. He was tired and anxious. He could hardly bring himself to look at the corpse of the blonde-haired man who sat slumped with his back to the side of the desk, one hand hanging down, the other up under his chin. He remembered Manning laughing and joking in a tavern or the palace refectory. All this had gone. All this was changed. All this was different. Manning looked crumpled, as if his merry, happy soul had been gouged out of him.

He drew a deep breath, murmured a prayer and picked up the large lanternhorn from the stool, placing it next to the corpse. Then he crouched down and stared pityingly at Manning. The dead clerk's eyes were half open, his mouth a gaping slit. A thin, creamy saliva stained his chin and chest. He had lost all that dignity that was rightfully his, nothing left but a crumpled, beaten, defeated man. Murder had brought him low. Corbett could only draw comfort from his own deeply felt belief that all he was staring at, everything that he could see, touch and smell, was the husk already beginning to rot. Manning's soul had broken free to begin its journey towards the light.

'Go bravely into the dark, my friend,' he whispered. 'May your angel take your hand. May the heavenly host greet you and save you from the clutches of the enemy, the Evil One, the Son of Perdition. I am sure that whatever sins you committed were simply born of that weakness that plagues us all.' He paused, feeling a surge of fiery temper. 'And I swear,' he continued, 'by all that is holy, I shall hunt your killer down and dispatch him for judgement.'

He fell silent at a knock at the door. Ranulf, carrying a chancery satchel, eased himself into the chamber. 'Good man,' Corbett murmured, getting to his feet. 'Ranulf, I want everything. Every scrap of manuscript you can find. Take everything.' He pointed to the narrow writing tray on the desk. 'And that includes quills, inkpot, sander and wax.'

Ranulf hastened to obey. Telling the others to stay outside, Corbett and Ranulf swept through that bleak chamber and gathered everything. Afterwards, they laid out Manning's corpse on the floor, making it as dignified as they could. Both clerks checked the dead man's wrists and hands, removing rings and bracelets, as well as purse, wallet and anything they contained. Once satisfied, they left the murder chamber. Corbett ensured that Benstead locked the room, and they all returned to their seats in the Hall of Secrets.

'What did you find?' Mepham queried.

'As yet, nothing of note.' Corbett pointed at Faldon. 'Tell me exactly what happened this morning.'

'I left my chamber and went to the Golden Aureole, where I waited for my master to join me in the taproom. Once he did, we attended mass in St Mary Bow. My master stayed for a short while afterwards, praying before the shrine of Our Lady of Walsingham. He lit two tapers, then we left for Westminster. A cold, hard journey. My master seemed subdued, preoccupied. We arrived here and broke our fast.' Faldon gestured across the hall at the buttery table.

'Mepham and Benstead, you were there?'

'Yes,' both men answered.

'One moment,' Ranulf interrupted. 'Manning ate and drank the same as you did? He had no wine skin, no linen parcel of bread or dried meats?'

'None,' Faldon retorted. 'My master did not have a sharp appetite at the best of times. This morning was no different. He picked at his food, sipped at his morning ale; indeed, he seemed to want to be away.'

'And then?'

'And then, Sir Hugh, he closeted himself in that chamber and asked not to be interrupted.'

'He took no food or drink with him?' Ranulf demanded.

'None,' Mepham and Benstead chorused.

'I would agree with that,' Faldon added.

Corbett turned to Ranulf. 'My friend, when all this is done – and it soon will be – have Ralph's corpse taken to the death house. Let him be dressed for burial. Take a sack for his clothing. We will take that, and the rest. I will ask Brother Philippe, principal physician at St Bartholomew's, to view the corpse on behalf of the Crown.' He pulled a face. 'At this moment in time, we cannot say how he was poisoned, why or by whom. Cicero, the Roman orator, asked, "*Cui bono?*" – who profits? So I ask you all, who would profit, in any way, be it money or revenge, by Manning's murder?'

The three clerks just stared silently back.

Eventually Faldon spoke up. 'As you are aware, Sir Hugh, my master was a most private soul. He kept strictly to himself, certainly over the last few months. You wish to interrogate me about what I know, but I swear I can tell you very little, whilst what I do know has no real evidence or proof. However,' he rubbed his face with his hands, 'I suspect Master Manning met a young lady in the city. I know he went out to the Convent of St Sulpice, to the north of London, on the heathland.'

'We know where it is,' Ranulf interrupted testily.

'What Faldon is saying,' Benstead intervened, 'is that Master Ralph worked very quietly here. He was a most loyal, industrious, competent clerk, but speaking for myself certainly, what I know about him outside this place is very little. As Faldon says, Ralph Manning was the most reserved of men.' He crossed himself. 'Of course there was the business of Daventry. You've heard the story, Sir Hugh?'

Corbett nodded, but kept his face schooled as he stared at the light pouring through the hall's one and only window. He wondered if Manning's spirit still hovered close in this place of dancing shadows and dappled light. He had heard the gossip. The royal precincts of Westminster were reportedly crammed with ghosts. Westminster was a place of intrigue, conspiracy, envy, jealousy and murder. Even more so now. He had sensed the tension as soon as he entered the royal enclosure. The king was absent, hiding with Gaveston. The great lords had summoned their troops, thronging into London and Westminster. If war broke out, the nobles hoped to seize the main departments of government and so control the sheriffs, bailiffs and other officials throughout the kingdom. Whatever he thought about Edward, Corbett was a king's man, body and soul, in life and in death. Oh, the nobles had approached him, promising all kinds of reward. Corbett, however, had remained steadfast, though he could not understand Edward's absolute absorption with the beautiful Gaveston. He had tried to advise the king, but to little avail.

'It will end in blood,' he murmured to himself. 'It will all end in blood.'

'Sir Hugh?'

He shook his head. 'My apologies,' he declared. 'I drift. Anyway,' he asserted himself, 'what truly happened this morning?'

'Manning left here for his chamber,' Faldon replied. 'He asked me to check what supplies we might need for the chancery. He said he would be closeted away for some time, but that at his say-so, I should be prepared to leave. Heaven knows, Sir Hugh, but I had the impression that we would leave the city. Manning added that I should see to our horses.' The henchman shrugged. 'Then he went into the chancery chamber. I heard him draw the bolts and turn the key.' He clicked his tongue. 'The morning drew on, I became concerned. My master had eaten and drunk a little here at the buttery table, but he'd taken nothing into the room with him.'

'Yet he was well?' Ranulf asked.

'Oh yes, he was planning to leave, possibly ride. He looked healthy enough and made no complaint whatsoever. But as I said, the hours passed. I became concerned.'

'So you knocked on the door?'

'Of course, Sir Hugh. I wanted to discover if he needed anything. There was no reply, so I left it for a time. I returned, knocked again, just silence. Now concerned, I dispatched a servant. Mepham and Benstead arrived. We knocked, shouted and tried the door, all to no avail.'

'We eventually forced it,' Mepham declared. 'We brought servants with a ram and cracked open the door. What you've just seen, we saw. I immediately dispatched a messenger to the Chancellor, then placed my seal wherever I could.'

Corbett drummed his fingers on the tabletop.

'Master?'

'Ranulf, we are finished here. Gentlemen, I thank you. Oh, by the way, I found this on Manning.' Corbett rose, opened his wallet and handed a key to Faldon. 'You recognise this?'

'Yes, it is the key to his chamber above the Golden Aureole.'

'Good.' Corbett picked up his war belt; Ranulf did the same. 'Gentlemen, once again I thank you, and I bid you adieu. However,' he turned back, 'you three worked closely with Manning. Did he ever say anything that provoked your curiosity?'

'In truth, Sir Hugh,' Mepham replied, 'and I think I speak for my colleagues here, what intrigued us most about him was his silence, his reserve, the way he kept to himself.'

'So he didn't confide in anybody?'

Mepham smiled and spread his hands. 'If he did, we don't know. He came here, he worked, he left.'

'But surely,' Corbett turned to Faldon, 'he liked the taproom, the bonhomie, the stoups of ale.'

'He once did. We are talking about the last few months. Ralph Manning kept to himself, and more than that I can't say.'

Corbett and his two companions left the inner sanctum of the Secret Chancery. They walked down the main gallery leading out to the icy wind-swept concourse that separated the various houses of state. All of these were overshadowed by the majestic dark pile of the abbey, with its soaring towers, spires, arches and buttresses, the stonework decorated with the carved faces of saints, demons and angels. Here and there the great windows caught the poor light and dazzled the eye. Corbett thought the place was magnificent. Ranulf, however, was slightly fearful of it, as the abbey held memories of how, on more than one occasion, he and Corbett had crossed swords with the powerful Benedictines within – the Blackrobes.

He was about to remind Corbett of this when his master suddenly paused and quietly cursed. Ranulf followed his gaze and saw the knot of young men, clerks, making their way towards them. He repeated Corbett's curse. The group of clerks were loud and unruly. Undoubtedly they had spent most of the afternoon roistering in some tavern, and were now set to loaf around the precincts to create as much disruption and chaos as possible.

Corbett immediately recognised Faucomburg, leading clerk in the household of Earl Thomas of Lancaster, the King's cousin and inveterate opponent. Striding beside this popinjay was Faucomburg's henchman Catesby, a sly villain of a man with a weasel mind and treacherous ways. This precious pair were entertaining the rest, who Corbett suspected belonged to the retinues of the other great lords, such as Pembroke, Arundel, Warwick and Badlesmere. If the king unfurled his banner and proclaimed an end to his peace, these clerks, with the host of armed men camped on the wasteland to the east of the Tower, would move to seize the great offices of state for their masters.

Faucomburg was the undoubted leader of the group,

a tall, blonde-haired ruffian with the slobbery face of an inveterate drinker and a temper to match. He walked with a swagger, the escutcheon of his master emblazoned on his jerkin and coat. His head was shaven around the sides, but the hair on his pate was carefully crimped and oiled. He delighted in playing the warrior, a helm on his head, his gauntleted hands ever ready to grasp dagger or sword, though he and the rest were not arrogant enough to carry weapons in the royal precinct.

Catesby, Faucomburg's shadow, small and lithe like the viper he was, had already recognised Corbett, and whispered heatedly to his master, who led his coven across the gallery to block the royal clerk. Languidly lifting a hand as a sign for his retinue to wait, Faucomburg stepped forward and bowed mockingly.

'I am glad you are not weaponed,' Corbett declared. 'Otherwise I would have arrested you. These are the royal precincts. I am a royal official, and you, sir, and your companions are drunk.'

'Hugh, Hugh, why are you so bellicose?'

'I am not bellicose. I am just reminding you, in my own way, of who you are and what you do, especially as you seem deep in your cups. I have little to say to you, sir, so please stand aside and I'll gladly walk on.'

Faucomburg gave a deep-bellied belch and stepped closer. Catesby followed.

Corbett studied both of them. He was sure they had weapons concealed. He was aware of Ranulf coming alongside him.

'Good day to you to, Ranulf-atte-Newgate.'

'Piss off, Faucomburg.'

'Now, now, Ranulf.' Faucomburg's face creased into a smile. 'Hugh, Ranulf, why are you here anyway?'

'King's business,' Ranulf retorted. 'So get lost. You reek of ale. You should go and lie down somewhere.'

'We are indeed on king's business,' Corbett declared. 'Stand aside.'

'Oh, you mean Manning, the quiet little clerk who loved the whores.'

'You've got a nasty mouth, Faucomburg. Watch your tongue or I'll pull it out.'

Corbett patted Ranulf on the arm.

'Watch your tongue!' Ranulf repeated.

'Perhaps Manning should have watched his.'

Corbett stepped forward, hand falling to the hilt of his sword.

'Poor, poor Manning,' Faucomburg sneered. 'The love-lorn clerk who lusted after perfumed flesh and now, I understand, lies dead in his chamber. Was he murdered, Hugh? Or was he rejected in love and took the coward's way?'

Corbett could take no more. He threw off Ranulf's restraining hold and struck Faucomburg across the mouth with his gauntleted hand, smiling as blood erupted from his opponent's fat face.

Faucomburg drew back. Catesby stepped between his master and Corbett, who threw his gauntlet to the ground. Catesby picked it up and glanced back at Faucomburg, now nursing his bruised nose. The Lancastrian clerk nodded.

'We accept.' Catesby thrust the gauntlet at Ranulf, who snatched it back. 'Three days' time, at the Angelus bell. My master will meet you in the tiltyard at Westminster, sword and shield to the death – *à l'outrance.*'

'Good,' Corbett breathed. 'Now get out of my way, and hold your tongue about a man better than you.'

Corbett, Ranulf and Chanson thrust themselves through the clerks thronging around Faucomburg, who quietly gave way. Corbett, still flushed with anger, strode on.

'Master,' Ranulf whispered, hurrying alongside. 'Was that wise?'

'Perhaps not,' Corbett snarled. 'But it certainly was necessary. Faucomburg and the rest of the pack are probing the king's defences. If they can insult me, the king's own personal clerk, here in the royal enclosure of Westminster, then walk away scot free, what hope is there for the likes of Benstead and Mepham? Believe me, my friend, the news of our little confrontation will soon be all over Westminster.'

'And?' Ranulf demanded. 'You're still to meet him in the list, sword and shield, yes?'

'Sword and shield,' Corbett agreed.

'He is skilled in sword and dagger play.'

'And so am I. I will kill him.'

Ranulf did not answer, but fell back to walk with Chanson. After a moment, he leaned down to the Clerk of the Stables and whispered, 'On that day, bring your crossbow. Should anything happen to the master, we will kill Faucomburg ourselves.'

They left Westminster and pushed up towards Fleet Street. The weather had turned icy, the ground hard underfoot, the wind biting, chafing at their skin. The day's business in the city was drawing to a close. Shops were shuttered, stalls withdrawn. Doors and windows were firmly closed. It was now candle time, when the good citizens retired into their homes. The beacons in church spires had been lit, and blazed through the darkness, the sign for all householders to fire the lantern-horns hooked next to their doors to provide light and comfort for those who had to trudge the streets.

These were many. A horde of journeymen and tinkers now surged towards the taverns, alehouses and cook shops, desperate to escape the cold. Not all could afford to pay for their food. The dispossessed and forsaken gathered about the great bonfires created out of the refuse that had been collected, doused in oil then set alight. These swiftly raging fires provided warmth and the means to cook the putrid food collected from beneath the stalls of nearby markets. The legion of the damned, the dwellers of the dark, as Corbett described them, were now emerging from their pits and cellars, the shabby tenements of London emptying as the day died and the light faded. The hunters of the night came out too, keen for any mischief that caught their eye.

It was a dangerous time, though no one accosted Corbett and his two companions. They were viewed as men of war, harnessed for any dagger play. More importantly, they were swiftly recognised as royal clerks; any violence against them would provoke the full wrath of both Crown and city. Nevertheless, Corbett remained sharp eyed as they made their way up Fleet Street, threading their way through the heralds of the dusk, the street people who made a living by offering to sing a carol, recite a poem or tell a story about fabled kingdoms to the East, where sorcerers lived in palaces built of jade and ivory. Chanson asked if they could pause and listen to a story about a place where the sea was always blue and horses played in the surf, basking in constant sunlight. Corbett and Ranulf obliged. Chanson was fascinated with anything to do with horses. Corbett stared around, half listening to the tale. The other troubadours, jesters and minstrels were now withdrawing to join the travelling tinkers in the many bustling taverns and alehouses, havens of warmth and light as the bitterly cold evening closed in. He knew that word of his confrontation with Faucomburg would soon sweep these places. The prospect of conflict sharpened every appetite. He did not regret his actions. He'd had to silence the man; if he hadn't, his opponent, greatly emboldened, would have sought out another opportunity to insult him.

He heaved a sigh of relief when Chanson said he'd heard enough. He wished to be back in St Bartholomew's. Soon the streets would be taken over by the Brotherhood of the Knife, the Fraternity of the Foist and the Sewer Squires of the Dark. The three men walked on, watching their step, as the filth and ordure seeping from blocked sewers had now frozen hard underfoot. Nevertheless, Corbett took comfort from the fact that, due to the freezing weather, the stench from the midden heaps was not so offensive. Despite his desire to reach St Bartholomew's, he paused abruptly and glanced up at a window, where a candle burnt fiercely. He stood and listened to a lucid voice singing a carol to 'Mary the most fragrantly beautiful Virgin of Walsingham'. The voice, some young girl's, not only pleasured the ear but touched the heart, despite the dirt and darkness of the night. Corbett, who loved nothing better than to sing in the choir of his parish church, waited till the singer had finished before striding on.

They turned into Ave Maria Lane. The Golden Aureole, a spacious, well-fronted tavern, was halfway down, a beacon light glowing fiercely beneath its garish sign. Corbett and his companions shouldered their way through the throng of prostitutes lurking at the mouth of the alleyways either side of the tavern. These hideous ladies of the night, hair dyed blood red, faces streaked with white paint, eyes dark ringed, moved in a cluster of colour in and out of the shadows, keeping an eye on possible customers, whistling at this man or that, whilst being very wary of the street bailiffs. These bully boys, if they caught the whores soliciting, would lash them brutally with their thin white splintered canes.

Corbett entered the taproom. Immediately the whisper 'king's men' was repeated time and again. A few of the customers immediately fled, one even pulling back the window shutters before leaping up and disappearing into the dark. The taproom was spacious and sweet smelling, delicious odours trailing from the kitchen yard beyond the great buttery table. Minehost Belstone greeted the clerks, bowing and scraping whilst wiping stubby bloodstained fingers on the thick cloth apron that covered him from head to toe. Of course, he declared, he had learnt about Master Manning's sad death, and yes, his chamber was still being guarded by one of the sheriff's men. Corbett said he held Manning's key, but was there another? Belstone said there was, and swiftly produced it from a long line of hooks on the wall behind the buttery table. He then led the clerks across the taproom, up some stairs and along the first gallery to where the sheriff's man sat dozing on a stool outside a chamber. Corbett paid the man a coin, said he could go, then waited for minehost to open the door.

The room inside was quite spacious and clean smelling. The taverner lit a lantern on a stool, as well as a three-branched candle spigot. He offered Corbett refreshments, but the clerk refused and the taverner left. Once he was gone, the three clerks searched the chamber thoroughly. Chanson went downstairs and brought up a leather sack for everything they could find. They lifted the mattress, shaking out coverlets and bolsters, taking jerkins and other clothing from their pegs. A second sack was needed, and eventually Corbett pronounced himself satisfied. He sat on the edge of the bed and gazed around. This had been the home of his friend, but now it was just an empty shell. He was satisfied that they had everything and that no one had entered the chamber since Manning had left earlier that day. They had collected manuscripts and sheaves of parchment, but he had also come across traces of a lady's touch: a small, delicate pomander, quite dried out but still fragrant, a posy of dried flowers, pieces of lace, a bracelet and a small heart-shaped pendant on a broken chain.

'Master?'

'Yes, Ranulf.'

'Faucomburg?'

'Pray for him.' Corbett grinned. 'Ranulf, in three days' time, I will meet Faucomburg in a combat to the death.'

'You are confident.'

'Confident in God's good grace. Never mind, never mind. Let's ignore that bully boy and concentrate on what we are doing here. We've collected Ralph's effects. Chanson, we will leave you here. See the taverner below, hire a cart and bring these sacks to St Bartholomew's.'

Chanson smiled and nodded. He was tired, sleepy, but he knew that once he reached St Bartholomew's, he could go to the stables and sleep with his beloved horses.

'Do what Sir Hugh says,' Ranulf teased. 'And for God's sake, don't sing.' He patted his companion on the shoulder and followed Corbett back downstairs.

Within the hour, the two clerks had reached St Bartholomew's. The great open field before the majestic priory had emptied for the day. The traders of cattle and horses, the fleshers and the tanners had gone, safely ensconced in the taverns that stood on the far side of Smithfield. Corbett and Ranulf went into the priory refectory, where they hastily broke their fast, then adjourned to the cells allocated to them, narrow closets though comfortable enough. Corbett immediately prepared himself for bed. Once ready, he opened his psalter and recited a psalm for the evening. He did not reflect on the day's events except to murmur a Requiem for Manning, and as soon as he'd learned that Chanson had arrived back safely, he retired to bed.

He woke early the next morning, the bells of the priory ringing out the summons to early-morning mass. He did not attend that celebration, but a second one held just before the local markets opened. Afterwards he lit some tapers before the statue of the Virgin, then he and his companions broke their fast in the buttery. They were joined by the tall, ascetic physician, Philippe, garbed in the grey robes of an Augustinian canon, a scholar who had studied in the medical schools of Montpellier, Salerno, Pavia and other illustrious places. Philippe quickly offered to view Manning's corpse and thoroughly sift through the dead clerk's possessions. Nevertheless he was visibly agitated, face anxious as he grasped Corbett's arm.

'I will do what you ask, of course, but, Hugh, I've heard stories that you've issued a challenge, a duel to the death in the tiltyard at Westminster. You intend to fight Lancaster's creature, Faucomburg. The news has spread swiftly, my friend. Surely you can—'

'Don't ask me to undo something that I cannot, Philippe. Faucomburg is dangerous, not because of who he is, but what he did. He cannot swagger through the royal precincts insulting the king's servants and officials with impunity.' Corbett put his blackjack of morning ale back on the buttery table. He smiled at the physician's worried expression. 'Oh man of little faith,' he teased.

'No, Hugh, a man of deep love. I care very much. So if you have to do what needs to be done, at least take care. Do not eat or drink either the night before or the following morning. Faucomburg will eat and drink to his heart's content and his own mortal danger. Anyway,' the physician picked up his travelling cloak, 'the corpse of poor Manning beckons.' He rose and left.

Corbett turned to the business of the day. He asked Chanson to go to the nearby market and buy whatever supplies they needed. Ranulf would keep watch whilst he himself closeted himself away to scrutinise Manning's papers. Ranulf offered to help. Corbett thanked him but declared that he wanted to read everything Manning had written.

He returned to his chamber and began his searches. Now and again he would pause to listen to the busy priory and hospital: cries, shouts, bells ringing or the lovely fading cadence of plainchant as divine office was sung. Servants hurried up and down the gallery outside as the guest house grew busy. Corbett was tempted to reflect on the coming duel, but he recognised the dangers of that. He had served in the royal array. He was aware of reflecting too much on every affray, be it a possible ambush in the steeply wooded valleys of Wales or a savage attack deep in the fog-bound glens of Scotland. He was determined not to grow agitated, confident that he would meet the threat as soon as it emerged.

He met Ranulf and Chanson for a light collation just

after the midday Angelus bell, and half listened to their conversation before returning to his studies. Daylight faded. The bells of the priory warned of the approach of dark; these calls were answered by the brazen braying of market horns proclaiming that the day's business was ending. Brother Philippe returned just before the priory gates were closed. He brought some ale and a tray of manchet loaves smeared with toasted herb-strewn cheese to Corbett's cell. He sat on the chamber's only stool, shaking his head as he sipped the ale and chewed on the freshly baked bread.

'A good day, Hugh, my friend. Interesting, though I found nothing amiss; no sign of poison, either on his fingers or on anything he may have touched.' He gestured at Corbett, who sat playing with a quill pen. 'Nothing,' he repeated, 'be it on the quill, the chancery satchel or the writing tray. Of course, he was definitely poisoned. I carefully examined the corpse, I noted the discoloration of the face, the mouth and the throat as well as the liverish stains on chest and stomach. Certainly a powerful poison was used. I would suggest a fortified dose of belladonna, nightshade or some other noxious potion. You see, Hugh, some poisons are as swift as an arrow.' He paused, clearly warming to his subject. 'They can act as soon as they're in the mouth. Take the abrin seed; the Venetians give it to the accused to determine innocence or guilt. You may have heard about this. Of course it is highly dangerous, but only if broken in the mouth. If the accused is wisely advised on what to do, he or she will swallow the seed whole.

The shell is so hard it simply passes through the body into the jakes. However, if the seed is chewed, the poison acts immediately. The purpose of my lecture, Hugh, is to demonstrate that poisons enter the humours through the mouth rather than the stomach.'

'Yet as far as we know, and I think this is correct, Ralph didn't eat or drink anything, whilst you say that any item he may have raised to his lips is untainted.'

'The answer to that is a blunt yes. Trust me, Hugh, I know what I saw and what I smelt. I will certainly check again but, for the life of me, I cannot determine how he was poisoned.'

Philippe left and Corbett returned to his manuscripts. He worked hard over the next two days. Now and again he dispatched Ranulf down to Westminster to the Exchequer and Chancery to search out certain records and transcribe the brief entries; occasionally he instructed him to borrow specific documents in their entirety. On the eve of the duel, he invited Ranulf into his chamber to review what he had discovered. Ranulf wanted to discuss the coming confrontation with Faucomburg, but Corbett resolutely refused. He served Ranulf a goblet of wine and toasted wafers of minced beef, declaring that he was intent on following Brother Philippe's advice. He would not eat or drink before the duel, nor would he dwell on it. Instead, they would concentrate on the matters in hand.

Once Ranulf had finished eating, Corbett, who had been staring through the narrow lancet window, returned to his chair and began to speak.

'So far, Ranulf, I have learnt the following, so make careful note of my conclusions. On one thing I am determined. Once tomorrow has come and gone, we shall, God willing, journey to the Convent of St Sulpice. However, we must first prepare ourselves for that, so let us begin.

'Item: Ralph Manning was a bachelor clerk in the Chancery of the Secret Seal: a good, honest, loyal servant of the Crown. I have nothing but praise for his work as a receiver.

'Item: from what I can learn, about a year to fourteen months ago, Ralph Manning became secretly betrothed to a young lady from the city, Katherine Ingoldsby, who lived near Pater Noster Row. An orphan, she had been entrusted to her only living relative, an aged aunt, the widow of a prosperous London merchant, and was, according to the sheriff's return, her aunt's heir in everything. Anyway, Katherine and Ralph became deeply infatuated with each other.

'Item: unfortunately, Katherine fell pregnant, and the poor girl suffered a miscarriage. Her aunt, that old virago, discovered this, and Katherine was packed off to St Sulpice. Her aunt, who has since gone to her eternal reward, or something like that, disinherited her niece, leaving all her wealth to the aforementioned nunnery, which now housed Katherine Ingoldsby.' He paused as Ranulf whistled beneath his breath.

'Item: some weeks ago, Lady Katherine, a novice at St Sulpice, simply disappeared. According to Manning's own papers, he visited St Sulpice time and again, only to be informed that Katherine Ingoldsby had apparently fled. He continued his search in and around the convent and, when he could, throughout the city. He never found her and had to face the possibility that she'd simply fled to somewhere in this kingdom or beyond.'

'And the nuns of St Sulpice had no knowledge of her whereabouts?'

'According to Manning, no. The young lady was gone, taking all her possessions with her; not a trace remained. The good sisters argued, and we must accept this, that the Convent of St Sulpice is a house of prayer, not a prison. They do not have guards patrolling the walls, nor would they detain anyone against their wishes. If one of the young ladies decides to leave, there is little they can do, or would want to do, about it.' Corbett scratched his chin.

'Item: there are certain matters I cannot understand. Manning makes reference to someone called "MM", and another abbreviation is "QN". I do not know what these mean.

'Item: even more surprising, Manning went to the archives at Westminster and began to investigate the case of Thomas Turbeville. Remember, Ranulf, we were involved in this. Turbeville became a spy for the French king. You and I trapped and exposed him. For some reason known only to himself, Manning searched the records for references to Turbeville and his family.' Corbett shook his head. 'Believe me, Ranulf, this is a deep mystery, a murderous one that swirls like a thick river mist. I intend to clear it and grasp the very heart of this problem, but not now. Tomorrow I meet Faucomburg . . .'

Early next morning, as the priory bells rang to summon the community to prayer, Corbett and his companions left St Bartholomew's. Ranulf was surprised that Corbett did not take any weapons or armour with him, yet when he asked why, Corbett simply grinned and shrugged. Nor did they make their way down towards Newgate, but instead across the mist-shrouded open field, the site of London's busiest market. Hours were yet to pass before the horns brayed to mark the start of the day's business. Nevertheless, the fog-bound silence was already broken by glowing pinpricks of light as torches and lanterns flared into life. Voices echoed eerily. Shouts and cries carried, drowned now and again by the neigh of horses and the lowing of cattle as they were herded down to the stalls for inspection and possible sale. Ranulf abruptly realised that they were heading towards the furthest end of Smithfield, where the great stone gallows reared up to the sky. At one point they had to pause as a gruesome procession broke through the mist. A massive dray horse, led by executioners, emerged silently out of the murk. The slaughterers were all garbed in black, faces hidden behind masks carved in the shape of animals: badger, monkey, dog and pig. The horse pulled a sledge on which the bloody remains of a traitor executed the previous evening lay heaped in a steaming mess. Corbett stopped, crossed himself and allowed the macabre entourage to sweep by them and vanish into the swirling mist.

'Master,' Ranulf pleaded. 'Why are we going towards the Elms?'

'You'll soon see, my friend.'

'What's that?' Chanson stuttered, fearful about where they were going and what he had just glimpsed.

'The Elms,' Ranulf retorted, falling back to walk alongside his comrade. 'It is the ancient name for the execution ground. In former times, when the elms grew thick and fast, they used to throw the hanging ropes over the branches of the trees and kick the poor bastards off carts.'

'And now?'

'You'll see, Chanson, a place of deep horror.'

They began to climb a low sloping hill. The mist broke and Chanson moaned at the horrid sight. The hill was topped by stone gallows about thirty feet high, with wooden cross beams connecting them.

'Enough wood,' Ranulf muttered, 'to hang an entire convent of priests.'

Chanson coughed and retched at the foul stench wafting about him. Ranulf, quietly enjoying himself, pointed to the corpses strung along each beam, all hanging by their necks. They twisted in the strong freezing wind.

'Next to these,' he declared, nudging Chanson, 'are the chains. You see them? They hold the baskets containing the quartered remains of traitors; their poled heads form a thicket above the entrance of London Bridge.'

Chanson stared in disbelief. He had never been here before, and he could only gape at the crowded skeletons swinging so high, making mournful music at every icy blast of wind that rattled the chains and sighed through the tangle of ropes. The hill was also the haunt of rats, crows and magpies. These scavengers and flesh-gobblers found plenty of food amongst the rotting corpses left to hang until plucked clean to the bone. Eventually the ropes would rot and the grisly remains would drop into the makeshift charnel pit dug deep into the hill beneath the gallows. The entire execution ground was ringed by a lofty palisade and a heavily locked fortified gate. Ranulf explained that this was necessary so relatives could not collect the remains of loved ones. Nor could the cadavers be stolen by the witches and warlocks who lurked around such places. These denizens of the dark were always eager to seize the remains of hanged men, as they believed such gruesome relics housed powerful magical powers.

'Oh yes, this hill of suffering is visited by many people, but why are we here?' Ranulf glanced at Corbett, who just stood gazing up the hill as if fascinated by the gruesome sight. 'Master?' he queried.

'Ranulf, Chanson, follow me.' Corbett turned to the right, going round the bottom of the hill into a deep tangled copse of great oaks and sycamore trees. Daylight was now strengthening. Weak sunlight shot like spears through the gaps and branches to afford some light in the cloying green darkness. Corbett followed a beaten track through the trees, now bustling with the noise and constant chatter of different birds. Chanson relaxed, relieved to be away from those ghastly gallows, but Ranulf immediately began to tense. Gibbets and places of punishment had been part of his childhood. He was a true child of the street, used to the flashing knife, the falling blade and the whirling arrow. He knew all about the horrors of a hanging, yet none of this frightened him. He was more concerned about this sea of greenery that clustered about him: the ancient gnarled tree trunks, their branches sweeping up and spreading out, taking on a life of their own. The rustling, scurrying and slithering in the undergrowth and along the branches above him put him on edge.

In the end they didn't walk too far, and Ranulf was relieved when Corbett led them into a glade where the light was stronger, a serene, peaceful place with a brook burbling its way past a pile of ancient rock. The face of this rock had been gouged out to carve a small cave or grotto, which contained a replica of the famous statue of Our Lady of Walsingham. Ranulf had visited the Norfolk shrine and he immediately recognised the carving, which presented the Virgin Mary as a crowned queen sitting on her throne dressed in flowing robes. The crowned Virgin held the Christ in the crook of her arm, whilst her right hand clutched a long lily stem. The statue had been carved out of costly wood, then treated carefully so as to protect it against the elements. The wood was clean and looked as if it had been recently polished.

Corbett led his two companions closer, until they

stood on the edge of the gurgling brook. Then he crossed himself and intoned the Salve Regina, chanting the lines, eyes closed. Ranulf just watched. He knew his master loved nothing better than singing this hymn to heaven's fragrant queen. Corbett reached the last few words, 'O dulcis Virgo Maria . . .', and his voice trailed away.

'Master, what is this? Why are we here, and why now?'

'Manning, my good friend Manning.' Corbett crossed himself and turned away, beckoning to the other two clerks to follow him. They left the glade, wrapping their cloaks more firmly around them. Corbett continued speaking. 'Five years ago, after I had left the royal service, Manning was promoted in the Secret Chancery. As you well know, Ranulf, I left all such matters alone. However,' he grinned, 'I kept my ear close to what was happening. Anyway, I heard rumours that Manning's sister Isolda was deeply smitten with a fellow clerk, John Daventry. They became lovers, but then quite abruptly the relationship turned bitter.'

'You mean between Isolda and Daventry?'

'Oh yes, Ranulf. In brief, Isolda accused Daventry of raping her in his chamber at the same tavern we so recently visited, the Golden Aureole in Ave Maria Lane. Their world turned very ugly. Manning, formerly Daventry's bosom friend, wouldn't accept his protestations of innocence. He publicly challenged him to a duel, to trial by combat, a fight to the death where God would decide who was in the right.' Corbett fell silent. 'Manning,' he sighed, 'killed Daventry in open and fair combat, and that should have been the sad end to a very tragic story. However, Isolda, frantic with grief and guilt, confessed within a month of her former lover's death that Daventry had been innocent and her accusation was born of sheer malice.'

'Sweet Lord,' Ranulf breathed.

'Yes, Ranulf, that revelation almost broke Manning. To a certain extent it changed him into the person we've heard about; quiet, reserved and contemplative. His sister's confession affected him deeply. He felt he had Daventry's blood on his hands.'

'And Isolda?'

'She hastily entered the convent we are going to visit, St Sulpice. Manning helped place her there, but from the little I've learnt, Isolda was fully consenting, feeling she had to make reparation for the death of her lover. Brother and sister never spoke to each other again.'

'And Manning?'

'He too wanted to make atonement for his slaying of an innocent man. He petitioned for a royal pardon for both himself and his sister, and received it, but he wanted to do more. Now, Manning – and his writings attest to this – was a tertiary in the order of the Friars of the Sack.'

'Tertiary?' Chanson demanded, stamping his feet against the cold and blowing on his mittened fingers. Ranulf too was rubbing his arms for warmth. Corbett, however, seemed impervious to the cold as he stood, narrow eyed, recalling the past.

'Tertiary,' he replied slowly, 'is when a lay person

becomes a member of a religious order. I enjoy the same privilege with the Franciscans. Anyway,' he hurried on, 'as you know, the Friars of the Sack have a unique ministry to those who are about to be executed. The good friars act as chaplains at the gallow ground we have just visited. Apparently Manning asked the friars what atonement he could make for Daventry's death. They advised him to go on pilgrimage to the shrine of Our Lady of Walsingham in Norfolk, and then erect the little grotto we have just visited. On execution days, the friends and relatives of the condemned go there to pray for them. Posies are left, candles lit during the spring and summer. And so you have it. I thought we should make a short pilgrimage here to pray for Manning, to pledge that I will fight for his name, and to petition him – if he has any influence in the court of heaven – for help in my imminent confrontation with Faucomburg. So let us return to the priory. I will arm, then we must leave.'

# PART TWO

Thomas Turbeville by name . . . came over to
England with traitorous designs.

An hour later, Corbett and his companions left St Bartholomew's, making their way through the maze of alleyways and runnels leading down to the river. Corbett was now harnessed for battle. Beneath his cloak he wore a light mailed hauberk, his favourite, a masterpiece created by Milanese craftsmen, light and comfortable but stronger than any armour or mail jerkin. For the rest he wore thick woollen leggings pushed into leather boots with a good grip on the sole and a small square heel. Despite Ranulf's protests, he refused to wear a conical helmet with its broad nose guard. All he took was his war belt, with its sheathed one-handed sword, along with two Italian stilettos, one pushed into a secret gap on his belt, the other into the top of his right boot. He also asked for a kite-shaped shield favoured by the Normans. He then pronounced himself satisfied, even as his two companions vociferously objected to the light armour he wore.

'Rest assured,' he declared. 'You will see soon enough why I am harnessed this way.'

Ranulf and Chanson had no choice but to accept, yet they remained worried as they trudged behind their master, now swathed in his military cloak and deep hood, along the streets and down to Queenhithe quayside. The Legion of the Damned, the night prowlers, still moved through the half-light. These citizens of the dusk watched from shadow-filled doorways and alley mouths as the three mailed clerks made their way down to the river. No one offered any obstacle or impediment. Beggars kept their clacking dishes silent. Whores and their pimps sheltered deeper into the murk, whilst the Brotherhood of the Knife simply melted away. The day was about to begin. Bailiffs and beadles, the men of the watch and heralds of the day, were busy enough, yet even these stopped to watch them go. Corbett strode on. He wondered what his wife the Lady Maeve would be doing now, whilst he quietly thanked God that she at least did not know what he intended.

At last they reached the riverside. Corbett hired a wherry to take them along to King's Steps at Westminster. They arrived just before the bells of the abbey began their insistent summons to prayer. The Blackrobes were already up and busy, dark shapes hurrying here and there across the abbey precincts. The news of the duel had swept the city, and already barges, boats and wherries were disgorging spectators eager to secure a good place, hours before the actual combat began.

Corbett kept himself well hidden, making his way

across the abbey grounds, down the narrow runnels that skirted the palace. He was intent on reaching the tiltyard as soon as possible. The broad tournament ground lay to the north of the monastic buildings, now becoming so distinctive as the day broke and the mist began to thin. Windows gleamed in the strengthening light; some of these were pure glass, others decorated in delicate colours. The sheer mass of stone, gilted wood and imaginative carvings was truly formidable. Corbett felt as if these sacred buildings were reasserting themselves in all their majesty over the pathetic world of men.

They reached the tiltyard, a bleak, stark place. A long, fenced rectangle of hard-packed earth, strewn with sand and sawdust and peppered with small pebbles to provide a firm grip. The lists had been taken down. Corbett would not even contemplate a tourney against his foe. Warhorses were far too valuable for a brutal fight to the death. On all four sides of the rectangle rose tier after tier of benches to cater for the hundreds, even thousands, who flocked to such occasions. At each end of the rectangle stood a gate leading to a small pavilion built of stone with a sloping red-tiled roof. Each of the pavilions housed a lavarium, a jakes pot and a cot bed as well as pegs driven into the wall on which the combatants could hang clothes, weapons and armour.

During his sojourn at St Bartholomew's, Corbett had sent Ranulf to meet the Herald of the South, who would act as master of arms throughout the combat. The herald was supported by four pursuivants, all five officials garbed in gorgeous tabards displaying the Crown insignia in a blaze of royal colours. They carried trumpets, but they also wore weapons to use against any combatant who refused to fight. Corbett raised his hand in greeting to them, after which he inspected the pavilion, warmed by braziers and furnished with a jug of wine and goblets as well as a platter of bread and dried meat. He pronounced himself satisfied. The heralds had displayed the Corbett arms, three crows on a golden background; the pennant was fastened on a pole thrust into the ground outside the pavilion. Corbett asked Ranulf and Chanson to inspect his weapons, whilst he, swathed in his cloak, sat on a stool and watched the arrival of the ever-increasing crowd thronging onto the tiers of benches.

The combat was set to begin after the noon-day Angelus bell. There was still plenty of time, but the citizens of London, despite the freezing weather, sullen skies and hard ground frost, were determined to secure a place around the tiltyard. Many brought small chafing dishes crammed with fiery charcoal to keep themselves warm. Of course the tribe of food and ale sellers had flocked in like crows swooping towards the feast. Hotpot boys, pastry pages, sugar squires and goblet girls wormed their way through the crowd offering a wide range of refreshments.

Faucomburg's entourage eventually arrived to noisy acclamation. The master herald and his acolytes became busy visiting the two pavilions and ensuring that the

family standards and pennants fluttering above the palisade were correctly unfurled. The daylight strengthened.
The warmth of the packed crowd could be smelt, and
the same applied to the various odours swirling across
the tiltyard. Voices shouted. Horns brayed. A relic seller
tried to sell a blade from the armour of St George and
was hauled away with catcalls, yells and a torrent of
half-chewed food. Whores slipped like eels through the
throng, ready to shepherd a customer into a darkened
corner for a hasty, feverish meeting. The crowd milled
about, thronging close.

Corbett just sat and watched. He kept remembering
that grotto, and he wondered about Manning. Ralph
had been a mailed clerk, a warrior who'd fought alongside Corbett. All such fighters, he concluded, suffered
soul shadows, wounds that arose to darken the spirits,
memories of previous conflicts. Manning had slain
Daventry in this same tiltyard. Isolda, his sister, must
have watched, then afterwards, consumed with guilt
and regret, confessed her sin. She had gone to St Sulpice,
as had Manning's lover Katherine, before she disappeared. Just as mysterious was the business of Megotta
the mummer. For reasons known only to himself,
Manning had visited Newgate and freed the moon girl.
She had been found guilty of two murders and been
sentenced to hang. Manning, however, had arranged a
royal pardon for her. There seemed to be some evidence
that one of the conditions of her pardon was that she
would enter the Convent of St Sulpice, a matter known
only to Megotta and Manning. So who was this

Megotta? And what was she supposed to do at St Sulpice?

'Sir Hugh?'

Corbett glanced up. Ranulf was staring anxiously down at him.

'Sir Hugh, I think it's time.'

Corbett stood up in surprise. He'd been so lost in his own thoughts he hadn't noticed that the benches on all four sides were now crammed with spectators. The prized seats had been allocated to members of the court, the College of Clerks and the leading officers of state. The master of arms had ensured that all the appropriate banners, standards and pennants be unfurled as if the king himself was in residence. The tiltyard was now ready. The four pursuivants took up their positions either side of the master of arms. Corbett had insisted that ceremony and pageantry be limited. The weather was freezing and the crowds could not be kept waiting for long. Faucomburg had agreed to this. Moreover, the tension between the king and his leading nobles now permeated court life, and in particular the busy precincts of Westminster. It was best if occasions such as this one did not linger long but were swiftly carried through.

Corbett stared across at where Faucomburg was preparing himself, surrounded by a colourful coterie. He narrowed his eyes as he studied his opponent, then turned and tapped Ranulf on the shoulder.

'Correct me if I am wrong, my friend, but has Faucomburg been drinking?'

'And still is.'

'And his armour, he's going to wear a helmet?'

'So it would appear.'

'Good,' Corbett whispered. 'And he's wearing mail gauntlets?'

'Yes, I can clearly see them, master. They are covered with sharp studs. You should watch those. Sir Hugh, where are your gauntlets?'

Corbett fished in the sack beside him and drew out a pair of soft doe-skin gloves.

'Sir Hugh, no!' Ranulf's protest was echoed by Chanson.

Corbett winked at them and grinned. 'Trust me, my friends.' He stretched out and clasped their hands, then pointed at the tiltyard. 'I was tutored there by no less a person than the old king, and, believe me, you couldn't get a better—' His words were drowned by shrill trumpet blasts repeated time and again. He strapped on his war belt and drew his sword. 'I am ready,' he murmured, and raised his sword in salute to his two comrades.

Ranulf stared back, his face full of worry. 'You be safe, master.' He pointed across the tiltyard. Faucomburg had already passed through the gate at the far end. The Lancastrian clerk wore half-armour and a conical helmet and carried a heavy siege shield as well as a broadsword, which he skilfully shifted and twisted, much to the enjoyment of the spectators, who revelled in such blade play.

'It's time.' Corbett spoke quietly and nodded at Ranulf, who opened the gate.

Corbett stepped through and raised his sword in reply to the muted greetings of the crowd, then drove the blade into the earth so he could adjust the kite shield properly. He gripped the sword and walked slowly to the centre of the tiltyard, where the master of arms and his pursuivants were waiting. Faucomburg joined them. Corbett stared at his enemy's fat red face, his blue eyes vibrant with hostility, the contemptuous smirk playing on his fleshy mouth. The master of arms instructed them to salute each other. Both combatants lifted their swords perfunctorily, blades flat against their faces. At the master of arms' bidding, the trumpeters blew three chilling blasts, then withdrew from the tiltyard. The herald flourished his staff of office. Corbett and Faucomburg stepped back, swords and shields raised.

The two men began to circle each other. Corbett watched intently. Faucomburg was already experiencing discomfort. Sweat coursed down his face, but because of his sharp-studded mail gauntlets he could do nothing about wiping it away. Corbett swooped in, swift and sure as any dancer, his shield thrust forward, his sword flickering like a serpent's tongue. Faucomburg aimed a slicing cut at his head, but Corbett had already moved back, and the blade cut aimlessly through the air. Corbett settled himself. He crouched before dodging to the right then stepping back. He repeated this, keeping out of his opponent's sword range, refusing to be drawn in, moving in a circle. Faucomburg followed, sweating and panting, desperate to inflict a blow that would hinder his opponent, who just refused to stay still. The crowd did not like this, but Corbett ignored the jeers and boos. He wiped his face with the back of his gloved hand and closely scrutinised Faucomburg, who was soaked in sweat and breathing heavily. Faucomburg advanced. Corbett withdrew. More catcalls and insults. Faucomburg himself was cursing loudly, yelling that Corbett was a coward.

'Very well, very well,' Corbett hissed. 'It's time. You brought me to the dance, and dance you will.' He lunged forward; Faucomburg rushed to engage, but Corbett swerved to his right, using his shield to deliver a hammer blow to his opponent's sword hand. The sharp rim of the shield struck just above Faucomburg's right gauntlet, a cutting, bruising blow, so hard he dropped his sword, screaming in agony. He then made the hideous mistake of trying to pick it up. Corbett was already moving. He slipped swiftly behind his opponent and delivered a vicious kick just above Faucomburg's right knee. Faucomburg collapsed, twisting desperately, his heavy shield becoming entangled with his harness. The wounds to his wrist and right leg were grievous; he arched in pain. Again Corbett closed, stamping hard on his opponent's left shoulder. Faucomburg screamed, even as Corbett bent down and tore his helmet off, sending it spinning across the tiltyard. He then lowered his sword, its tip resting against Faucomburg's exposed throat whilst Corbett's shield pressed down hard on his chest.

The crowd, which had watched in fascinated silence, now erupted in shouts, laughter and noisy applause. Corbett, staring down at his fallen opponent, knew that the fight was not what the spectators had wanted, yet he had fought the same way as he had on many a battlefield and against better men than this. The fallen clerk gazed up bleakly, eyes flickering. He dared not move, wary of antagonising the victor. Corbett pressed gently and his sword drew a bead of blood.

'Do you,' he demanded, 'withdraw all insults to me and my beloved comrade Ralph Manning?'

'I do,' Faucomburg rasped. 'Unreservedly.'

'Do you apologise for any grievance caused?'

'I do, unreservedly.'

Corbett ignored the growing cries from the crowd of 'Kill, kill!' and 'Let him have it!'

'Do you solemnly promise that no hurt or injury will be offered to me and mine?'

'I do, unreservedly.'

He withdrew his sword, lifted it in salute, to the thunderous acclamation of the crowd, then left the arena.

Inside the stone pavilion, he sat down on the stool. Ranulf and Chanson, loudly praising their master's victory, served a little wine and fingers of slightly hard honeyed bread. Corbett listened to their congratulations, then shook his head.

'Faucomburg made terrible mistakes. He ate and drank too much. His battle harness was too heavy, and . . .' He paused at a knock on the door. He was surprised at being disturbed, because Ranulf had specifically asked the master of arms to keep all supporters and well-wishers away. He glanced at Ranulf, who just shrugged. Again the harsh rapping.

'Open it,' Corbett ordered. Chanson did so, and a much humbled Faucomburg limped through the door. Ranulf made to block his way, but Faucomburg raised his injured right hand.

'*Pax et bonum*,' he murmured through his bruised mouth. 'Sir Hugh, once again please accept my apologies.' He closed his eyes and winced at a spasm of pain in his sword arm. 'I have come to explain.'

Corbett got to his feet and insisted Faucomburg take his stool. The man smiled his gratitude and sat down nursing his injuries.

'I talked about Manning and whores.' Faucomburg smiled thinly. 'A true case of the pot calling the pan black. My friends and I arrived in the city. We lodged at comfortable taverns and of course we wanted to savour all that London could offer.' He took a deep breath. 'We made enquiries and eventually discovered the delights of a most opulent brothel or whore house in Coppergilt Street in Cheapside, a quiet thoroughfare. Now this house of pleasure is very discreet. It's called the Queen of the Night, and its owner is a lady who proclaims herself Mother Midnight. We went there to pleasure ourselves; my lord of Lancaster is a very generous patron. He has furnished us with silver and gold and promised to pay all our expenses in the city.'

'I am sure he has,' Corbett interrupted drily. 'But be careful, my friend. If Lancaster becomes undone, so are you. You watched the mob today at the tiltyard; the same voices who cheered also shouted at me to kill you. But continue.'

'The girls at the Queen of the Night are French and know a great deal more than the local whores. Anyway, on at least two occasions I glimpsed Ralph Manning there. I recognised him immediately because I have seen him a number of times in the Chancery offices at Westminster.'

'And what else?'

'Well, I saw him deep in conversation with Mother Midnight. I had the distinct impression that he was not there to relish the joys of that place. I suspect he was making enquiries, investigating some issue.'

'How do you know that?'

'Sir Hugh, he looked serious and he was deftly questioning Mother Midnight in a fashion she visibly did not like.' Faucomburg pulled a face. 'But as for the what, the why and the wherefore, I cannot say. I know you are investigating Manning's death. Anyway, in view of the compassion you showed me, I thought I should tell you what I know and what first prompted my insults. Now,' he grimaced, 'I need to leave.' He rose, then turned, hand on the latch. 'Sir Hugh, why did you spare me?'

'In God's name,' Corbett retorted. 'I never wanted your life, just an apology, and I got that. God save you, Faucomburg.'

The Lancastrian clerk left and Corbett began to busy himself.

'Now what, master?'

'Why, Ranulf, safe journey back to St Bartholomew's, then let me wash, change and feast on some good food and wine in the buttery. Once we have done that, we shall visit St Sulpice.' Corbett abruptly paused. 'Oh sweet heavens . . .' he whispered.

'Sir Hugh?'

'Faucomburg has resolved one mystery. As I sifted through Manning's memoranda, I came across those references to QN and MM. Now I know what they mean: Queen of the Night and Mother Midnight. So . . .' He drew up his hood. 'St Bartholomew's it is.'

They returned to the priory. Corbett washed, changed and ate a nourishing meal of spiced veal stew served with luce wafers, a very delicate fishcake. The Keeper of the Secret Seal had intended to leave for St Sulpice, but the day was drawing on and he felt suddenly weary after the excitement of the last few hours. He slept for a while and, after he woke, he met with Ranulf and Chanson in the buttery to sup evening ales before returning to his chamber. Once comfortable, he laid out his documents on the table and began to revise and amend the conclusions he had reached.

'Item.' He stopped nibbling on the end of his quill pen. 'Ralph Manning,' he continued, talking to himself as he wrote. 'Yes, Ralph Manning, a chancery clerk, falls in love with the Lady Katherine, who becomes pregnant. The poor girl loses the baby as well as the support of her only living relative, an aged but very wealthy aunt. This beldame disinherits her in favour of the Convent of St Sulpice, where Katherine is lodged well away from clacking tongues. In truth,' Corbett wrote swiftly, 'a common enough practice for young

ladies who fall from grace. They are put out of view,
hidden away, forgotten. Now,' he continued, 'St Sulpice
is an ideal place, I have studied the records. It claims
to follow the rule of St Benedict, but in fact it is a
well-furnished, comfortable residence for ladies who
wish to withdraw from society.

'Item: this case, however,' he went on, 'is truly unique.
Manning's lover entered St Sulpice only to disappear.
Manning's sister, Isolda, also entered the convent; is she
still there? Suppose she is not; was Manning involved
in both disappearances?' He tapped the end of his quill
against his lips. 'Are these disappearances the reason
for Manning visiting Mother Midnight at the Queen of
the Night? Was he searching for the two ladies? Or had
he used that high-class brothel to hide them? But then
what? Did he murder the two women?' Corbett recalled
his own musings about Manning. The clerk had been
a soldier, a warrior, who had ruthlessly taken the life
of a close friend in order to defend the honour of his
sister. He had been a man of war, a man of violence.
He certainly had blood on his hands, but whose?

'Item.' Corbett dipped his quill into the inkpot and
continued to write in that cipher known only to him.
'Even more mysterious is Manning's use of a mummers'
girl, Megotta. Apparently convicted of a stabbing
outside an Essex tavern and arrested whilst fleeing,
Megotta was found guilty and sentenced to hang.
However, Manning intervened, Megotta was released,
and, if Manning's notes are correct, the girl assumed a
new name, Isabella Seymour, and enough money to

place herself in the Convent of St Sulpice.' He shook his head. 'You spent your own money to ensure this. Why, Ralph? What were you looking for? What happened at that convent? Were your investigations so dangerous that someone decided to poison you? But how?'

Megotta, or Sister Isabella as she was now known, slipped out through the narrow postern that led onto the small cloisters. Night was falling, and those heralds of the dark, the owls, were hooting mournfully high in the trees. A cold wind blew. Sconce torches spluttered, their flames leaping up against the cold. Candle-shine glowed from this window or that. The convent was settling down after the work and prayer of the day. The offices of terce, sext and vespers had been sung in the chapel, and now the good nuns were allowed leisure time to chat, mingle and above all gossip about the community.

Manning had given Megotta strict instructions on how to act: not to search for anything in particular but to look for something untoward or amiss in this enclosed community. She had certainly settled down swiftly and serenely. She had been allocated her own cell, a comfortable, clean chamber with a polished wooden floor and lime-washed walls. There were pegs driven into the plaster to hang her clothes; also a writing desk, chair, stool and a cot bed boasting a thick mattress, bolsters, coverlets and clean linen sheets. Like other sisters, she was given a lavarium along with a Turkey carpet for the floor. Candle spigots and a lanternhorn had been supplied. In truth, the convent was most comfortable, the food much better than Megotta had eaten on her journeys along the highways and byways of the kingdom. St Sulpice was luxurious, fragrant and most welcoming. Indeed, for Megotta, that was the problem: there was nothing to report. She certainly acted the part of the pious and obedient novice. She had been educated in her horn book, so she easily engaged in singing the divine office and making the responses during the daily mass, celebrated by a local priest. She ate delicately in the refectory and participated in the various works of the convent, be it embroidery, gardening, tending the livestock or keeping the buildings fresh and clean. She loved nothing better than working in the kitchens. She had a natural flair for cooking, her baking skills honed during her long years of travelling. The kitchener, Sister Constantia – at least until her mysterious murder out on the carp pond – had actively encouraged her to cook farced chicken, baked lamprey or roseye, fried loach with almonds.

She had certainly been made very welcome. The good sisters, during the leisure time between vespers and compline, had soon discovered her talent for mimicry and acting. They had been enraptured by her accurate imitation of a snobbish court lady and even that of a strict abbess; this certainly made Mother Eleanor laugh behind her fingers. No, life at St Sulpice was calm and harmonious, and Megotta had taken to it like a swan to swimming. Yet that posed a real difficulty. What could she report to Manning? He had asked her to study and scrutinise the convent and these ladies playing at being Benedictine nuns. She had worked hard to achieve this. She prided herself on her accurate observation yet, for the life of her, she could find nothing wrong at St Sulpice. True, the nuns liked their comforts, but why shouldn't they; after all, didn't God want them to be happy? Megotta, to use her own phrase, poked her nose into this and that, like a pig snouting for a truffle, but she could not unearth anything suspect.

She paused under the shadow of some trees, pulling her hood and cloak tighter about her. Two matters now concerned her. First, what had happened to Sister Constantia in that boat on the carp pond? Was it true, about a dagger blow direct to her heart? Yet surely no one could swim in that freezing water? And if they had, Sister Constantia would not simply have sat there and waited for them. If the gossip was true, if Constantia was stabbed whilst the boat was moored next to the jetty, then who rowed it out to the centre of the pond, and how would the assassin have got back to shore? Rumours raced through the community like March hares through a cornfield. Manning would certainly be interested in this. But that posed further mystery.

Megotta was supposed to meet Manning at this hour when the chapel bells sounded the beginning of leisure time. She was supposed to cross the convent grounds to Devil's Tower, housed deep in a thick copse close to the lofty curtain wall. The brickwork on the outside wall was loose; the gaps created provided a foothold for Manning to clamber up, then drop down silently and smoothly as a shifting shadow. But not recently. Megotta had sat in the dusty stairwell of the tower, the door to the steps leading up firmly locked by Sister Marie, the Lady of the Halls. The stairwell was comfortable enough and housed a jakes cupboard that could prove useful during a long wait. However, Manning had stopped coming. Perhaps he would be here tonight?

Megotta now knew her way around the convent buildings, so the darkness posed no problem as she hurried across the grass. She reached the clearing that stretched down to a fringe of bushes and trees and hastened on, hoping Manning would already be there, that she'd glimpse the glow from the small shuttered lanternhorn he always brought with him, its flame winking through the dark. But she could hear or see nothing. As she reached the entrance to the tower, the darkness was deepening. She went inside and stood listening to the various sounds, the cracking and snapping as animals pushed their way through the undergrowth outside, along with the last tired calls of the birds.

Abruptly she tensed. One sound was different. The snapping of twigs under something heavy. Somebody was edging closer to the entrance to the tower. Manning never made such a sound. Again the blood-chilling snapping. Megotta, now fully alarmed, recalled the legends about this place, how demons prowled here. Another sound; there was someone behind her. As she turned, dark shapes filled the doorway. She stepped back, but they pursued her. She saw the sack being thrown over her and struggled violently, but a sharp blow to the head stunned her, and she fell into a dead faint.

'St Sulpice is at least a hundred years old; we follow the Benedictine rule.' Sister Marie, Lady of the Halls, smiled apologetically as she raised bejewelled fingers to touch the snow-white coif that cupped her sweet, soft face. Once satisfied that the wimple was in place, she adjusted her fur-rimmed brown hood to protect her cheeks against the cold, then lifted her cowl, a rich brown colour that contrasted starkly with her ivory skin, pert little nose, soft eyes and merry mouth. 'Oh, I do chatter.' She giggled, fingers going to her lips as she stared at this dark-faced, powerful royal clerk. Corbett gazed back, a searching look, then smiled and spread his hands.

'Sister Marie,' he declared, 'you have shown us St Sulpice in all its glory, yes, Ranulf?' He turned and glared at his henchman, who had been mimicking the good sister as she had led them on what she called a 'thorough visitation' of the nunnery. They had certainly seen everything: the exquisitely well-furnished refectory, the comfortable library and scriptorium, even the farm-yard, rich in poultry ripening for the table.

'Is there any other place you wish to see?' Marie's face became all serious. 'Lady Abbess and the others will meet you in the chapter house. We've been there; you've seen it,' she gabbled on. She was highly nervous but determined to hide it. The arrival of these royal clerks armed with their warrants and licences had certainly caused consternation. Corbett, with his dark good looks and deep-set eyes, was regarded as the king's own man. Ranulf, his henchman, with his slanted green eyes, pale face and spiked red hair, had set some hearts a-flutter. Prioress Margaret had put an end to such nonsense.

'The world of men,' she had declared caustically, 'has entered our world, so let's be prudent and watch.'

Sister Marie fully agreed and had volunteered to escort the clerks around the convent. One of them, who looked like a farm boy, had chosen to stay with their horses in the stables.

'Sir Hugh, is there any other place?' she said again.

'Oh yes.' Corbett, who had been staring around, stepped closer. 'Sister Marie, I thank you for your help, but I need to see the jetty, the boat and the carp pond where Sister Constantia was murdered. Once I have seen that, I need to view her corpse.'

'But Sir Hugh, Constantia was a lady, a nun, a woman consecrated to God.'

'All true.' Ranulf now joined his master. Marie tried not to flinch at the smell of sweat and leather and above all at that feeling of danger; these were royal clerks but they were also men of war. 'We need to see her now.' Ranulf pushed his face closer. 'Constantia may have been all you say she was, but she was also the victim of murder. We must investigate that.'

'But there's no hurry,' Corbett declared. 'First.' He pointed at the soaring foursquare tower that reared up high above the trees. A red-brick donjon with its turreted top. 'What is that?'

'Devil's Tower, Sir Hugh. These lands were once owned by Geoffrey de Mandeville, Earl of Essex. It was in reparation for his many sins – and they were deeply scarlet – that they were given to the Benedictine order. You have heard of Mandeville, Sir Hugh?'

'Of course, of course.' Corbett narrowed his eyes to study the tower's crenellated top, then glanced at Ranulf. 'Geoffrey de Mandeville, Earl of Essex, was regarded by many as the devil incarnate. Over two hundred years ago, a savage civil war raged in England.' He crossed himself. 'Pray God that never happens again. Anyway, they called it "the season of perpetual winter", "the age when God and his saints slept". Mandeville certainly didn't. He used the breakdown of the king's peace to terrorise East Anglia. No one and nothing was safe. Churches were pillaged, abbeys sacked, monasteries burned. Mandeville died excommunicate. He was denied burial in consecrated ground, so his coffin had to be hung from the branches of a tree, stuck between heaven and earth.'

'Is it still?'

'No, Ranulf, the Templars, God bless them, eventually accepted the coffin for burial at their church in London. So,' Corbett added, 'the tower remains.'

'It has to,' Sister Marie declared. 'It's part of the land grant. Every evening Sister Fidelis, our sacristan, fires the beacon light, a sign, a help and a comfort to travellers, especially when the mist swirls in. They say,' she added darkly, 'that the beacon also summons Mandeville, who comes riding up from hell on Satan's own horse.'

'Do they now?' Corbett laughed.

'They also say that his spirit, like a demon rattling in a bottle, haunts the tower. Anyway,' she sighed, 'gentlemen, let us view the jetty and the boat.'

As they walked on across the grounds, the gardens, herb plots, flower beds and vegetable furrows gave way to a broad stretch of uncultivated ground. Corbett reckoned they must be approaching the curtain wall. The Devil's Tower now stood to their right. He stopped and looked back, as if memorising where he'd been. He idly wondered if any of the nuns they'd glimpsed was Megotta the mummers' girl, now disguised as Sister Isabella Seymour. However, that would have to wait. He had already planned what he intended. He and his companions had risen early. Corbett had felt a little stiff after the previous day's exertions. Nevertheless, they attended the dawn mass, broke their fast, then, once ready, rode briskly through the city and out towards St Sulpice. Oh yes, the day was planned. This recent murder was not a distraction; it might well be part of the mystery around this so-called House of God. Corbett was determined to immerse himself in this convent, to capture its very essence, and only then would he ask to see Megotta.

He glanced up at the sky. The weather was fine. The sullen grey clouds had broken and a weak sun provided some light and meagre warmth, a welcome relief to the freezing temperature and face-stinging breeze.

'Sir Hugh,' Ranulf murmured, 'I think Sister Marie is getting cold.' Corbett apologised, and they hurried through a copse of trees, following a path down to the broad carp pond and the slightly raised wooden jetty.

Corbett walked to the edge and stared across the water. He had seen such a facility in many a manor, a means of providing fresh fish for a truly delicious meal. Carp could be easily managed, fostered and fed to a full ripeness. The pond was certainly wide enough, and would be at least four yards deep in the centre. Weeds and other growth provided nourishment for the fish, which grew so fat and plump they could be easily caught.

Corbett hitched his cloak about him and walked onto the jetty. This was extremely well built, with sturdy wooden pillars and broad planks specially honed and treated to provide a good grip underfoot. To the left of it, embedded into the bank and half covered by water, was a small sluice gate. He went across and crouched down. The sluice was a thick wooden slat reinforced with iron plates either side and managed by a pulley, lever and the toughest cord. It looked well oiled, and he reckoned it could be easily raised to allow more water from the underground spring that undoubtedly fed this pond. Water levels would rise and seep into the soil around. In winter this could pose a problem, but a strong summer sun would soon bring the water under control. On the right side of the jetty were two stout bum boats, well fashioned with three benches, the oars held fast in their locks. Corbett rose, went across and studied each of these before turning and beckoning Sister Marie to join him. She hurried, lifting her gown as she walked daintily along the jetty.

'Sir Hugh?'

'Which boat did Constantia use?'

Sister Marie pointed to the boat that was moored further along the jetty. She and Corbett went as close as they could.

'So,' Corbett murmured, 'Constantia used this boat.' He paused. 'And the second?'

'Oh, that was chained and padlocked, the benches covered by canvas sheets, the oars stowed away in the boathouse. Many of our community, including Stigand our principal labourer, will confirm that the second boat had not been used, not even disturbed.' Corbett turned and smiled at the nun. 'Stowed away? That's how you described the oars. You must have some knowledge of boats to use a phrase like that.'

Sister Marie laughed prettily behind fluttering fingers. 'My husband, now gone to God, was a master mariner. John Abingdon sailed his cog out of the Cinque ports, though we lived quite a distance away in a house overlooking Southampton Water.' She laughed again. 'Sir Hugh, I must confess, even though my husband was a sailor, water frightens me.'

'Even more so now,' Corbett replied, gesturing at the boat. 'A gruesome, cruel death.'

'You can see where myself and another sister scrubbed the bloodstains clear, or at least we tried to.'

'Yes, yes, the blood must have dried and become

ingrained in the wood. Sister Marie, please join my good friend Ranulf whilst I reflect on what I am seeing.' Corbett clambered into the boat and sat down on the middle bench. He stretched out and grasped the oars, though of course he couldn't swing them out, trying to imagine what had happened in this cold, bleak place. The assassin, he reasoned, must have climbed into the boat to be with his or her intended victim. He or she must have sat facing her, then lunged forward with a dagger, a blow direct to the heart. But then what? The mooring ropes must have been loosened, the boat freed to be rowed across, but surely not by a dead woman? If the killer had guided the boat out into the centre of the pond, how did he or she get back? In such freezing weather, swimming would be highly dangerous, and someone soaked to the skin and shivering could hardly walk unnoticed through a busy convent.

Corbett glanced up. Ranulf and Sister Marie had now left the jetty. Ranulf caught his eye and raised a hand. Corbett responded, then went back to leaning on the oars, staring at the mooring ropes.

'Of course,' he whispered to himself, 'you must have got into this boat knowing you were going to leave once you had murdered your victim. So you did, but you made sure the dead woman's hands were on the oars. Rigor mortis would soon set in, the fingers turning hard, a process the freezing cold would intensify. So your victim was sitting there slumped with a dagger to the heart. You got out.' He rose and stepped back onto the jetty and stared down at the mooring rope. 'You loosened that, but then?' He shook his head. 'The pond has no current. Wait a while, wait a while, I have not asked a very important question. Sister Marie,' he called. 'Why should Constantia go out onto the carp pond so early in the morning? In other words, what was she doing here?'

Sister Marie walked back onto the jetty, grasping one of the poles. 'They claim it is easier to capture carp at the beginning of the day, and of course the kitchen needs to gut and clean it and then cook it for the table. It's all in a day's work. Carp swimming in the pond in the morning should be swimming in sauce by the evening, or so the cooks tell me.'

Corbett smiled at the lilt in the nun's fresh voice. 'But if that was the case,' he retorted, 'surely she would have taken nets, a line, a hook, possibly even some bait. She would fish for one carp, yes?'

'Two at the very most, Sir Hugh. But from what I gather, only one was needed that day. As for the fishing tackle, this was in the boat but removed along with poor Constantia's corpse.'

'Thank you, thank you. Now to the main problem. This pond has no current, so how did that boat get out there?' He turned, swiftly scrutinising everything before going back to the sluice gate. He crouched down, undid the rope tied in a figure-of-eight knot. He then grasped the lever and slowly turned it. He heard Sister Marie's exclamation as she hurried to investigate. Corbett, however, continued winching back the cord, watching the sluice gate lift and, as it did, a swirl of gushing water ebbed out. He observed the ripple effect strengthen and spread out across the lake and beneath the jetty. He quickly reassured Sister Marie that all was well, then carefully lowered the sluice gate, making sure it stayed in place and tying the rope with his own special knot. He got to his feet clapping his hands against the cold, pleased that he had at least resolved one small part of this mystery. He did not share his conclusions with Ranulf and Sister Marie; he needed first, at the appropriate time, to test his hypothesis and so turn it into a strong probability.

'Master.' Ranulf stamped his feet. 'Are we finished here?'

'Yes, for the moment, but one thing nags me.' Corbett gestured back at the jetty. 'Why? Why the masque, the mummery, the drama? Ranulf, you are a dagger man. If you wanted to kill a member of this community, surely you would wait in ambush or strike in some dark lonely corner?'

'Yes, yes,' Ranulf agreed. 'Why all this play-acting and mystery. Stabbing someone to death on a boat in the middle of a carp pond?'

Corbett smiled at Sister Marie, who was staring at him curiously. 'Sister Marie, I know you are not a dagger man, but wouldn't you agree?'

'Yes, Sir Hugh, and several members of the community have voiced the same. Why here? Does it have some significance?'

'Well if it has,' Corbett whispered, 'it fully escapes me.' He stretched himself and winced; the previous day's conflict had jarred his body as well as his mind. He took a deep breath and looked down at Sister Marie's sweet face.

'My lady, I am sorry, but we really must view Constantia's corpse.'

They left the jetty and quickly made their way back to the convent. They arrived at the small chapel, a beautiful jewel of a building, founded and raised according to the new ideas and designs now sweeping northern France. The cemetery, a well-tended stretch of God's Acre, lay to the south of the church, with the death house, a grey-brick building with narrow lancets and a red-tiled roof, in its centre. Sister Marie took the keys fastened to the belt around her waist, opened the smartly painted door and led them into a sombre chamber.

Lime-washed walls gleamed in the torchlight, decorated with only a crucifix and a broad painted cloth depicting Christ's descent into hell and his harrowing of the underworld. The chamber held eight tables, all slightly sloping. One of these was covered by a gold-edged purple pall. Corbett waited while Sister Marie removed the cover, then the white sheet beneath, so that Constantia's plump but aged corpse lay naked for inspection. He approached the table, crossed himself, then stared down at the blue-black wound deep in the left side of the chest.

'Look, Ranulf,' he whispered. 'A true killing blow direct to the heart. Constantia must have died in a few breaths.' He glimpsed the long-bladed bone-handled dagger that lay beside the corpse. He picked this up and examined it carefully.

'Mother Abbess asked for the knife to be buried with her,' Sister Marie declared, 'so that when the resurrection of the body occurs, Constantia can leave the grave holding the means of her murder to demand justice against the damned soul who used it.'

'At the final resurrection,' Corbett retorted, 'Constantia will join a multitude demanding justice, but God doesn't want us to wait that long. Justice has its own force, its own compulsion; it will not be thwarted. Rest assured of that, Sister Marie. God's ways are not our ways, but they are His ways and so they cannot and will not be impeded. So what do we have here? A nun, a kitchener, who went out at first light to catch a carp so it could be cleaned, cooked and made truly delicious before the sun set. She fully intended to fish, but on the way down to that jetty suppose she met her assassin. You can imagine it would be difficult to see, two nuns dressed in dark brown making their way through the swirling mist. Constantia must have been comfortable with her companion. She apparently made no objection, no alarm was sounded, nothing at all until Sister Fidelis glimpsed that corpse in the boat in the centre of the lake. Sooner or later I will establish how Constantia was murdered, though the why and the wherefore will be more difficult to establish.'

He took one last look at the corpse, scrutinising it delicately but very carefully, examining the wrists and ankles, the back of the head and the shrivelled breasts.

He could find no trace of a blow, or the binding of any ligature. 'There's nothing,' he whispered, 'nothing at all to suggest that Constantia was forcibly restrained. So the assassin must have drawn very close and stabbed, swift as a lunging viper. Ah well.' He paused at a knock on the door, and a servant came hurrying in.

'Sister Marie, Sister Marie,' she gasped. 'You must come. Abbess Eleanor demands it. Sir Hugh,' she turned to the clerks, 'you and your companion are also summoned.'

'Are we now? Well if that's the case, let us not keep the lady abbess waiting.'

They left the mortuary, going round the chapel, which fronted one side of the great cloisters. The chapter house stood directly opposite across the cloister garth, in the centre of which a straggling bush, all spiked and rambling, displayed clusters of spring roses. The inside of the building was well lit by large glass-filled windows on either side, some of which were exquisitely decorated to depict scenes from the life of Scholastica, the sainted Benedict's sister. The far wall was rounded like the apse in a church. In the centre stood a throne-like chair flanked by three heavy oaken stalls either side. Abbess Eleanor had already taken her seat on the throne. The leading officers of the convent were seated either side.

Corbett and Ranulf bowed to the abbess, then sat down on the two cushioned chairs just below the dais on which the throne and stalls were situated. Sister Marie, fluttering around like a butterfly, whispered that if they wished to eat and drink, they could do so from the buttery table at the side, but both clerks refused. A servant who acted as porter closed the door of the chapter house from the outside. Corbett glanced at Ranulf, a gentle warning to remain prudent.

The abbess sat erect, hands on her lap, head slightly turned. Once she heard the door click fast, she sat back in her huge ornate chair and smiled thinly at her two visitors. Abbess Eleanor, Corbett concluded, was a harsh, rather imperious woman. He glanced at the other nuns. They all looked the same, with their starched white wimples, brown veils and earth-coloured hoods. They were strong-faced, sharp-eyed women who viewed the world as a distraction or even a temptation to be endured rather than enjoyed. The only exception to this austere group was Sister Marie. Indeed, she sat smiling so serenely that Corbett wondered if she might be slightly fey. He studied the rest as Prioress Margaret introduced them.

Margaret herself was a tall, lanky woman, thin-featured, with long, bony fingers so that her hands looked almost claw-like. She explained how, subject to Mother Abbess, she administered the convent, with a special responsibility for novices. She then named her companions. Sister Marie, Lady of the Halls; Sister Perpetua, in charge of the gardens; Sister Callista, who looked after the guest house and all their visitors; and Sister Agatha, the young-faced infirmarian. Corbett studied the latter and wondered whether they had met before. Agatha was pretty but bland, as if hiding behind her schooled expression. Lady Margaret, however, was now in full flow. She apologised that one of her companions was missing: Sister Fidelis, the sacristan. The prioress's annoyance at this was obvious.

'Does anyone,' she snapped, 'have any idea where Fidelis might be?'

Sister Marie spoke up. 'I believe she may be tending to the beacon light in Devil's Tower.'

'If that's the case,' the prioress retorted, 'send someone to fetch her here now.' Marie did so, hastening out of the chapter house before returning to her seat.

Once she was assured of silence, Abbess Eleanor lifted a gloved hand, around which she had wound ivory Ave beads.

'Sir Hugh, I appreciate that you are here on certain business. Rest assured that I and the senior ladies in this convent will do all in our power to assist. I understand you have already visited both the jetty as well as poor Constantia's corpse in the death house?'

'I have.'

'And?'

'Mother Abbess, Constantia was stabbed to death. A quick, deep thrust. She must have died immediately. I suspect her murderer then opened the sluice gate to create an eddy. On reflection, I also believe the assassin did more. Constantia was apparently intent on snaring a carp for the convent table. She would have taken with her a long-poled net to achieve this, yes?' A murmur of agreement answered him. 'Very well,' he continued. 'The assassin untied the boat and used the long netting pole to push it as far along the jetty as possible. He or she then threw the net into the boat, which was driven forward by the eddy created by raising the sluice gate. The assassin probably waited for a while, then closed the sluice gate and left.' Corbett shrugged. 'Of course I could be wrong. More importantly, I cannot lay any allegation against anyone. However, Constantia was murdered; her death was unlawful and malicious. Whoever was responsible should hang.'

His words were greeted with silence. Abbess Eleanor leaned over and whispered heatedly in the prioress's ear.

Corbett turned to Ranulf. 'Remember what is said here; make a good accurate record.' Ranulf nodded his agreement.

'If it would help, Sir Hugh,' Prioress Margaret spoke up, 'Sister Fidelis believed that when she was on the jetty, she glimpsed something untoward, something amiss, but for the life of her she couldn't recall what it was.'

'That's just typical of Fidelis.' Perpetua, the gardener, shouted so loudly Ranulf bowed his head to hide his smile. This nun was definitely short of hearing.

'What do you mean, typical?' Corbett demanded, eager to divert attention from Ranulf.

'God be praised,' Abbess Eleanor replied, 'but Fidelis prides herself on her powers of observation and memory. Indeed, quite recently she claimed to have met Sister Marie some time ago.'

'And I assure you, Sir Hugh she certainly didn't.' The Lady of the Halls smiled. 'I am a widow who joined this community two years ago. I had never met anyone here before I arrived. Anyway—'

'Ladies,' Corbett declared sharply, cutting Sister Marie short, 'I am not here for convent gossip. Sister Constantia, your friend, your companion, lies murdered. Does anyone here know why she should be killed in such a way and in such a place? Did she have any enemies? Was she caught up in anything that would explain her brutal sudden death?'

Again, silence.

'Another matter,' Corbett continued remorselessly. 'Mother Abbess, I know of one novice, perhaps even two, who have mysteriously disappeared from St Sulpice: Katherine Ingoldsby and Isolda Manning. The only connection between them is that they were both related to Ralph Manning, a clerk in the Secret Chancery at Westminster.'

'If you are keeping a tally,' the abbess intervened, 'there is a third and most recent. Sister Isabella Seymour was last seen yesterday evening. However, this morning she is not to be found in her cell and, despite our best efforts, we cannot find her.'

Corbett kept his face impassive.

'Mother Abbess,' Ranulf spoke up sharply, 'you must have heard the rumours, I mean about Manning.'

'We certainly have,' Abbess Eleanor replied. 'Sir Hugh, tradesmen flock to St Sulpice, they bring us gossip. We have heard the news about Manning's death, and about your duel with Lancaster's clerk. Please accept our congratulations. Thanks be to God you emerged as the victor.' The abbess folded back the broad silken cuffs of her gown. 'Sir Hugh, you talk of young women going missing from St Sulpice, but you must realise we are an open convent, not a prison; a house of God, not Newgate or the Fleet. Young ladies come here for a myriad of reasons.' She smiled icily. 'Nor must you believe what you are told about this situation. Ralph Manning is now dead. He came here looking for both his beloved and his sister. Matters are not as simple as they appear.' The abbess turned and beckoned Sister Agatha. The young nun rose from her stall and came to stand close to Corbett.

'Tell him,' Prioress Margaret barked. 'Tell our royal clerk who you really are.'

'Sir Hugh.' Agatha tapped the clerk on the back of his hand. 'Look at me. What do you see?'

'A pretty face,' Corbett replied. 'Indeed, a lovely face, though you have been crying, I can see that. I am sorry for your grief over Constantia.'

'I thank you, Sir Hugh, for what you did.'

'What do you mean?'

'For avenging Ralph Manning's good name. I heard what happened. The slurs cast on his reputation.'

'And why should that concern you?'

'Look at me, Sir Hugh.'

Corbett studied Agatha's face even more intently. 'God be praised,' he whispered. 'You look like—'

'Ralph Manning, Sir Hugh? Of course I do. I am his sister Isolda. Or so I was in a previous life.' The nun turned, bowed to her superiors then crouched like a penitent next to Corbett, a pleading look in her eyes. 'I know about you, Sir Hugh. Ralph was always singing your praises. I am very grateful for the way you championed him. I know you will hunt down and catch his assassin. You will, won't you?'

'I promise I will see justice done. But you, mistress, why the mystery?'

'I was – I still am – deeply ashamed of what I did. In truth, a hideous sin, malicious and deeply grievous. I could not bear to meet Ralph. Every time I did, I would catch his soul-haunting stare. I felt as if I was dead to him. Indeed, we vowed never to meet, yet my guilt remained. I could tolerate it no longer. In the end, it was an easy step. I consulted with Abbess Eleanor, I assumed the veil, took a new name, and in reparation . . .' her voice quavered, 'I became infirmarian. I can serve the sick. I know something of physick and I am skilled in the properties of herbs. For the rest of the world, and that included Ralph, Isolda Manning lay dead and buried, and Sister Agatha emerged out of the dark.'

'What you hear is true,' Prioress Margaret sang out. 'Isolda Manning is no longer here. Sister Agatha, however, is an excellent infirmarian, skilled in all aspects.'

'Sir Hugh,' Agatha got to her feet, 'again I thank you for what you did. Please accept me for what I am. No longer Isolda Manning, but Sister Agatha, infirmarian at St Sulpice.' She turned and walked back to her seat.

Corbett leaned forward, rubbing his hands together

as he stared down at the polished elm floor. 'And Katherine Ingoldsby, Lady Abbess?'

'Sir Hugh, you must know that Katherine came here sick in mind and body after she lost her child. A sad creature whom Ralph Manning regularly visited, sometimes openly, on other occasions secretly, or so we suspect. I cannot speak for her. Perhaps her wits dulled, perhaps her mind turned fey, but one morning she was gone. Of course we searched both within and without, but to no avail.'

'And her possessions?'

'We are a convent in the Benedictine tradition; we try to live as poorly as we can. Personal possessions are few. Small keepsakes. Items that can be tied up in a fardel. Sir Hugh, you have walked St Sulpice: it is open, the walls can be scaled, doors can be opened. Once you leave the convent, it is a short walk into the city, and of course, once there, it is easy to hide, to disappear, to vanish.'

'But what would Katherine do, where would she go?'

'God knows,' Prioress Margaret retorted. 'Your guess is as good as anyone's.'

'And you have heard no more about her?'

'Nothing.'

'And Isabella Seymour?'

'We still have to investigate, to search.'

'What was she like?'

'A little wayward, even provocative in her mimicry, but we liked her. Sister Isabella deeply amused us. She certainly seemed happy enough. Perhaps like others, she felt constrained, constricted.' The abbess shrugged. 'Sir Hugh, you are most welcome to visit her cell. Speak to anyone you wish.' Again she played with the cuffs of her gown. 'You see, novices who begin their lives here often change their minds. They come full of good intentions, but then flinch at the demands of the religious life. Some leave formally: they come, they thank me and they depart. Others just vanish. If you wish, you can question two ladies who left the city for St Sulpice and then returned.'

'I would appreciate that, Mother Abbess. If you can provide their names . . .'

'Agnes Sorrell, who lives along Rolls Passage off Cheapside, and Mathilda Blackbourne, whose house can be found on the corner of Tapestry Lane in Farringdon ward.'

Corbett glanced at Ranulf. 'You have that information?' His henchman faithfully repeated what the abbess had said. Corbett turned and stared at Lady Eleanor, who coolly held his stare. The abbess was undoubtedly haughty, arrogant and used to having her own way. A woman confident of herself and the world she lived in. Nevertheless, Corbett sensed that not all was well with this powerful lady. She betrayed her hidden mood in sudden glances, and abrupt changes of expression. He believed she was fretful, uneasy.

'I thank you—' He was interrupted by a frantic knocking on the chapter house door. Sister Marie hurried to answer it. She exchanged hasty whispers with a servant, then slammed the door shut, leaning against it.

'Mother Abbess,' she gasped. 'Some of the sisters went looking for Fidelis, as Lady Margaret asked. The door leading to the steps of the Devil's Tower is locked. The good sisters have pounded on that door, shouting her name, but Fidelis has not replied. Moreover, they have done a thorough search of the convent. She is not to be found. She must be in the tower, and something must have happened to her.'

Abbess Eleanor rose. She declared the meeting ended and asked Corbett and Ranulf for their help. The two clerks immediately agreed and followed the prioress and Sister Marie out across to Devil's Tower.

Someone had already summoned the burly Stigand and his comitatus of labourers, who, dressed in their soil-stained leathers, stood in the stairwell of the tower waiting to be told what to do. At Corbett's bidding, they pounded the door, shouting Fidelis's name. As they did so, Corbett gazed round the cavernous stairwell. He went across and opened the door to the narrow jakes closet, no more than an empty cupboard with space enough to squat. He closed the door, then glanced down and glimpsed an iron grating beneath the rushes strewn on the floor. He kicked away the thick, dry coating and stared at the grating, just over two yards long and the same in width.

'What is this?' he asked.

'A relict from Mandeville's days,' Marie replied. 'They call it Hell's Pit.'

'It certainly is,' Ranulf declared. He squatted down and pulled back the grating. It came up slowly, the dirt-encrusted hinges creaking. Corbett crouched and peered down into the darkness.

'You are correct, Ranulf, it is indeed a hell pit. Captives would be lowered by ropes, God help those poor souls,' he murmured. 'Thrust into the darkness, with only what was thrown down at them to eat and drink.'

'Sir Hugh,' Marie demanded. 'What shall we do now?'

Corbett and Ranulf replaced the grating and ordered Stigand and his comrades to fetch a log. Once they had done so, Ranulf supervised the battering that ensued. A constant crashing against the thick, heavy door. Now and again they would pause. Sister Marie and the other nuns went to stand outside the tower. Conversation was futile, as the crashing and banging became incessant. Eventually Prioress Margaret dismissed the nuns, saying their presence was not necessary. Corbett, swathed in his cloak, also left. He just hoped the battering would not take much longer.

Outside, he glanced up. The day was strengthening and he wondered what it would bring. He was about to take his Ave beads out of his purse when he heard the sound of wood cracking, creaking and splintering. Shortly afterwards, the door collapsed, wrenched back on its hinges. Curses and cries made Corbett hurry back into the stairwell, shouting at Ranulf to clear the place. His henchman ushered the labourers out, asking the prioress to order stoups of ale for them from the buttery.

Once he was assured that no one would follow him, Corbett stepped over the broken door and stared down at Sister Fidelis, nothing more than a crumpled heap, her head and face one bloody wound. She lay sprawled like a broken toy. Corbett noticed the vomit, and pinched his nostrils at the foul smell. He knelt down beside the corpse and crossed himself.

'Master.' Ranulf stood in the doorway. 'The prioress is now maintaining order, but they've glimpsed Fidelis, they suspect what's happened.'

'They mustn't see this,' Corbett murmured over his shoulder. 'This poor woman fell; as she did so, the shock to her humours must have made her vomit.' He glanced around and noticed a stout, heavy key lying close by. He picked this up and asked Ranulf to test it in the lock of the ruined door. Ranulf did so and reported that it fitted, although the lock like everything else was severely damaged.

Corbett rose to his feet and murmured a prayer for the dead woman. Fidelis now looked so pathetic. A busy little nun, her life had been extinguished as swift and as sure as any bright candle flame. She had suffered a ghastly death. He crossed himself once again. 'I do wonder,' he whispered, 'if you can hear me, Fidelis. If your soul still hovers close. I promise you I will avenge your death, so let me begin.'

He touched the hilt of his dagger and began to climb the steep spiral staircase. It was an arduous task; the steps were high, clustered close, and they wound around in quite dizzying turns. There was a rope hold fastened to the wall. Nevertheless, the ascent was difficult. Corbett felt himself sweating, and he winced at the stiffness in his legs. Now and again the steps paused at a narrow platform built just beneath a lancet window, nothing more than a place where a bowman could loose one shaft after another.

At last he reached the top. He clambered up a set of wooden stairs and pulled himself through the hatch, the trapdoor flung back, then crouched to catch his breath. Once calm, he rose and walked gingerly to lean against the battlements and stare out. The tower, which seemed to rise to a lofty height, provided a clear view of the surrounding countryside and, despite the mist, the lights of the city.

He turned slowly, steadying himself against the battlements. The top of the tower was broad, the ground covered in a thick carpet of sand and pebbles to provide a firm grip underfoot. The beacon light, a massive lanternhorn, stood on a high-legged table. On a shelf beneath this was tinder, small flasks of oil, bowl and knives, all the materials needed to prune the wick and fire the huge tallow candle inside the large four-sided lantern. The beacon light, with its opaque glass panels, was a veritable work of art, and Corbett recalled being able to detect its glow even from the heart of the city. Next to the table stood a wicker basket, the lid firmly closed and tied with a secure knot in its clasp. He peered down and realised it contained fresh candles for the beacon. He patted the basket absent-mindedly, then walked slowly around the tower. In the far corner was a small table and stool; apparently Fidelis would sit there wrapped in her cloak, which now hung from a hook driven into one of the crenellations. Corbett also noticed a linen parcel containing breadcrumbs and cheese fragments, as well as a small wine skin and goblet, both now emptied. The crows, ravens and other birds had also feasted, but apparently with no ill effect.

'No, no,' he murmured to himself. 'Fidelis did not die here, but down those steps.' He took a deep breath. 'So you came up here, Fidelis.' He paused as the wind whipped his hood. 'Are you there?' he continued. 'Do you ride the air? Do you hover where your last breaths were taken? God rest you, Fidelis, you came up here, you enjoyed it. You used the excuse of trimming and tending the beacon to revel in a cup of wine and a few tasty morsels to eat.' He glanced at the trapdoor. 'So what truly happened here? I suspect you liked to be alone. You locked yourself in, then climbed those steps. You reached the top, where you rested and enjoyed your refreshments.'

He paused in his whispering as he heard footsteps. Ranulf, sweating and cursing, clambered through the hatch onto the tower. For a while, he just sat and fought for breath before pulling himself up.

'Sir Hugh, a steep climb.'

'And an even steeper fall. What is happening below?'

'Rest assured, master, the prioress is laying about her, ordering this and that. She has a tongue like a whip. And here?'

'Here, Ranulf, you have nothing remarkable. A jug of wine, a goblet, and a piece of linen with crumbs and scraps of food.' Corbett picked up both jug and cup and sniffed at them. 'And the birds of the air can have them.' He paused. Someone else was coming up the steps. Both he and Ranulf drew their daggers, then relaxed as Sister Marie, veil slightly askew, pushed her head through the gap and grinned mischievously.

'Sirs, I assure you this is a terrible climb, one I always find difficult. God knows what happened here.' She paused to grasp Ranulf's hand, and he pulled her gently through the hatch. The nun tried to maintain her dignity, dusting herself down and carefully adjusting her veil as she walked across to the battlements.

'A fine view,' she murmured. 'Fidelis loved to come up here, caught, so she said, between heaven and earth. Poor woman. She had her weaknesses, which I am sure the Lord will ignore.' She turned and pointed at the small buttery table, and was about to continue when Prioress Margaret and Sister Agatha emerged onto the tower roof. The prioress seemed not the least discommoded by the climb, but full of what was happening below. Agatha caught Corbett's gaze, smiled and gently rolled her eyes heavenwards.

'One question.' Corbett raised his voice against the chatter. 'It would appear Fidelis came up here as accustomed. She then seems to have left in a hurry, grasping the key to the door below, and running down those steps. It is hardly surprising that she tripped and fell to her death; the steps are hard and sharp edged. They would cut as deep as any dagger.'

'Your question, Sir Hugh?'

'An obvious one, Lady Prioress. Why would she be in such a hurry?'

'She was late for chapter,' Sister Marie replied. 'We did send servants to call her name, to seek her out.'

Corbett nodded in agreement, then, accompanied by Ranulf, went back down the steps. He walked cautiously, asking Ranulf to study every step as well as the wall alongside. They moved slowly in their careful scrutiny, but could find nothing that would explain Fidelis's fatal fall. They reached the bottom. Fidelis's corpse had long been removed and the effects of her fall, the blood and the vomit, thoroughly scrubbed away. The air was still sharp with the reek of pinewood, the astringent used to cleanse the stairwell. Corbett scrutinised the jakes cupboard but found nothing amiss. He gazed once more round the stairwell, then went out to join Ranulf, who was sitting on the battering log chatting to Chanson. The Clerk of the Stables looked sleepy eyed and, despite Ranulf's teasing, he asserted that he'd seen nothing amiss.

'A beautiful place,' he murmured. 'They have a fine stable and the palfreys are well trained and obedient.'

Corbett heard him out, then adjusted his cloak and stared up at the sky, now a light blue and scored with broad wisps of white cloud.

'An accident, Sir Hugh?'

'I would like to say so, Ranulf, but,' he tapped the side of his head, 'here in my mind there is a nagging doubt. It's like the yapping of a guard dog in the dead of night. An irritation. It might be nothing, or it might be that great danger lurks nearby.'

'Sir Hugh! Sir Hugh!' A servitor, her apple-cheeked face flushed with excitement, came hurrying up, one hand lifting her smock, the other flailing the air. 'Sir Hugh.' She gasped, fighting for breath. 'Abbess Eleanor needs to speak to you on a most urgent matter.'

# PART THREE

Turbeville attempted to send a certain letter to the King of France.

Megotta stirred, moaned, then opened her eyes. She ached and throbbed from head to toe. She couldn't move her arms, these being firmly lashed above her head. She twisted and turned on the mattress and, despite the pain, tried to look around. The chamber, cellar or pit where she was imprisoned was pitch dark except for the pools of light thrown by small lanternhorns placed around the rank-smelling room. She peered through the murk, lifting her head to get a better view. She recalled that hideous moment in the stairwell of Devil's Tower. The heavy black sacking floating like a cloud to cover her. The desperate struggle, followed by that jarring blow to her head that sent her into a fitful faint. Afterwards, the nightmare of lying in a cart and listening to the crack of a whip, the clop of horses' hooves, the boards jolting beneath her.

She drew a deep breath as she tried to calm herself. She must take stock of where she was. She heard sounds.

Pools of water seeped across the hard-packed earth and, despite the rank odour, she was sure she could smell the tang of the river: salt, brine and the pervasive stench of rotting fish. She again recalled that jolting, jarring ride. She must have been taken into London, close to the Thames. She'd heard voices, names shouted – Sherwin, Brasby and others – noisy chatter in the slang of the streets, the patois of the slums along the river. The word 'Picardy' was repeated time and again. Was this a ship, or the name of one of the rifflers who had abducted her?

She closed her eyes. What had happened to Manning? Why had he stopped coming to visit her at St Sulpice? Was he behind the present mischief? Who were these people? Why had they abducted her? What did they intend? She feared the worst. She had travelled the roads long enough and had heard numerous stories about young women being kidnapped and sold to this brothel or that whorehouse. Would she be kept in London, or put aboard some cog berthed along one of London's quaysides?

She strained at her bonds, then tensed as she heard female voices chattering in French. There was a cry, an exclamation. Doors were thrown open, then banged shut. As she was wondering what was happening, the door to her cell was kicked open. Two men, dark figures against the light. One came across and moved the lantern closer to Megotta. He leaned forward, a sweaty bearded face with fleshy lips and watery eyes. He drew his dagger and cut her robe, slicing the fabric so he could pull it free off her, then roughly removed her linen shift and padded loincloth. He knelt back on his heels and studied her, mouth slightly open, eyes blinking. Then he stretched across and, ignoring her pleas and cries, began to feel her body, squeezing her breasts, poking between her thighs. 'Very nice,' he slurred. 'Look at the way she squirms. These full round breasts and long legs. She will be a fine ride and I intend to enjoy a gallop.' He abruptly lunged forward and smashed his fist into her cheek.

'Stay still while I prepare to mount.' He stumbled to his feet and, at his companion's urging, began to undo the points on his hose.

Corbett and Ranulf sat before the chancery desk in Abbess Eleanor's elegant chamber. A well-furnished room with wood-panelled walls, soft Turkey rugs, chafing dishes, and a merry fire leaping in the broad hearth. The walls above the panelling were painted a delicate light pink and decorated with small triptychs and other devotional images. To the right of the abbess, a lectern for the Book of the Gospels, and on her left, a carved lavarium with snow-white jug, bowl and towel. The two clerks had already washed their hands in the perfumed water. Ranulf could still catch the fragrance on his fingers.

The abbess did not look as calm or as confident as she had done earlier. She leaned her elbows on the table, sighed noisily, then picked up two scraps of parchment and pushed them across.

'Sir Hugh, of your kindness please read these. The one on your right is the first.'

Corbett picked up the scrap of stained, weathered vellum. The words upon it were written in a distinctive bright red ink: *Across the water in a borrowed boat towards realms unknown, so shall judgement be awarded.* He read it again and passed it to Ranulf, then picked up the second scrap: *Down the tower a fall like Lucifer, never to rise again, and so shall judgement be awarded.* He held up both messages to make out the signature scrawled faintly in the bottom corner of each.

'MM,' he murmured. 'Mother Midnight.' He glanced up. 'Lady Abbess, Mother Midnight is a whore-mistress who owns a tavern or brothel known as the Queen of the Night. A place for high-class courtesans who cater to men who really should know better. What could such a woman have to do with a convent like St Sulpice? Or indeed, as the messages attest, with the two murders committed here?'

'Sir Hugh, I don't know, that is why I am now pleading for your help.'

'The messages are important,' Corbett declared. 'I will keep them and scrutinise them again: they refer directly to the two murders here. Sister Constantia out across the water in that boat, and Sister Fidelis falling to her death in Devil's Tower. I would say it's logical that the person who wrote these messages carried out the murders. When did they appear?'

'I cannot say, except that they were pinned to my door shortly before or shortly after each of the murders.'

'So it must be someone here,' Corbett murmured. 'Somebody who can move around, leave a message pinned, then vanish.'

'Or it could be a joke.' Ranulf spoke up.

Corbett turned. 'A joke?'

'Master, the murder of Sister Constantia was complex, very mysterious; it would take some plotting and careful preparation. The same is even more true of Fidelis's fall: there was no one in that tower apart from the victim.'

'So?'

'Constantia was definitely murdered, but there is a very strong possibility that Fidelis's death was an unfortunate accident. In other words, we have two tragic deaths here and someone exploits this by mischievously pinning notes to the abbess's door.'

'It's possible,' Corbett agreed. 'Both messages were supposedly signed by Mother Midnight, yet she lives miles away. In addition, I doubt very much whether she would visit this hallowed place. Even if she did, she would certainly not sign any threatening note. So you believe,' he pointed to the scraps of parchment, 'this is simply the work of some mischief-maker taking advantage of what has happened?'

'In a word, yes.'

'Is that possible?' Corbett turned back to the abbess.

'Sir Hugh, we are a community of many souls. A few of these would take to such mischief as a bird to flying. I do agree with you. Why were the notes signed "Mother Midnight"? If you confront the whore-mistress, which I am sure you will, the woman will strongly deny any involvement in what's happening here. Wouldn't you agree?'

'Of course.'

The abbess leaned across the table. 'Sir Hugh, Master Ranulf, come and stay at St Sulpice. Our guest house is empty. Our kitchens serve delicious food. Our grounds are delightful and, in the main, there is harmony both within and without. You are royal clerks. You can walk the convent grounds, speak to our sisters, grasp the very essence of this place. Above all, you can resolve these killings.'

'My lady,' Corbett bowed, 'I thank you for your most generous offer, which I gratefully accept. I shall move my baggage and that of my companions from St Bartholomew's to here. I shall confront these mysteries and, God willing, resolve them. However, we must be aware of the real danger of our situation. First, a killer prowls this convent: who and why?' He shrugged. 'That's the mystery. Second, I do believe our assassin will strike again, or at least try to. So,' he held up the two scraps of parchment, 'I shall keep these, and should there be any more such messages, you must tell me immediately. Your community must be vigilant. Now, to return to Fidelis. When I met you in the chapter house, there was mention that she glimpsed something amiss down at the jetty. Do you know what that could have been?'

'God be my witness, Sir Hugh, but we don't.'

'In which case, Lady Abbess, I will leave you. I need to scrutinise Fidelis's corpse, where she died, as well as her chamber. I take it I have your permission to do both?'

'Of course.'

Corbett and Ranulf left the abbess's lodgings, where a servitor waited to lead them to the death house. This dark, sombre building was now well lit. Inside, Sister Agatha, the infirmarian, was busy dressing Fidelis's corpse for burial. She glanced up as the clerks entered and courteously beckoned them closer.

'Sister Agatha, you have dressed the corpse; have you found anything amiss?' Corbett pinched his nose at the conflicting smells of corruption and the strong tang of pinewood.

Agatha gestured them closer and pulled back the corpse sheet. Corbett stared down and murmured a prayer. Fidelis's body, now stripped of all clothing and ornamentation, was a mass of injury from head to toe. Gashes, bruises and bloody rents where the steps had cut and sliced her soft body. He glanced across at the infirmarian, who stood, hands joined, looking as composed as if she was ready to sing vespers in the choir.

'My lady,' he asked, 'have you found anything that would explain this woman's death? Any bruise or wound to the leg or shin that might suggest more than the fall?'

'Sir Hugh, Fidelis was the widow of a city merchant; she lived a comfortable life and looked after her body. Her skin was soft and supple but easy to bruise. I am more than convinced that every wound to her was

caused by the fall. I understand that you lodged at St
Bartholomew's Priory. If you doubt me, any physician
there is most welcome to come and view the corpse.
Or indeed, I can arrange for it to be sent to the Smithfield
Hospital as soon as possible.'

Corbett shook his head. 'That won't be necessary.'
He glanced around and noticed the robe and other
clothing heaped on a table.

'Sister Fidelis's,' Agatha declared, following his gaze.
'That's the clothing she was wearing.'

Corbett walked across, picked up the robe and carefully went through the deep pockets either side. He
pulled out a small wax candle and pieces of string all
knotted and tied. Apart from that, nothing else. He
thanked Sister Agatha and left the mortuary.

'Master?' Ranulf, who had kept very quiet, now
tapped Corbett on the shoulder. 'Master, what is it, what
are you searching for?'

'I don't know,' Corbett replied. 'Ranulf, I have scrutinised numerous deaths. I have, God be thanked,
resolved many mysteries, but I truly believe that Fidelis's
murder must rank as one of the most cunning I have
ever encountered. Indeed, if it wasn't for that note
pinned to Mother Abbess's door, I would conclude that
it was a simple accident. But it was not, so let us visit
the dead lady's chamber.'

A servitor led them across into the dormitory hall of
the convent. Fidelis's chamber was on the ground floor.
A simple, stark chamber. Corbett and Ranulf carefully
scrutinised everything, but apart from collections of

string, tied, knotted or rolled into a ball, they could discover nothing untoward. They then left and made their way to Devil's Tower. Both the door to the stairwell and that leading to the steps hung open. Corbett, ignoring Ranulf's muttered protests, began to climb, using the guide rope pinned to the wall. Once again, he scrutinised every step, every turn and twist, but could find nothing of interest.

Breathless and sweating, he climbed through the hatchway and stood for a while allowing the cold wind to cool his head and face. He glanced around. The beacon lantern still stood primed and ready, its long wick greased for the flame. Next to it the wicker basket had been opened, and two fresh candles lay on the ground. Corbett realised that the tallow candles burned fiercely and had to be regularly replaced. He walked around the top of the tower, allowing the wind to whip his hair and tug at his cowl. Satisfied, but simply shaking his head at Ranulf's questions, he went back down the steps.

'Where to now, master?'

'Why, Ranulf, the jetty.'

They walked across the convent grounds, muffled against the freezing cold and the frost. A sombre place, where the cawing of rooks was a constant harsh, scraping sound. Lonely and desolate, the heathland gave way to a small copse of trees. Corbett and Ranulf, aware of the darkness on either side, walked quickly. Ranulf kept a hand close to his dagger, sharp eyes glancing to left and right, ears pricked for any sign or warning of danger.

They left the copse and came out onto the jetty. Corbett walked carefully along it. He stood for a while staring at the two boats, then walked back. He crouched down and studied the sluice gate, which had now been opened, allowing the spring water to flood the small lake and saturate the ground around it.

'What are we searching for, master?'

'Something out of the ordinary, Ranulf. I'm trying to follow Fidelis's footsteps. Do you know, I believe she did see something amiss. She made the mistake of proclaiming it to her community and paid the price. The assassin who killed Constantia, a subtle, devious soul, also took care of Fidelis.' He got to his feet. 'However, for the life of me, I cannot glimpse what Fidelis saw. I cannot understand why she said what she did.'

The two clerks made their way back to the guest house. Corbett asked Ranulf to fetch Chanson, and they all met in Sir Hugh's chamber, a comfortable, pleasant room with a glass-filled window, the furnishings polished to a shine, the air sweet with the fragrance of beeswax candles.

'Very well.' Corbett made himself more comfortable in the cushioned chancery chair. Ranulf and Chanson sat on the edge of the bed. 'There will be more killings, I am sure of it. Something malignant lurks at St Sulpice. We are here, so we must deal with it. I want you both to go into the city, collect our possessions from St Bartholomew's and give Brother Philippe my kindest regards. Then, Ranulf, I want you to visit those two ladies the abbess mentioned who left St Sulpice to return to the secular life. Question them closely. If you discover anything suspicious, I shall return with you. Afterwards, call in at Westminster just to ensure that all is well. Seek out Mepham and Benstead. I want to know when poor Ralph Manning is being buried.'

'Will you be safe here?' Ranulf demanded. 'Sir Hugh, we are dealing with an assassin who seems most skilful and has all the impudence and arrogance of Satan.'

'We certainly are.' Corbett half smiled. 'But I'll be vigilant. I know the devil wanders like a lion, seeking whom he may devour. I am also aware of the terror that stalks at midday and the monsters that lurk just beyond our sight.'

'Poetic!'

'Poetry perhaps,' he retorted, 'but it's still the truth. Now, my friends, if you wish to break your fast in the buttery, please do so. Take care, and look after each other.'

The two clerks left. Corbett took off his cloak, unstrapped his war belt and eased off his boots, then lay back on the bed, staring up at the ceiling. He thought of Constantia floating out across that carp pond, rigid fingers clutching the oars, head bowed as if staring down at the knife thrust deep into her heart. The assassin watching her go, standing on that mist-cloaked jetty until the boat disappeared into the mist.

'Then there's you, Fidelis,' he whispered. 'You are at the top of that tower. You fear nothing. You left the hatch open. But what changed all that? What made you grasp the key and rush down the steps? Hurry, hurry, little nun. And then you tripped, bouncing off the stone, your flesh gashed by the sharp edges, your body racked by pain so that you vomited whatever you'd just eaten and drunk. The key slipped from your hand, but by then you were past caring. Dead to this world and alive to the next.'

He reflected on what he'd seen and heard. He let his mind drift. Manning, slumped across the chancery desk. Faucomburg all arrogant. Those two nuns caught up in violent death. And the other mysteries? Where was Megotta? He closed his eyes. Perhaps he'd left it too late, but he should have asked to search Sister Isabella's cell. There again, what was the use? Undoubtedly a killer prowled St Sulpice; he or she would remove anything suspicious.

About to drift into a warm sleep, he was roused by a furious rapping on the door. He sat up. The day was drawing on, but it was still too soon for Ranulf and Chanson to have returned from the city. Again the rapid knocking, a hollow sound that sent a cold tremor up his back, a feeling of danger. He got up, drawing his dagger from its sheath on his war belt.

'Who is it?' he called, but there was no reply. He walked to the door, turned the key and drew back the bolts, then opened it cautiously and peered to the left and right. The gallery was deserted, though he was sure he'd heard the sound of footsteps. He was about to close the door when the rapping began again, this time further down the gallery. Intrigued, he grasped his dagger and softly made his way towards the sound. A window at the far end showed that the daylight was dying; the only real light was provided by lanterns that hung on hooks next to each guest chamber. Corbett recalled Abbess Eleanor's words, how the guest house was empty, so who could be here playing such games?

Again the loud knocking noise jarred him. He was now certain it was coming from the last chamber along the gallery. He edged forward. He could hear no other sound. He paused before the door, dagger at the ready, and waited. Sure enough, the rapping came again; someone in the guest room was knocking insistently as if eager to get out. He put his hand on the latch, then stopped. The lantern hanging on its hook provided a pool of light. If he opened the door, he would be a clear target. He crouched, drawing deep breaths to compose himself, then got to his feet, flattened himself against the wall, pressed down the latch and pushed the door open. It had hardly swung back when he heard the click of a crossbow, and a bolt sped through the air to smash into the wall just beneath a lantern. If he had been standing there in the light, he would have been killed instantly.

His attacker must still be in the room. Perhaps he or she had a second arbalest primed and ready. It would be futile and foolish just to rush in. He backed down the gallery seeking the shelter of his own chamber. When he reached it, he stood in the doorway, peering out. He heard sounds, then silence. He took a deep breath. He knew what he would do; there was no rush, he would wait. He stepped back into his own chamber, locked and bolted the door and lay down on his bed, trying to stay composed.

About two hours later, Ranulf and Chanson returned with the baggage they'd collected from St Bartholomew's. Corbett let them into his chamber, closed the door and told them exactly what had happened. At his bidding, they went out into the gallery, down to the last chamber. The door was still open. Chanson went in first, lifting a lantern. Corbett followed and stared around. The chamber was no different from his, simply yet comfortably furnished. But it was cold. The shutters over the window had been pulled back. The window itself, filled with stiffened oiled parchment, had been flung open. He cautiously peered out. The gallery was on the ground floor, with a stairwell leading down to the cellars beneath.

'Whoever it was,' he said over his shoulder to his two companions, 'waited here to kill me. When he or she failed, they left through this window, an easy enough task, dropping quietly to the ground below. Anyone could do that without danger of injury or hurt.'

'But why?' Ranulf asked.

'I don't know. Why kill a royal clerk? Unless, of course, the assassin here wishes to create as much chaos and murderous mayhem as possible. The impression I have, Ranulf, is that the person responsible for the murders of Constantia and Fidelis is at war with this nunnery; they want to punish the place. But why, eh?

'Oh, and before I forget, Chanson, seek out Prioress Margaret or Sister Marie. I want to examine Isabella's cell, the girl who disappeared last night.'

Chanson hurried off. Corbett made himself ready, then turned to Ranulf.

'You visited those two ladies in the city – Sorrell and Blackbourne?'

'Sir Hugh, I did. Both women are merchants' daughters who believed they had a vocation to the religious life. Both entered St Sulpice only to discover that they did not, so they left. They were quite categorical, and I met them individually: they had no complaint to make about their stay here.'

'Good, good,' Corbett whispered. 'So let's discover a little more about Megotta.'

A short while later, an aggrieved prioress, accompanied by Sisters Maria and Agatha, came to the guest house and led Corbett and Ranulf across into the convent proper, up some stairs to a long gallery. To the left, the outside wall; to the right, a row of narrow-doored chambers. She opened one of these and ushered Corbett in, telling Marie to put the lantern she carried onto a table so he could clearly see around the room. It was tidy and neat, bleak yet comfortable enough for a young novice. There was a bed, table and chair, two chests and a coffer for possessions, clothes pegs driven into the wall underneath some shelves, a lavarium with jug, bowl and napkins and a prie-dieu for prayer beneath a crucifix. The bed was made, coverlets pulled up. Corbett searched the chamber but found nothing of value: it seemed that Megotta, or Sister Isabella as she called herself, had simply packed her possessions and quietly left the convent.

'This is how we found the room,' Prioress Margaret declared. 'As you see, Sir Hugh, it would almost appear as though Sister Isabella never existed, although she certainly did live here.'

'Would the chamber be left like this if she had simply decided to go for a walk, for example, intending to return?'

'Of course,' the prioress snapped. 'This is the way the rooms should always be, neat and tidy. Although I must admit, her personal possessions – probably just a few items – do seem to be missing.'

Corbett stared around. He glanced at the crucifix, closed his eyes and tried to imagine Megotta, pretending to be a novice, leaving this chamber. He was certain the girl had been abducted. However, was this abduction the result of a conspiracy involving persons within the convent walls? Had she been taken, then someone had stripped the room of all personal possessions so it would look as if she had left of her own volition?

He opened his eyes at the sound of footsteps outside. Sister Perpetua, all a-fluster, appeared in the doorway.

'There are men at the gate,' she declared. 'They sport the insignia of Lancaster. Two men, one Faucomburg and the other Catesby, his henchman. They demand entrance. They wish to speak to you, Sir Hugh.'

'Do they indeed?' Corbett murmured. 'Why should

Faucomburg ride out here to see me? Let's find out!
Prioress Margaret, with your permission, I would like
to meet your unwanted visitors in the guest house
buttery.'

A short while later, Faucomburg and Catesby slouched
into the buttery. At Prioress Margaret's insistence, they
had unstrapped their war belts and any other battle
harness and left them in the porter's lodge. Faucomburg,
however, was pleasant enough. He smiled at Corbett's
two companions as he sat down and accepted the blackjack of ale the servitor offered. He sipped at the thick
frothy drink, then toasted Corbett with his tankard.
    'Sir Hugh, thank you for seeing me. I'll be brief and
blunt.'
    'I would appreciate that.'
    Faucomburg smiled faintly. 'Sir Hugh, I am in your
debt, you know that. I want to talk to you about Faldon,
Manning's henchman. First, he was often seen at the
Queen of the Night, and has been since his master's
death. He appears to be a very keen devotee of Mother
Midnight.'
    'And second?' Corbett demanded, Faucomburg's
words provoking a growing unease.
    'Sir Hugh, when we met in combat at the tiltyard in
Westminster, I was escorted there and supported by the
likes of Catesby and other friends.' He held up a hand.
'I mean no offence, but on your part there was only
you, Ranulf and Chanson. Where was Faldon? His
master had been murdered and, I admit, his name

besmirched by me. You were determined to challenge me and make me recant, which you did. Surely Faldon should have been there?'

Corbett stared hard at his visitor, then leaned over and gently squeezed the man's hand.

'Faucomburg, you are a man of honour. Is that why you've come here?'

'Yes, it is, Sir Hugh. I am in your debt. Manning died in mysterious circumstances, yet his henchman does not seem the least perturbed, neither mourning for his master and friend nor seeking justice on his behalf.' Faucomburg nodded at Catesby, and both men rose to their feet. 'Sir Hugh, I have done what I came to do. Use what I told you, and remember,' he stretched out his hand, which Corbett clasped, 'I am your ally and not your enemy.'

Once Faucomburg and Catesby had left, Corbett let Chanson return to the stables. For a while he sat in silence, slowly rubbing his hands together as he stared at the floor.

'And so we have it,' he murmured, 'eh, Ranulf? Poor Manning murdered. Katherine, the love of his life, still missing, although the poor wench is probably dead. At least Isolda survived, and she looks happy and safe enough to me. Of course there's the mysterious Megotta, known to the convent as Sister Isabella. We searched her chamber and discovered nothing remarkable. Yet the shadows are beginning to gather.' He closed his eyes as he recalled that ominous, sinister knocking at his door, the way it was repeated further down the gallery;

that secret assassin waiting for him to show himself against the light.

'Sir Hugh.' Ranulf eased off his boots. 'The attack on you? I have searched that chamber and the outside. It cannot have been one of the nuns.'

'Why do you say that?'

'Master, your assailant would have had to move quickly. Knocking on your door, then hastening to the room at the far end, where they loosed a bolt at you before escaping through a window. Think of those pious nuns in their long flowing robes! They'd have all the swiftness of a snail!'

Corbett grinned at his henchman.

'And they are all quite delicate,' Ranulf added. 'I doubt any of them are quite strong enough to wield a crossbow. Anyway, Sir Hugh, what do you make of Faucomburg's visit and what he told us?'

Corbett closed his eyes as he experienced that familiar spasm of unease he felt when something deeply troubling him was about to surface.

'Faucomburg is correct,' Ranulf insisted. 'Faldon was Manning's henchman. We met him when we viewed the corpse, but since then he's played the will-o'-the-wisp. Why hasn't he approached you? Has he been involved in the preparations for Manning's funeral tomorrow morning?' He caught Corbett's look of surprise. 'I am sorry, I'd overlooked that. Brother Philippe gave us the news. Manning's requiem mass will take place at the priory an hour before midday, followed by swift burial in God's Acre. As for the tiltyard, you'd have expected

Faldon to be there, wouldn't you, to see justice done for his master? Even if he was delayed, why hasn't he approached you to thank you, to congratulate you? Faucomburg may be an arrogant bastard, but he's a clever one. We should question Faldon, even if it is only to get answers to the questions I've listed.'

'Not to mention,' Corbett intervened, 'why he so often frequents Mother Midnight's and the world of the Queen of the Night. We have been distracted by matters here. Once Ralph's funeral mass has finished, we'll go hunting Faldon. Now, Ranulf, fetch Chanson; he shouldn't really sleep in the stables. I'll have one more small goblet of wine, say my prayers and prepare for bed.'

Ranulf left. Corbett busied himself around the chamber, putting things as tidily as he wished. He undressed, washed at the lavarium, donned his nightshirt and sat on the edge of the bed cradling a small goblet of wine. He sniffed and sipped carefully and closed his eyes in appreciation of the rich, full flavour of Bordeaux. He thought of Manning and lifted his cup in ghostly toast. 'God be with you, my friend. God speed your journey into the light, but I must discover who sent you there.'

He glanced across at his chancery satchel, buckled and fastened on a small side table. He thought of Manning working in that chamber. His gaze fell on the disused quill pen that he had removed from his satchel earlier in the day. The sharp nib was now blunted, the end of the quill pen slightly tattered where he had placed it in his mouth. He sat up, putting the wine cup down, and picked up the damaged quill. 'Sweet angels!' he breathed. 'Is that what was wrong? The quill pens!'

He sat for a while sifting through all the possibilities, certain he was now on the path to the truth. He just needed to ask certain individuals blunt, specific questions. He walked to the window, opened the shutters and stared out. The sky was still clear of cloud, though a frost was coming. He strained his ears, but could hear nothing, not even the chatter of the crows. It was as if the deepening cold had frozen all sound. He closed the shutters and prepared himself for bed.

After Manning's requiem mass and funeral the following morning, Corbett extended his condolences to Sister Agatha, who came and went like a ghost in the night, then he and his two companions met Brother Philippe in the sacristy to thank him for all he had done for the murdered man. Brother Philippe just shrugged and quickly blessed himself.

'Hugh, it's the least I could do. Manning sometimes came here when he wanted to be free of Westminster. Now, I want to show you a patient brought in last night.'

Corbett held up a hand. 'Philippe, excuse me, but I cannot. I have very urgent business I must attend to. Something I have discovered. You received my message before mass?'

'Yes, Yes.' Brother Philippe swiftly divested, then led Corbett and Ranulf out of the church and into the small guest room just inside the entrance to the hospital. He served them hot possets, then brought out a sealed chancery bag. He broke the seal and shook the contents out onto the table.

'You recognise these, Ranulf?' Corbett asked. 'They're what we took from Manning's chamber. I now think I have the truth.'

'What do you mean?'

Corbett picked up a quill pen. 'There were two of these, both allegedly used by Manning.'

'Oh sweet God,' Philippe breathed. 'I see what you mean, Sir Hugh. Something so obvious I overlooked it.'

'And so did I,' Corbett retorted. 'Ranulf, these quills were supposed to have been used by a very busy clerk, yet their nibs and points are totally untouched. No stain of ink or any sign of being pressed down onto a piece of vellum or parchment. Moreover, I can't think of a single scribe who wouldn't confess to nibbling the quill stem of his pen.'

'We all do it,' Brother Philippe agreed.

Corbett examined both quills again. 'Both new,' he breathed, 'both unused.'

He walked across the chamber and stared at a triptych fixed to the wall. The painting celebrated the martyrdom of St Laurence, Deacon of Rome, who was grilled to death over a bed of coals. The artist had picked out the glorious martyr in gold and silver paint. His tormentors, however, had blood-red skins, bright orange hair and small popping black eyes. Above these hovered demons with the faces of rat,

badger, pig and fox. Corbett concentrated on the detail
in the painting, for it was no different to the problems
confronting him now. He must sit, study and reflect
on every item, however petty it might seem to be.
He'd made a terrible mistake when he first went into
Manning's chamber. What he now knew, he should
have seen then. 'Sharpen up, sharpen up,' he whispered
to himself.

'Ranulf, I want you to hasten to Westminster. On
second thoughts,' he picked up his cloak and swung it
about him, 'I'll go myself.'

'Hugh, I must tell you—'

Corbett strode across, grasped the physician by the
shoulders and kissed him on each cheek. 'Philippe, I
shall return. I now know how Manning was murdered;
I must still discover by whom. Chanson will stay here
with our horses. Ranulf, down to the quayside as swiftly
as we can.'

They hurried out of the hospital and into the city
streets, now busy after the Angelus bell. The merchants
and traders, tinkers and chapmen had broken their fast
in the many alehouses and taverns and were ready for
business. The streets were crammed with people taking
advantage of the cold yet clear weather. The two clerks
had to push their way through the crowds, constantly
refusing the hotpot girls, sausage squires and pastry
pages who offered wine and food or tried to entice
them into some bothy hastily set up for that purpose.
The air was rich with various smells: ale, wine and
sizzling meats as well as the usual stinks from the sewers,

cesspits and laystalls. Justice was also busy. Whores were being birched for daring to tout for business beyond their own street. Petty thieves, naps and foists were being fastened in the stocks or doused in the many dirty, ice-encrusted horse troughs. Beggars whined for alms, and all the counterfeiters were out prowling for victims, some soft-hearted passer-by who would believe their concocted tale of woes. Travellers from across the sea offered stories. Two singers chanted a hymn to St Michael the Archangel. Dogs and cats scrounged amongst the midden heaps. Children shrieked and played whilst dodging horse and cart.

Corbett kept an eye on what was underfoot as well as the dangers of slops tossed from the windows above him. At last they reached Queenhithe, where he ordered a six-oared barge to take them down to Westminster. They arrived at King's Steps to find the royal precincts as raucous as the city. A gang of river pirates had been taken for trial before King's Bench. They had been found guilty, but had broken free while being led away. A violent, bloody struggle ensued, but in the end, all six pirates had been cut down, their bloodied, gashed corpses left gibbeted on scaffolds either side of King's Steps. A disgusting, macabre sight, the white flesh displaying an array of gruesome wounds.

Corbett had to use his pass and warrants to get through the cordon of men-at-arms and archers, but they eventually reached the path leading to the House of Chancery, where the scribes, clerks and scriveners worked from first light to the vespers bell. Again a very busy place. The king had moved north to confront his barons, so a constant stream of messengers came and went. Corbett was recognised. Some of the clerks wished to have words with him about what was happening at court, but he simply shook his head and pressed on. They reached the offices of the Secret Chancery. Corbett went into a small waiting chamber whilst Ranulf went searching for Mepham and Benstead. He eventually returned with both clerks.

'Sir Hugh.' Mepham's cold face broke into a smile. 'To what do we owe the honour? We were informed that you'd moved to St Sulpice. You want to see us about certain business?'

'Murder,' Corbett replied. 'I want to visit Manning's chamber again.'

'There's nothing there.' Benstead sounded flustered. 'It's been cleaned and cleared. We are waiting for it to be blessed and the walls anointed so the foul sin committed there can be exorcised for good.'

'I'll do better than that,' Corbett retorted. 'God's justice!' he added. The two clerks gazed back, mystified. 'Come!' he urged. 'Let us summon up the ghosts.'

Mepham shrugged, and they led Corbett out of the Hall of Secrets and down to Manning's chamber. The door was locked. Mepham opened it and ushered Corbett in. The room had certainly been cleared of everything but its furnishings.

'Very good, very good.' Corbett sat down on the chancery chair beside the table. 'Gentlemen.' He lifted his head and stared at the two clerks, who both looked rather nervous with Ranulf standing so close, a silent, threatening shadow.

'Sir Hugh,' Benstead pleaded. 'What is this?'

Corbett pointed to the wall bench. 'Sit down and close your eyes!' The two clerks stared back in surprise.

'Sir Hugh Corbett is the Keeper of the King's Secret Seal,' Ranulf intoned in a deep, carrying voice. 'Do what he asks.'

Both men hastened to obey.

'Now,' Corbett began, 'I want you to reflect on the moment you forced the door to this chamber. Try to recall what you actually did. Precisely where you were and what others did. You must do this separately. Mepham, please leave. Benstead, stay.'

Once Mepham had gone, Benstead, at Corbett's urging, got to his feet and tried to replicate what had happened on that fateful day. When he was satisfied, Corbett asked him to leave the chamber. Mepham came in and was invited to do the same. Corbett then called Benstead back in and asked them to repeat exactly what they'd done, though this time Ranulf would play the role of Faldon. He sighed in satisfaction when both men solemnly assured him that whilst they tended to Manning's corpse, Faldon had been busy about the dead clerk's desk. At the time they had thought this appropriate.

Corbett laid out the quill pens Brother Philippe had kept at St Bartholomew's. He explained what had happened. 'I believe,' he declared, 'that Faldon murdered his master. No.' He raised a hand to still their objections.

'The ends of the quill pens were heavily laced with a deadly tasteless poison. Like any clerk, Manning sucked at the end of these and basically drank the poison. He'd be totally unaware that he was drinking his own death with every sip on those poisoned feathers. Remember, Faldon knew his master and his ways. He would know that Manning would sit here reflecting and writing, the tip of his pen between his lips. Manning died. The chamber was forced. You gentlemen took care of the corpse. Faldon, however, was secretly busy concealing the cause of his master's death. He brought in a fresh batch of quill pens, replacing the ones Manning had been using, which he secreted away in his wallet. Of course their tips were drenched in ink. I am sure they would have stained his wallet; they certainly did his fingers. I noticed that when we first met him in the Hall of Secrets.'

'Are you sure, Sir Hugh?' Mepham gasped. 'Why should he do that?'

'I cannot answer for the why; that is something I have yet to discover. But as for the how, think, sirs! You are in here, shocked by Manning's corpse. You concentrate on that. You are aware of Faldon moving about. It would take, what, a few heartbeats to pick up a clutch of pens, hide them away and replace them with a fresh batch. Faldon made one terrible mistake, however. The quill pens he brought in here had not been used. The nibs were sharp and free of all ink. How could that be if Manning had been closeted away for so long, scribbling his notes? What other explanation is there for his death?'

Corbett turned to Ranulf. 'Start counting slowly, one to twenty.' Ranulf glanced back in surprise. 'Do so,' Corbett urged. 'Now.' Ranulf began to count. Corbett picked up the quill pens he'd brought in, pushed them beneath his cloak, then brought them out again, placing them on the writing tray as Ranulf reached number nine. He spread his hands. 'You see how it was done, gentlemen, swift and sure. Now, tomorrow morning, I want you to go before the justices in Westminster Hall and swear out warrants for the arrest of Luke Faldon on suspicion of treason and murder.'

'Treason, Sir Hugh?'

'Manning was a royal clerk. Ask the justices to give the sheriffs these warrants and for the most rigorous search to be carried out. Faldon must be taken alive.' Corbett paused at a knock at the door. A servant pushed it open.

'Sir Hugh Corbett, we have received an important message from St Bartholomew's that Brother Philippe needs urgent words with you on the matter in hand.'

Corbett repeated his instructions to Mepham and Benstead, then he and Ranulf left the royal precincts. They made their way down to King's Steps, where Corbett commandeered a royal barge to take them up the swollen, turbulent Thames. So forceful was the river, he was pleased they could hug the shoreline. He and Ranulf sat close together, swathed in their cloaks, watching the lights glinting through the mist, their ears assailed by the incessant bray of horns as the craft warned each other off.

When Corbett disembarked, he gratefully touched the base of the patron saint of that quayside before they made their way up the city streets. The day's business was drawing to a close. Stalls were taken down, shops boarded up, lanterns lit and hung either side of every doorway. The beacon lights of scores of churches now flared against the night sky. Once again Corbett thought of that sinister Devil's Tower and Sister Fidelis tumbling down the spiral staircase – one she was very used to. Surely, he reflected, she would have grasped the guide rope. To all appearances it was an accident, yet that note pinned to the abbess's door was proof of deliberate, vicious murder, but how?

He walked on lost in his own thoughts as they made their way through the web of twisting streets. The dung carts had rolled out. The night walkers, dark dwellers and tribes of twilight also appeared. Whores clustered, pimps hovered. Taverns and alehouses threw open their doors to provide funnels of flickering light. Prisoners were being released from the stocks. Burial parties stumbled back full of funeral ale. Cooking smells wafted heavy and cloying, vying with the stench of cesspits and open sewers. A cohort of moon walkers had entered the city, faces painted white, garbed completely in cow hide with bull's horns fastened either side of their shorn heads. These travelling magicians looked even more grotesque in the light of their dancing torches as they made their way to a campsite near Blackfriars.

Corbett and Ranulf now turned into a maze of even narrower, meaner streets, nicknamed 'the Galleries of

Hell'. These runnels were needle thin and bereft of all light, so dark and desolate Corbett hired a link boy to go before them with a lantern. Corbett and Ranulf followed with both sword and dagger drawn, and the sinister shapes staring from the darkness turned away. At last they reached the approaches to St Bartholomew's. The lane leading to the priory's imposing gatehouse blazed with the dancing flames of cresset torches lashed to long lines of poles either side. They gained admittance through a postern door, where a breathless lay brother gasped how they must accompany him into the hospital, where Brother Philippe was waiting.

They went up some stairs into a long, high-ceilinged room. Philippe had studied with the Moorish physicians, who insisted that cleanliness was vital in the care of the sick. The long hospital hall, his own creation, reflected such teaching. Its walls were scrubbed and lime washed, no carpets or rushes on the floor. The wooden panelling was clean and polished. A row of cot beds was ranged on either side, each cordoned off by a white sheet, whilst the beds and their coverings looked clean and fresh. Every so often they passed braziers and smoke jars crammed with herbs to fragrance and cleanse the air. In addition, the brothers who tended the sick had constant recourse to jugs of hot water, laced with some powerful astringent, to cleanse their hands and arms up to the elbows.

Brother Philippe was waiting for them in a small, gloomy chamber at the back of the hall. He was sitting on a stool next to a bed where a patient lay with his hands by his sides. The man's fingers were heavily bandaged but, even so, blood had seeped through to stain the crisp white sheet, whilst the mask covering his face was also deeply bloodied. Brother Philippe rose to clasp hands with his visitors. He then waved them to stools on the other side of the bed. Corbett and Ranulf took their seats, and Brother Philippe dug into his purse and handed across a hardened wax seal displaying the insignia of the Secret Chancery.

'In sweet heaven's name!' Corbett exclaimed. He pointed at the masked patient. 'Is this who I think it is? Faldon?'

Brother Philippe nodded. 'I tried to tell you this morning, Hugh. I had my suspicions, but once you left, I made my own enquiries.' He paused. 'Let me tell you. This poor unfortunate was found on the steps of St Michael and All the Angels. Now the parish priest there is an old man who was once a royal clerk. He realised from the victim's clothing that he was a man of some means. He searched but could find nothing except this seal lodged deep in the corner of one of the man's pockets. Now as you know, royal clerks have the privilege of being treated here. The parish priest, God bless him, realised that the man he had found needed urgent medical attention. Once he was brought to me, I made enquiries at the Chancery. One clerk had been reported missing for at least two days – Luke Faldon. Of course, I realised the implications of all this, but the information only came in after you had gone. In fact I only learnt it myself about an hour ago.'

He leaned over and skilfully removed the blood-stained veil.

'It's Faldon, but Lord save us.' Corbett peered down at the face, a gruesome mask despite Philippe's best ministrations. The mouth hung open, lips parted. Corbett glimpsed blood frothing there, with more seeping down through the nostrils. Faldon was unconscious, eyelids fluttering.

'He's had his tongue removed,' Philippe whispered. 'Wrenched out. The whole inside of the mouth is a deep open wound. I cannot stop the bleeding, and there's this . . .' He undid the bandages around the hands.

Corbett flinched. All four fingers on either hand had been neatly clipped off, leaving nothing more than bloody stumps.

'Cruelly shorn,' Brother Philippe explained. 'Bleeding from mouth and hands. He's getting weaker by the moment, and of course there's the sheer shock of what happened to him.'

'In other circumstances,' Corbett replied, 'I would be arresting Luke Faldon for the murder of Ralph Manning. Not only murder but, because Manning was a royal clerk, a hideous act of treason. Brother Philippe, I will go on oath. Faldon undoubtedly poisoned Manning's quill pens. He probably did so early on that fateful morning. He prepared the writing chamber then left. God knows what poison he used or where he bought it; however, do I understand that there are poisons that can kill in a few heartbeats?'

'There certainly are. Some poisons take time, but others are like the bite of an adder. Death comes swiftly.'

'The murder was set,' Corbett declared. 'Manning happily obliged. I have described this before, but it's worth repeating to see if you agree with my conclusions. In brief, Manning went into that chancery chamber, locked and bolted the door and, like the good clerk he was, became immersed in this problem or that. He would think. He would reflect. He would nibble the end of his quill pen, as we all do. Luke Faldon must have watched him. He must have realised that such a mannerism could be exploited. I am sure Ranulf could imitate the way I sit, the way I write,' Corbett glanced sideways, 'and even what I look like.'

Ranulf, a little embarrassed, looked away.

'Manning died. Of course he could not be roused, so the door was forced. Faldon would make very sure that he got into that chamber as quickly as possible. He did, and the rest was easy. Mepham and Benstead would be shocked, distracted; all they could see was their friend and colleague sprawled dead. They would think of nothing else except Manning. Faldon exploited the situation to swiftly change the tainted pens for new ones. He made one mistake. A terrible error. The pens he exchanged had not been used. The nibs were pristine, unscratched, not even dipped in ink. He thrust the poisoned pens into his wallet and, in doing so, he stained his fingers. He did his best to remove the stains, but I glimpsed them that morning shortly after Manning's corpse had been found.

'So,' Corbett rubbed his hands together, 'we now know the who and the how, but as for the why, the motive behind Manning's murder, I am still very much in the dark. Manning was a good clerk, a kind master. I always thought Faldon was his comrade. So what happened, eh? Who suborned Faldon? Why should he poison Manning and, after he did, why this?' He gestured at the wounded man.

'Sir Hugh.' Ranulf shuffled his feet, pushing back the stool. 'Undoubtedly someone took Faldon prisoner. They must have done to inflict such gruesome wounds. I strongly suspect that this abduction and torture is in some way connected to Manning's murder. Yes?'

'I would agree.'

'Perhaps Faldon was persuaded to commit the murder by someone else?'

'And then what?' Corbett asked.

'Some sort of falling-out? Was it over money? A fee paid for Manning's death? Or something else? Yes, Sir Hugh, it must have been something else. Faldon could hardly threaten others with exposure. He'd simply hang with them. So the mystery deepens.' Ranulf scratched his head. 'If Faldon's attackers wanted him dead, why not just slit his throat and have done with it? Why all this blood, the torture?' He paused. 'Except . . .'

'Except what?'

'I know the riffler gangs of London. Faldon's injuries are those I'd expect a gang to inflict. But again, why? I suspect he was interrogated, tortured, then left on the steps of a church, where he was supposed to bleed to death. However, due to the sheer compassion of that priest, and you, Brother Philippe, he was not left to die alone.'

'But as you said,' Corbett pointed out, 'why didn't his enemies just slit his throat?'

'Ah.' Ranulf chewed the corner of his lip. 'He was left as a warning.'

'To whom?'

'Perhaps to us, Sir Hugh. Is that why they left the seal in his pocket? And maybe they chose that particular church because they knew what the priest would do. Anyway, master, that is what I believe. One royal clerk being used as an example of what could happen to others.' Ranulf sighed noisily. 'That's all I can offer.'

'Very plausible,' Corbett replied. 'So we have Faldon suborned to kill Manning. We arrive to investigate Manning's murder and other mysteries. Faldon is abducted, interrogated and tortured, his body tossed onto the steps of that church. I do wonder . . .'

'What, master?'

'Did they interrogate Faldon to find out about us? Here we are in God's own hospital,' Corbett nodded towards Brother Philippe, 'but outside, the chaos grows and the darkness deepens. The king is not in his royal precincts but hiding in some palace desperate to save the life of his favourite; or, as some would have it, his royal catamite. The Palace of Westminster is deserted. The great offices of state limp along. In the city, the gang leaders flex their muscles. Perhaps someone didn't want Manning snooping around, and if they resented

Manning, they will certainly detest me. Oh yes, there's a mystery here, but we will solve it. Now.' He pointed at the patient. 'Is he dying?'

'In a word, yes.' Philippe crossed himself. 'Hugh, there is little more I can do.'

'Does he come out of his death sleep?'

'Yes, and he will continue to do so, then the sleep will be forever. But not yet. He is not ready to make the journey.'

'Then I will wait,' Corbett replied.

Ranulf left. Philippe continued to sit close to the patient, whilst Corbett dozed in a chair in the corner. When he was shaken awake, the room seemed colder, darker.

'He's awake,' Brother Philippe hissed. 'Be swift now, Hugh. In God's name, he needs to be shrived.'

Corbett went and knelt by the dying man. Faldon's face was as white as driven snow, his eyes dark pools of hopelessness and pain.

'You are dying, Faldon. We cannot do anything to save your body, but your soul, yes.' Corbett leaned closer. 'Brother Philippe is both priest and physician. He can listen to your sins and shrive you and, once you are absolved, he will prepare you for your journey to judgement. Afterwards, I promise you, I shall pay a chantry priest here at St Bartholomew's to sing requiems for your soul. Heed now, Faldon. The darkness deepens. The demons gather, crowding around you like wild dogs crouched ready to spring. So I ask you, on the fate of your immortal soul, you murdered Ralph Manning, yes?'

Faldon, face all sweat soaked, gave a bloody gasp but nodded.

'You prepared that chamber, you coated the plumes of Manning's quill pens with a most powerful poison. Yes or no?' Again the nod. 'And when you broke into his chamber and Manning lay dead, you exchanged the poisoned pens with untainted ones. Again on your immortal soul, yes or no?' Faldon blinked. 'Why?' Corbett demanded. 'Why did you kill a good man, a good clerk, a good friend in such a fashion? Manning was your comrade. You were both mailed clerks, you stood together in the shield wall. Why?'

Faldon, wild eyed, tried to rise but fell back. He gazed round the chamber as if searching for a way out of this deepening nightmare. Then he gave a deep sigh, raised his arm and pointed to the far corner. Corbett followed his direction, but there was only an hour candle on its stand, its broad flame eating away the wax towards the next red ring. He gazed back at Faldon, eyes narrowed.

'What is it, man, what is it?'

Again Faldon pointed to the corner, making some sound in the back of his throat.

'Tell me,' Corbett urged. 'Those who attacked you and left you for dead had no mercy. No one needs their tongue and fingers more than a clerk. You were tortured and maimed in a fashion to end your calling. You owe such people nothing. So why?'

This time Faldon pointed towards the hour candle then moved his mangled hands to tap his own chest.

Corbett rose and, wetting his fingers, extinguished

the flame. He let the wax settle for a while, then brought the candle across, placing it on Faldon's chest. The clerk glanced beseechingly at him, then began to dab the candle with his bandaged hand, time and time again. Corbett picked the candle up. The wax was divided by red rings, but the one denoting midnight, the one Faldon was indicating, was a deep purple.

'Midnight?' he asked.

Again Faldon nodded.

'Mother Midnight?' Corbett declared. 'Are you saying she is responsible?' He could almost feel Faldon's relief as he nodded vigorously. Corbett placed the candle on the bedside table. He could see that Faldon had little time left; he was already exhausted by his exertions.

'You'd best go,' Brother Philippe whispered. 'He can tell you no more. Mother Midnight certainly has the power and the means to carry out such an attack and inflict gruesome wounds on a royal clerk. She is well protected and patronised by Thomas, Earl of Lancaster, leader of those nobles bitterly opposed to the king. For the moment we must leave that. Faldon needs absolution.'

Corbett left the chamber and stayed outside, sending a servant to search out Ranulf and Chanson. Both clerks arrived just as Philippe came out of the room.

'Faldon is shriven and has now gone to God. Hugh, is there anything I can do?'

Corbett opened his purse and took out two silver pieces, handing them to Philippe. 'You will see to the burial and the requiems, yes?'

'Of course.'

'Interesting,' Corbett declared, 'what you said in there, Brother Philippe, about Mother Midnight. The king and his faction are absent from Westminster, well away from the city. Lancaster, Hereford, Pembroke and the rest have their troops ready to march at a moment's notice. We have already done business with Faucomburg. I'm sure before the week is out, Lancaster's influence will be paramount in London. The leaders of certain gangs will be favoured, and malignants like Mother Midnight given generous patronage in return for services offered. It's time we visited her.

'But first . . .' He clapped Chanson on the shoulder. 'My good friend, Ranulf and I will return to St Sulpice, but you must go to Westminster and seek out Mepham and Benstead. Tell them to search the records for any mention of the traitor Thomas Turbeville, hanged in chains until he rotted some seventeen years ago. Yes?' Chanson nodded. 'Ask them to discover anything they can about Turbeville's family. Tell them I'm intrigued that Manning's scribblings make regular reference to Turbeville. I want to know why. In addition, I want them to make careful search about young women disappearing in the city, any corpses found. God knows poor wretches are slaughtered every day, their bodies left on quayside steps, cadavers floating in puddles or washed up by the Thames.' He paused. 'I cannot resolve every problem, but I can deliver justice whenever I am able to. We must always do the right thing at the right time. There are crimes here, hideous sins crying out to God for vengeance, and we, my friends, are that vengeance. So do what I ask.'

Chanson faithfully repeated the message and, with Ranulf's warnings about not forgetting what Sir Hugh wanted ringing in his ears, the Clerk of the Stables hurried off to his beloved horses.

# PART FOUR

The tenor of Turbeville's treasonable letter was as follows . . .

egotta the moon girl stared bleakly into the blackness of the filthy cellar where she was imprisoned. She struggled against the ropes binding her wrists above her head to an iron clasp driven into the wall. She had been raped time and again; her body was one constant bruise, but her pleas for pity had fallen on deaf ears. Her tormentor seemed to revel in her distress and hit her hard to make her squirm. He had practised his filth upon her until she prayed for deliverance. Hours had passed since his last visit, but Megotta, straining her ears, had heard whispers. *The Picardy* was a cog; it was preparing to leave and she was to be taken aboard. She had also heard other details, including names.

Moving to ease the pain in her back, she abruptly glimpsed her salvation: a piece of thick slate, jagged along the edge, serrated like a dagger with the sharpest of points. Because of its dark colour, it was almost invisible, a relict perhaps of tiles stored there over the years. She blinked and wondered how she could grasp it.

The door was abruptly flung open and her abuser came in. He crouched down beside her.

'Are you ready, wench, because I and my comrade want to ride you like the soft, plump palfrey you are.'

'Untie me,' Megotta pleaded.

'Never.'

'Please, let me use my hands. I can show you tricks I have learnt to give you even greater pleasure. Honestly.' She forced a smile at the malevolent demon crouching beside her. 'A woman from the East, who claimed to have worked in the harem of the great Cham, taught me a particular skill—' She broke off as the man slapped her across the face. She steeled herself. 'It does involve a beating,' she whispered. 'But you inflict it, and you will enjoy yourself immensely.' She could have cried with joy. The torturer, watery eyes blinking, wetted his lips. He was tempted.

'That smack,' her abuser grated, 'just a warning. No other tricks. Don't try to escape. My friend waits outside.'

'I know, I know,' Megotta gasped.

Her tormentor drew his dagger and cut the ropes, then sawed at the bonds around her wrists. Megotta breathed out in relief, then stretched her arms and hands to ease the throbbing stiffness. She smiled coquettishly at her tormentor and leaned forward. He lifted his dagger to prick just beneath her chin.

'Be careful,' he warned.

'Never mind that,' Megotta replied. 'Come closer, with your back to the wall.' Her tormentor did so. She lifted her torn shift and sat astride him, moving forward to whisper in his ear even as she stretched out and grasped the piece of slate, its edges so sharp they cut her soft fingers. Her tormentor pulled her closer.

'Show me,' he breathed.

'I certainly shall.' She thrust the pointed slate into the man's throat, ignoring the pain in her hands as she pressed down, driving it in so deep his blood spurted out like a fountain. So shocked, so surprised, he could only shudder and tremble as his life blood spilled out. Megotta pressed harder, watching the life light fade in his eyes.

'Go down to hell,' she hissed. 'A host of devils await you.'

The rapist gave one last shudder as more blood spurted out, then he sprawled still, eyes staring sightlessly, bloodied mouth gaping.

Megotta got up. She grasped the man's dagger and moved to the door. She was no longer tired or frightened. She felt as if she was ablaze with life and energy. She stopped by the door and rapped on it. A voice called. She rapped again as her tormentor would when summoning his accomplice to take his turn. The door opened. A dark shape against the light. She lunged with the long-bladed dagger, a killing blow direct to the left side of the chest. Her opponent had no chance. It was almost as if he had walked directly onto the blade. He fell to his knees, hands flailing, unable to utter more

than a gargle. Megotta slipped behind him, kicking the
door shut with her heel. She grasped the man's greasy
hair, pulled his head back and slit his throat, which
opened like a second mouth from ear to ear.

'I am your nemesis,' she whispered. 'Your punishment
incarnate.'

She shoved the man away and watched him shudder
as he slipped into death. Then, putting the knife down
on the battered chest, she crouched, leaning against the
wall, and stared round the cellar, allowing her sweat to
cool and her breathing to become calmer. After a while,
she got to her feet, picked up the dagger and went out
into the dark cobbled passageway that ran between the
building where she'd been imprisoned and a high grey-
stone wall. She walked towards a stool beneath a
lanternhorn where her second tormentor must have sat.
He'd left his arbalest there, a small crossbow, as well
as a leather quiver crammed with feathered bolts. Like
the rest of the moon people, Megotta had been trained
in the use of arms in order to protect the tribe against
the outlaws and wolfsheads who infested the highways
and lonely coffin paths across the kingdom. She picked
the weapons up and hurried back to the cellar.

She primed the arbalest, then found the sturdy sandals
she'd been wearing when she was abducted. Stripping
both corpses, she dressed herself in their clothing, taking
the best war belt with its sword and dagger, then
searched the wallets. She was delighted to discover that
both men had bulging purses. Once she was ready,
garbed in quilted jerkin beneath a leather jacket and

thick woollen leggings, she picked up and strapped on the war belt, swinging a heavy military cloak around her to provide warmth as well as to hide the arbalest. She felt hungry and pained, but she was ruthlessly determined.

She left the cellar and was walking down the passageway when she heard a voice behind her.

'Is all well, Bryn? Is the wench giving trouble?'

Megotta shrugged back her cloak and turned. She lifted the arbalest, and, before the surprised man could react, she had released the clasp, loosing the quarrel to shatter his face.

Corbett and Ranulf made themselves comfortable in what the doorkeeper of the Queen of the Night called 'the waiting chamber'. Corbett opened his chancery satchel and, using the small, exquisitely carved table before them, took out pen and ink and began scrawling a message. He was not to be disturbed.

While his master worked, Ranulf stared around the room and whistled under his breath, astonished at its wealth and opulence. This chamber was one of the most luxurious he had ever sat in, a place of warm comfort and blatant richness. The walls were covered in finely woven tapestries, a brilliant array of colours celebrating famous love scenes: Dido's infatuation for Aeneas and Lancelot's for Guinevere. They were a moving sea of colour. The ceiling was raftered, the plaster between the gleaming black beams a soft pink. The thickest Turkey rugs covered the floor. The furniture was the finest wood, polished so it caught the glimmer of the host of beeswax candles burning fiercely on their silver-chased spigots. He was about to draw his companion's attention to the luxurious throne-like chair opposite when Corbett thrust a scrap of parchment into his hand.

'*Tolle et lege* – take up and read,' he whispered.

Ranulf looked at the scrap and slowly translated the Latin. '*Tace atque vide* – stay silent and watch – because *muri aurent oculos auresque* – the walls have eyes and ears.' He grinned and passed the note back, then stared at the far wall, wondering where the peepholes might be. He watched the hour candle burn down, its flame close to the next red ring, and recalled their meeting the previous evening with Brother Philippe. Afterwards, Corbett had thanked the physician, and then the clerks had returned to St Sulpice.

They had risen early, attended the dawn mass, broken their fast in the buttery and travelled back into the city. Corbett was determined to confront Mother Midnight. Ranulf wondered what this sinister whore-mistress was like. He glanced at his master. Corbett sat playing with the chancery ring on his finger as he gazed at the gorgeous tapestry opposite, celebrating the love of Jupiter for Juno.

The door quietly opened and both clerks rose to greet the woman garbed in the dress of a nun who swept into the chamber followed by a maid dressed identically to herself. She offered her ring hand for Corbett and Ranulf to kiss, then smiled dazzlingly at them. In a soft, cultured voice, she asked them to take their seats whilst she sat in the throne-like chair opposite, her escort standing obediently behind her. She introduced herself as Mother Midnight, laughingly adding that that was what people called her. Corbett was tempted to ask her real name but realised that whatever this woman said would be a lie.

They were offered refreshments. Corbett refused. He scrutinised this elegant woman with her soft face framed by a starched white wimple, her head covered with a deep blue veil, the same colour as her gown. She had a blood-red cincture around her slender waist, thick-soled sandals on her feet, her only concession to luxury her finger rings and a gold bejewelled bracelet circling her right wrist. He found it difficult to believe that she might well be responsible for the murder of Manning as well as Faldon's gruesome death.

He raised his hand to cover the bottom half of his face. Mother Midnight gazed at him, smiling with her eyes, then glanced away. Corbett continued to watch her. He lived by logic, but he also conceded that the human soul could pluck sensations, thoughts and feelings out of the air. He was certain that he was in the presence of a woman capable of great evil. He could not articulate that feeling, he had no evidence or logic to substantiate it, but he truly believed he was looking into the face of real wickedness.

'Sir Hugh, you are staring at me.'

'Madam, I apologise, but my reason for coming here is not the most pleasant of tasks. Let me be brief, blunt and succinct.' He described what had happened at St Sulpice, the murders and the notes pinned to the abbess's door. He related in great detail Sister Constantia's death on that freezing carp pond and Sister Fidelis's fatal fall down the steps of Devil's Tower. He openly conceded that there was nothing he had seen or heard that connected these deaths to the Queen of the Night or to Mother Midnight herself. Nevertheless, those two notices had been pinned to the abbess's door and had to be taken seriously. He apologised for any distress he might cause, but he needed answers to certain questions.

Mother Midnight heard him out, a look of complete incredulity on her face. She appeared so startled that Corbett, whatever his suspicions about her, instinctively felt that this whore-mistress, schooled as she was to maintain composure, was genuinely surprised at what he'd said. Once he had finished, she sat shaking her head.

'Nonsense,' she whispered. 'Absolute nonsense.'

'So why should someone use your name?' Ranulf asked.

'God knows, Red Hair, but when you catch the culprit, let me know. I would dearly love to question him or her.'

'As you did Luke Faldon? Or did others do it for you?' Ranulf taunted.

'I beg your pardon!' Mother Midnight leaned forward, face all concerned, yet Corbett caught the shift in her dark eyes, a fleeting change of mood.

'Luke Faldon,' Ranulf insisted. 'You know him, or

you did. Ralph Manning's henchman, and you must have heard about Manning as well.'

'Let me explain.' Corbett intervened. 'Let me describe things as they are so you'll know.' He gave a succinct description of Manning's murder, what had been found on his desk, the disappearance of Faldon and the henchman being found mortally wounded on the steps of the church. Mother Midnight's only reaction was a constant playing with her finger rings. When he had finished, she turned to the young woman standing behind her.

'Janine,' she spoke in French, 'fetch me my chancery coffer, the one emblazoned with a silver dragon curling along the lid.' Janine bowed and hurried out as silent as a ghost.

'Well, Sir Hugh.' Mother Midnight turned back, her face wreathed in a fixed false smile. 'I know very little about all this. Ralph Manning came here searching for the love of his life, Katherine Ingoldsby. From what I learnt, she was a foolish young girl, admitted to St Sulpice, but then she disappeared. A common enough occurrence. Young women all over London, not to mention the shires beyond, are desperate to escape the drudgery of their lives. I suspect Katherine was one of those.'

'Why should Manning come looking for her here at the Queen of the Night?'

'I asked him the same question.'

'Please listen carefully, madam. I am a royal clerk, now investigating the murder of two other royal clerks, not to mention killings that might be linked to the murders of these same clerks.'

'Oh yes, you are royal clerks.' Mother Midnight's voice was rich with mockery. 'Tell me, what did you find to link me to Manning or to this Katherine Ingoldsby?'

'Just your name and your brothel,' Ranulf replied heatedly. 'We went through Manning's papers. He mentions your name and this whore pit. Why should he do that?' He paused as Corbett gently touched him on the shoulder. Sir Hugh sensed that his henchman had also taken a deep dislike to this arrogant woman.

'Now *you* listen well, clerk,' Mother Midnight retorted, her voice almost a snarl. 'You have come here. You have hinted that me and mine could be connected to the deaths of two silly nuns out at St Sulpice. We are not! For the love of God, can you imagine me or one of my ladies sauntering up to St Sulpice, gaining admission, then being allowed to wander such holy precincts, pinning up warning notes before we saunter off again. Take that before any justice and you'll be the laughing stock of Westminster.' She paused, breathing in deeply. 'And then there's Manning, searching for his young woman. He believed, for God knows what reason, that Katherine Ingoldsby fled St Sulpice to come here. I concede, Sir Hugh, that a number of young ladies of good stock do knock on our door for shelter, but we take very few in. Most of our novices are French. Go on,' she flailed her hand, 'wander this place to your heart's content. Ask any of those who dwell here. They are here of their own volition. They are happy and they do not want to leave. I don't really know,' she continued, 'why Manning came here. He loved Katherine Ingoldsby, she disappeared, and he came hunting for her.'

'And Faldon?'

She held up her hand. 'Just wait for a while,' she murmured. They did so. A short while later, Janine returned carrying a small gold- and silver-embossed coffer. She placed this on the desk before her mistress and would have stepped back behind the chair but Mother Midnight caught her by the hand.

'Janine,' she said, still speaking in French, 'tell our visitors about Master Faldon.'

The young woman with the smooth, beautiful face of an angel blinked then shook her head.

'What is it, Janine?' Corbett asked gently.

'Master Faldon. I met him, or rather he met me when Master Manning came here. I admit we were friendly. He came back without his master. He lay with me and I with him. But then there was a descent into hell. Master Faldon returned time and again. He kept asking for me, and when I was alone with him, he urged me to leave, to set up home with him, to leave my life here to be alone with him, husband and wife. Of course I was flattered, but I knew it would not work. Master Faldon became more and more insistent, at times even violent. On at least three occasions my mistress's guards threw him into the street. Sir Hugh, we have many people visit here, some very powerful. Faldon was abusive and insulting.'

'So you're saying he could have brought about his own death?'

'I am.'

Corbett shifted his gaze. Mother Midnight sat with her head bowed, hands joined in her lap. He was tempted to tell her that he didn't believe a word of what he'd heard, but now was not the moment. Instead he leaned over and tapped the coffer. 'You sent for this; what does it contain?'

Mother Midnight drew a host of keys from a pocket in her gown. She unlocked the coffer and gently moved back the lid, then took out a scroll and handed it to Corbett, inviting him to undo the red ribbon. He did so and carefully unrolled the parchment.

'What does it say, royal clerk?'

Corbett glanced up, then returned to deciphering the clerkly script, which proclaimed that Edith Poppleton, otherwise known as Mother Midnight, was a most loyal subject of the Crown, that she enjoyed the full support and favour of Thomas, Earl of Lancaster, the king's royal cousin and leader of the Council, and that whatever she did, she did for the good of the Crown and the Commonweal. Accordingly, she was not to be troubled in any form whatsoever. The letter was personally signed by Lancaster and sealed with his household insignia.

He reread the manuscript and thrust it back. 'So,' he declared, 'you know nothing about Manning's murder. You have little or no idea about what he was searching for or why Faldon should be killed in such a horrific fashion. In fact, mistress, you know nothing at all.' He got to his feet and stared hard at Mother Midnight. He could feel the anger seething within him. This smug, conceited woman, who made a fortune out of perfumed flesh, had sat here and baited him. He had no doubt that she had had a hand in Manning's and Faldon's murders. She hid behind a tissue of lies and, when pressed, invoked the support and patronage of people who really should know better. He could not walk away from here and leave the impression that he was weak or frightened. He put on his cloak and fastened the clasps. Mother Midnight rose. Corbett abruptly lunged forward and grasped her by the shoulder.

'Remember this,' he hissed, 'I believe you are an assassin, a murderer, a woman steeped in many crimes. Manning's blood cries for vengeance and so does Faldon's. Now listen to me, you sweetened hussy. I am going to hunt you. I will trap you and I shall see you hang. And you can produce papers from the Holy Father in Avignon, supported and sealed by the College of Cardinals but, believe me, I will pin them to the filthy shift you will wear when you hang on the common gallows outside Newgate. Madam, I shall be back.'

Ranulf made himself comfortable in Corbett's chamber in the convent guest house and gazed sorrowfully across at Sir Hugh. Old Master Longface had left the Queen of the Night quietly fuming, and Ranulf knew this was highly dangerous. Corbett rarely gave vent to his anger, and when he did, he would become withdrawn, his mind teeming, seeking for a way to resolve any deadly challenge confronting him. Mother Midnight was such a threat. In truth a highly dangerous woman, the whore-queen openly revelled in the patronage and favour showered on her by the high and mighty. She undoubtedly enjoyed the full protection of Thomas of Lancaster. If she was dangerous, so was the king's wayward cousin, who could whip up the other lords like a huntsman would his hounds. Little wonder Lancaster had sent a cohort of mailed clerks under Faucomburg into Westminster. He was determined to make his presence felt, be it in the Chancery or the pulsating life of the city. Corbett had said the same during their return to St Sulpice. And what could they do to confront such a challenge? They could call on the garrison of the Tower, its archers and men-at-arms, for support. In the end, however, any attempt to arrest and detain such a powerful and malevolent woman could well end in sword and dagger play in the streets of the City. Corbett had been asked to do what he could to maintain harmony and peace in London. He had fought Faucomburg because he had to, but any further violent confrontation had to be avoided.

Ranulf decided to break the silence. He shuffled his feet and cleared his throat.

'Master, we are back now and the blood has cooled; what can we do?'

Corbett stretched his mittened fingers towards the fiery brazier. He stared into the blazing coals, then smiled at Ranulf. 'My good friend, my humours have been restored. I have now met Mother Midnight and she knows me. But for the present, all we can do is what we are skilled at: define the problem, analyse it and apply logic.'

'Shall I draft a memorandum?'

'Certainly.' Corbett pointed at the chancery desk. 'Come, my friend, let us begin.'

Once Ranulf was prepared, quill sharpened and steeped in ink, Corbett rose and walked up and down the guest chamber.

'First, my learned Clerk of the Green Wax, we have Ralph Manning, who worked with us in the Secret Chancery. He fell deeply in love with Katherine Ingoldsby. She became pregnant, but, God save her, lost the child. In the eyes of her aged but not so venerable aunt, Katherine had brought disgrace on the family name, whatever that might mean, so she was taken out of harm's way and lodged as a novice here in St Sulpice. Manning, deeply smitten, followed her here. They met, sometimes secretly, to plan their future. Second, this truly innocent affair seems to have gone well, but everything was shattered when Katherine went missing. She could not be found either here or in the city.

'Now Manning was an excellent clerk. He had the stamina of a hungry ferret and immersed himself in a most rigorous search for Katherine. As he did so, he made notes, really nothing more than elliptical references, the most intriguing being that to Turbeville, who, as you may recall, Ranulf, was a royal knight, a member of the king's household. Turbeville was captured by the

French and, in return for money and favours, became Philip of France's spy at Edward of England's court. He was eventually apprehended – I had a hand in that – and was tried, found guilty and hanged, his corpse left in chains to rot. Mepham and Benstead are now busy on that reference, for it is most mysterious. What can a traitor executed almost seventeen years ago have to do with Katherine Ingoldsby or St Sulpice?

'Anyway, third, Manning apparently did not believe that Katherine had fled but suspected that she had been abducted. However, there is no real proof for that. Of course reality exists in the mind of the beholder. Manning was a trained clerk, skilled in logic. He concluded that Katherine had no reason to flee and hide from him. So he scoured the City, eventually concentrating on a high-class brothel, the Queen of the Night, and its owner, that lady of the dark, Mother Midnight. Manning certainly visited that house of ill repute, as did his henchman Faldon. Deep in his searches, he probably didn't realise the dangers confronting him. A mailed clerk, he thought he was safe. A fatal mistake, and the poor man was poisoned. Why?'

'To silence him?'

'Of course, and his killer was his own henchman, Faldon. We now know what Faldon did and how he achieved it. But why would a man like that be so easily suborned? He was Manning's henchman, friend and confidant. Why the change? Why commit that brutal mortal sin? In answer, I can only suggest those two

great demons that hunt and haunt human souls –
avarice, that deep love of money, and lust, the love of
all that is fleshly, including the very pretty Janine. One
of these, or possibly both, prompted Faldon to commit
the unspeakable.

'So Faldon murdered Manning, but then life took
one of its strange twists. Faldon himself was attacked,
grievously wounded and, I suspect, left as a warning.
And do you know, Ranulf, I agree with you: that
warning was directed towards us. Mother Midnight
must have learned of our arrival both here and in
Westminster. She must have heard about my confrontation with Faucomburg and she would know that I
would become involved. She is deeply confident that
she can warn us off. You saw how she flaunted her
privileged status. She sees herself as above the law.
Manning tried to flex his muscles at the Queen of the
Night, using his authority to demand certain answers,
and he was murdered. Faldon also had to be removed.
A stark warning to other inquisitive clerks. In her eyes
we are to leave well alone. Well, Ranulf, we shall see
about that.

'Fourth, we now arrive at what I call the root of all
this murder and mayhem. I have mentioned it before.
In my view, Manning truly believed that Katherine had
been abducted. A fine young lady whom any brothel
might covet. He visited Mother Midnight and challenged
her. She of course would plead her innocence and,
according to all the evidence, she was correct. She made
a similar offer to us. She invited us to tour her brothel,

to question the girls, most of whom are French. Manning must have been told the same, but what prompted him to go there in the first place? At this moment in time, I cannot answer that question.

'Fifth, and just as important, Manning believed there was something rotten, or at least highly irregular, here at St Sulpice. Did he suspect that other young women like his Katherine were being abducted? But again, there seems to be no evidence for that at the Queen of the Night. Moreover, Mother Abbess Eleanor provided the names of two novices who had left the convent. You did a careful search and, according to what you discovered, both girls simply returned to their family home. However,' Corbett added ruefully, 'I made one terrible mistake, an oversight that I want to address. Ranulf, when we are finished here, go to Prioress Margaret or the abbess. I need to see a list of all novices who have left St Sulpice in the last three years. I need their full names as well as precise information about where they lived before they entered the convent.'

'And if they refuse?'

'Tell them that you will hasten to Westminster and obtain a writ of search and seize from the royal justices and return here with a cohort of court bailiffs to enforce it.'

Ranulf grinned. 'So, master, why do you want this list?'

'I've been reflecting, Ranulf. Manning's Katherine had no kin outside these walls and she disappeared. Megotta, a moon girl, a convicted felon, had no close kin and she too has vanished from St Sulpice. We need to concentrate on this, so get that list sooner rather than later.'

Corbett sipped from the tankard of ale he'd brought from the buttery. 'Now, to return to these mysteries. Sixth, the young woman Megotta. Manning must have been truly desperate. He obtained a pardon for this convicted killer and somehow placed her here as a novice. Why? The obvious answer is that Megotta was his spy, though she was given little time to do anything.'

'She was a convicted felon. She might have fled.'

'I doubt that. I believe she was abducted.'

'So seventh,' Ranulf intervened, 'Manning believed something was very wrong in this convent. I suspect he also saw some link, strange as it must be, between St Sulpice and the Queen of the Night.'

'The obvious answer to that is the hypothesis that young women were abducted from St Sulpice and forced to work as prostitutes at the Queen of the Night. But,' Corbett shook his head, 'that's too simplistic, and there's not a shred of evidence that even hints at it.'

'Nevertheless,' Ranulf retorted, 'Mother Midnight seems determined not to allow anyone to meddle in her affairs. Manning and Faldon did, and they paid a heavy price, which she was keen to share with us.'

'True, Ranulf, and that's as far as we can go at the moment. So we begin a second schedule – the murders here at St Sulpice. Let us see what we know. First, there have been two murders, though the why, the how and the who are a mystery: two nuns murdered in quite eerie circumstances. The only loose thread we have detected is a casual remark by Sister Fidelis. She was the one who found Constantia stabbed on a boat in the middle of the convent carp pond. We know how the assassin arranged that. However, Fidelis seems to have mentioned to others that when she discovered Constantia, she also glimpsed something amiss. We do not know what that was, but the question begs a further one – was Fidelis murdered because of her remarks? Indeed, her death intrigues me; it's almost the perfect murder. I would have dismissed it as an accident if it hadn't been for those messages left pinned to the abbess's door. And where did those come from? Mother Midnight actually spoke the truth. Although the messages were allegedly signed by her, I cannot imagine anyone from her brothel secretly entering the convent to display such warnings. So, Ranulf, we must conclude that the writer of those two proclamations is also the assassin, and possibly a member of the community at St Sulpice.' Corbett fell silent.

'Sir Hugh, one further problem.' Ranulf pointed to the door and windows. 'We are secure here, but let me warn you, Mother Midnight is a highly dangerous woman. We know she killed Manning, or had him killed. We saw what she did to Faldon. She doesn't give a damn about anything or anyone. To quote the words of scripture, she fears neither God nor man.' He paused, hands tapping the hilt of his dagger lying on a stool next to him.

'Spit it out, Ranulf.'

'Sir Hugh, you seized Mother Midnight today. You grasped her shoulder and shook her like a dog would a rat. You promised that you would see her hang. I was watching her face: that woman is murder incarnate. You insulted her before her maid.' Ranulf laughed sharply. 'You showed you didn't care either. You were like a knight in the lists. You are involved in a fight to the death. I am very worried about you, master: either she dies or we do. You know I speak the truth.' Corbett nodded in agreement. 'Mother Midnight will have her revenge. Now it could come from some street assassin or down some darkened alleyway when the shadows close in. However, to be brief and to the point, if I was Mother Midnight, I would strike to kill you here at St Sulpice. We are distant from the city, we cannot call upon the watch or the royal archers at the Tower. If an attack is launched, and I believe it will be, they will come here in the dead of night and it will be sooner rather than later.'

'I agree,' Corbett conceded. 'Perhaps I shouldn't have lost my temper but, for the love of God, tomorrow morning somewhere in the city some poor bastard will be hanged for stealing a loaf of bread or money to feed his children. Yet that bitch killed my friend Manning and dismembered poor Faldon. Mother Midnight is steeped in sin. She is the cause of so much wickedness and now she thinks she can crow like a cock on a shit heap, protected by the sword of Faucomburg and the letters of Thomas of Lancaster. I will remind her about all this when I put the noose around her neck and kick the ladder away. I truly believe that woman has caused widespread, deep unhappiness. Hell awaits her.

'Now, I have given vent to my feelings. Ranulf, you are correct. I could ask for a cohort of Tower archers to be dispatched here, but that might take time. In the meanwhile, we will each stand guard: four hours' duty each. I'll take the first watch.'

Megotta felt her prayers had been answered. Using the money taken from her abusers, she had bought new clothes, dressing like a man in a hard leather jerkin, woollen hose and good stout boots. She had escaped the cold and hired a narrow chamber in the Inglenook, a small, quiet tavern not far from where she had been imprisoned and within walking distance of the Queen of the Night, a tavern mentioned so often by Manning. She had washed herself carefully, changed, and eaten a full hot meal in the shadowy corner of the tavern taproom. She had reflected on what had happened to her. Sometimes she was on the verge of tears. She knew about the sexual games played between men and women; she had flirted with other travellers, she had kissed beneath a full moon and made promises she knew she wouldn't keep, but that had all been child's play. What had happened to her in that cell had violated her soul and started a fire that would not be quenched. She wanted vengeance. She had changed and become another person, acting the part of a young man-at-arms slouching through the city.

She had decided to discover what had happened to

Manning, and journeyed to Westminster, where she had received the dreadful news. A street herald, one of those well-known informants who collected gossip and proclaimed it to anyone who paid him, had informed her in hushed tones how the clerk Ralph Manning had been foully murdered in his chamber, whilst his henchman Faldon had been found grievously wounded on the steps of a church. At first Megotta could not believe this. Manning was so confident, so capable, a man of integrity whom she had trusted. True, the thought had crossed her mind that he could have been involved in her abduction, but she had quickly rejected that. She had hoped that he would help her obtain justice, but now he was gone, and that eerily taciturn Faldon was also dead.

She had paid the street herald another penny to provide her with more news. He had declared how Sir Hugh Corbett, a royal clerk, the Keeper of the King's Secret Seal, a man to be truly feared, had arrived in Westminster to pursue Manning's killers. How he had clashed with Faucomburg, Thomas of Lancaster's henchman and leader of a cohort of mailed clerks. Megotta had listened to his lurid description of the duel between Corbett and Faucomburg and its unexpected outcome. She had then slipped the street herald a further coin and said she wanted to know as much as he did about Sir Hugh Corbett. What he had told her had convinced her. Corbett was of the same mould as Manning. A royal clerk, a man of integrity, someone she could trust. She was determined, in her own time and in her own place, to speak to Sir Hugh Corbett.

In the meantime, she spent most of her daylight hours in her narrow chamber. At night, however, cloaked and harnessed for war, she'd take up position where she could keep the Queen of the Night under close scrutiny, waiting to see if anything sinister occurred. Yet during the hours she spent there, she glimpsed nothing amiss, except the fact that many who frequented the tavern came hooded and visored, determined not to be recognised by anyone else. The only exception was a cohort of mailed clerks sporting the insignia of Thomas, Earl of Lancaster. Megotta had seen similar escutcheons when she wandered the highways north of the Trent. These bully boys had no difficulty crowding through the majestic door of the Queen of the Night. But for the rest, nothing.

She did leave her chamber occasionally, to buy necessities. She also plucked up courage to go down to Dowgate, where she had learnt that a merchant cog, *The Picardy*, had recently berthed. Wrapped in her cloak, she had wandered the quayside and, whenever possible, studied the sturdy one-masted, big-bellied sea cog. She immediately noticed how the gangplank was closely guarded, both on the quayside and on the deck above. She waited and watched. Eventually she glimpsed the ship's master, a tall, thin-faced, sour-eyed rogue garbed in leather with a broad war belt strapped around his waist. She studied him and his henchman, together with any members of the crew who came ashore.

She also made careful note of what the very garrulous taverner at a shabby alehouse fronting the quayside told her. He informed her that *The Picardy* was an English cog out of Dover and did constant business with Boulogne and other ports on the other side of the Narrow Seas. Interestingly, he also explained how the ship had been due to sail but had been delayed, perhaps even for days.

Megotta, with her hair all shorn, acted the part of a young man looking for work, though she soon decided that her presence on the quayside would eventually be noticed. She was more than aware that whoever had organised her abduction must be beside themselves with fury. She had killed three of the coven, plundered their corpses and escaped. Her description would be carefully noted and disseminated to the legion of professional informants, street spies and runnel rats, ever hungry for the rewards being offered for information. Now and again she glimpsed people staring at her. She was a stranger, and that in itself was dangerous. She decided to leave. She had learnt enough.

She returned to watching the Queen of the Night. For hours she experienced the same freezing boredom as before, but this was abruptly interrupted by the arrival of a cart, two men on its seat. She watched as the horses, blowing noisily and scraping their hooves, stopped before the huge gate that sealed off an alleyway running along the side of the tavern. Sconce torches coated in tar and pitch flared either side of the gateposts. The carters had to wait for the great wooden doors to be opened. One of them pulled back his deep hood, and Megotta caught her breath. 'The first!' she exclaimed quietly. 'The first link in the chain.' She stared again, but she was certain. The lead carter was undoubtedly the master of *The Picardy* and, when the second man pulled his own hood back, she immediately recognised the captain's henchman.

The moon girl studied the cart in the dancing light of the torches. It looked empty, so why was it here? To accept something? Its abrupt appearance at such a late hour made her deeply suspicious. She settled down to watch, rubbing her arms and legs and moving to keep warm. The hours passed. Now and again the front door of the tavern would open. Customers would slip out like shadows, scurrying into the dark. The Lancastrian clerks, however, were boisterous in their departure, slapping and pushing each other and breaking into raucous laughter.

At last lights were doused both within and without the tavern. Abruptly the gates were pulled back, squealing on their hinges, and the cart emerged. From where she stood, Megotta thought it seemed heavier, but it was impossible to determine what it contained. She decided to follow it, an easy enough task along the darkened streets. She kept herself muffled and hooded against the cold. She also drew the sword she'd seized from one of her tormentors. The glint of light on its broad steel blade made sure the shadow-watchers and dark-dwellers kept their distance. Others were more importunate. Beggars shuffled forward with their clacking dishes and hideous injuries, be it the removal of an eye, an ear or nose, a missing leg, a withered arm

or an injured hand. Some were genuine, others the work
of the masters of deceit. The whores, their faces
grotesquely painted, heads covered in flaming blood-red
wigs, whispered, murmured and enticed from doorways
and alley mouths, one eye on potential customers, the
other on the watchmen wandering the streets, sharp
white canes at the ready.

Megotta thought the cart would return to Dowgate,
but it kept to the main thoroughfare stretching past the
dark mass of Castle Baynard, staying within bowshot
of the Thames. She followed it out onto the lonely
stretch of wild countryside bordering the river, where
it abruptly turned left and made its way along the coffin
paths and tinker tracks down to the riverside. Here and
there were gaps in the sprouting vegetation, the coarse
grass and bushes already tinged with frost as the cold
night turned freezing. The cart emerged from the heathland and stopped at a lonely stretch of riverbank.

Megotta made herself secure as she wondered what
the carters intended. They sat for a while staring across
the river, and she realised that they must be making
sure no skiff or fishing smack sailed close. Eventually
they climbed down. The night was now clear, the sky
frosty with stars. She watched as they took something
from the cart, laid it on the ground and began to pound
it with what looked like heavy hammers or mallets. She
could hear their gasps and curses wafting on the cold
night breeze. Eventually they finished and picked up
the bundle. She shivered. It looked like a corpse, a
woman's body, naked, its white flesh catching the light,

long hair trailing. The carters swung it backwards and forwards like a sack, then tossed it into the river with a noisy splash. Megotta whispered a prayer.

The two men stood for a while watching the Thames, now in fast flow, catch the corpse and carry it away. Megotta had seen enough. It was time for her to leave.

Corbett spent the next two days going over the notes he and Ranulf had made. He also wandered the convent, taking careful note of everything, which reaffirmed his conclusions that St Sulpice was exactly what it claimed to be. A retiring home for ladies who wanted to forsake the world in return for comfortable, devout service to the gospel. The nuns he encountered were pleasant and cheerful and fully committed to their religious life. He closely questioned Sisters Marie and Agatha; both seemed very happy with their lot.

Ranulf eventually returned with a list of young women who had left St Sulpice over the last three years. Corbett carefully studied their particulars. He asked Ranulf and Chanson to scrutinise each one and establish where they lived.

On the third day after Corbett's return from the city, Mepham and Benstead arrived at St Sulpice. Both clerks were muffled against the cold, complaining bitterly about their journey. Corbett met them and their hooded, visored companion in his chamber at the guest house. He told his guests not to stand on ceremony but to make themselves comfortable on the stools and chests he'd arranged around the braziers. Once everyone was settled, he served them mulled wine and toasted manchet loaves coated with herbal cheese. Their companion, a lank-haired, mournful-looking character with a perpetually dripping nose and protruding red ears, now introduced himself.

'My name is Raul Briscoe.' When he smiled, he looked pleasant enough.

'Ah.' Corbett nodded. 'I have heard of you, both your name and your reputation. In fact, I've seen your petitions, which flow into the Chancery. I have not been as attentive as I should be, as I've been absent for some time from Westminster. Anyway.' He glanced at Mepham and Benstead. 'Raul is here because?'

Briscoe tapped the medallion on the chain around his neck. 'As you know, Sir Hugh, I am the Harrower of the Dead, an officer of the city council. My task is to collect and store corpses found throughout the city, a truly macabre task. I and my collectors comb both the streets and the river. We pluck corpses from here and there. We make no apology for what we do, because our work is essential. Now in the normal run of things I would not challenge you in this way. However, I am concerned.'

'About what?'

'Sir Hugh, I have petitioned the Chancery, I have asked for their help, but officers such as yourself are absent on this business or that, whilst the king seems only interested in his favourite.'

'Good government grinds on,' Corbett murmured. 'And we must use whatever is given to us. So, my friend?'

The Harrower drew a deep breath.

'Sir Hugh, over the last two years, perhaps even longer, I have fished corpses out of the Thames. I take them to the Paradise, the great death house, the public mortuary not far from St Mary atte Bow. The corpses remain there before being blessed and committed for burial. However, increasingly I am being asked to bury the corpses of young ladies who have been brutally murdered. Now these are not street walkers or common whores; the flesh of these cadavers is delicate, their nails, both hands and feet, carefully manicured. We bury them, but I am intrigued. Sir Hugh, as you know, women disappear every day in the city – God forgive us men for the violence and abuse we show them. Nevertheless, the corpses I am talking about are soft, supple, perfumed, carefully tended. But that's only half the mystery. What is truly intriguing is that neither I nor any of my officers have ever been approached or questioned.'

'In a word,' Corbett demanded, 'nobody claims these corpses?'

'Sir Hugh, you have it, yet the mystery remains. Why should such delicate young women be found in the streets or the river, a mallet blow to the back of the head, another to the face, wiping out whatever likeness you might see there?'

Corbett gazed at the Harrower of the Dead. 'So you are bringing these matters to my attention. Young women, perhaps of high status, murdered with a blow to the back of the head, their faces smashed beyond recognition, their bodies tossed away like rubbish?'

'I am.'

'And the other matters?' He pressed on. 'Perhaps Master Briscoe should leave us.'

'No, no.' Mepham waved a hand. 'Let him stay. Listen, Sir Hugh, we have established that Thomas Turbeville was a traitor to the Crown. He was hanged at Tyburn, his corpse left to rot in chains. You took a leading part in hunting and exposing him. You know that the old King Edward was furious, seething with rage at such treachery. Turbeville's wife, Mathilda, made the hideous mistake of thinking they would win some mercy or compassion from the king. They were brutally disappointed. As you may know, Sir Hugh, in Paris the shoulders of whores are branded with the fleur-de-lis, a symbol of control. Turbeville's widow and two daughters came before the king; they pleaded for mercy and were rejected. Edward said they were traitors as guilty as Sir Thomas, that they were French whores and should be branded as such.' He shrugged. 'Sir Hugh, you knew the old king. He could be good and compassionate, but he had a ruthless streak, a profound lack of kindness that turned him chilling.'

'Too true,' Corbett agreed. 'I fought with him in Scotland. I saw what happened during the sack of Berwick. Men, woman and children cut down like flowers of the field. In some streets the blood ran ankle deep. Edward was a great but terrible king. I am sorry.' He gestured at Mepham. 'You were saying.'

'Mathilda Turbeville and her two daughters, Edith and Emma, were branded with a red-hot fleur-de-lis high on their backs. A gesture of contempt and rejection. Edward personally arranged it. Afterwards, they were told to wander the streets and beg for what they needed. No one knows what truly happened to them. I have searched the records, but there's nothing to be found.'

'How do you know about the branding?' Corbett demanded.

'Ah.' Mepham clapped Briscoe on the shoulder. 'Our good Harrower of the Dead searches for corpses, but he is also a royal clerk. In a word, Sir Hugh, Master Briscoe was an apprentice hangman when Turbeville was executed some seventeen years ago. He listened to the chatter about what happened to Turbeville's family.'

Corbett rose and walked up and down the chamber. 'We have,' he declared, 'a real problem. Manning and Faldon have been taken care of. We know what happened to them and why. We also know how they were killed, but there's a lack of hard evidence, real proof. They were certainly murdered by Mother Midnight, yet how do we press the case?' He paused in his walking. 'We must also accept that we live in very dangerous times. The king has fled north and the city is under the control of the likes of Faucomburg and his coven. We are not safe here. We are vulnerable to attack. Gentlemen, for the moment, we are finished.'

Corbett thanked Mepham, Benstead and the Harrower of the Dead. He assured them that they had done well. He escorted them to the convent gate, then returned to his own chamber. He sat for a while allowing his mind to drift, but time and again he returned to that violent confrontation with Mother Midnight. Ranulf was correct. She would not let such an insult pass. She would soon retaliate.

The following night, Corbett took the first watch, just after the bells tolled for compline. He sat in the small waiting chamber on the ground floor of the guest house, the door closed and locked, and watched through a narrow window as the lights of the convent faded. Ranulf came down to ask if he wanted anything to eat or drink. Corbett refused. He told his henchman to go back to his chamber and remain vigilant.

Darkness descended. The convent fell silent. Corbett sat listening to the sounds of the night. Nothing extraordinary: the hoot of an owl, the shrieking cry of some forest creature. He dozed, waking abruptly as the arbalest he held clattered to the floor. He rubbed his eyes, picked up the weapon, then froze. Just for a brief moment, a matter of heartbeats, he'd heard a whisper. Someone was outside, creeping close to the guest house. He checked the arbalest and hoped that Ranulf and Chanson on the floor above were vigilant and watchful. He moved over and peered between the shutters, catching the glint of torchlight, dark shapes moving. They were under attack!

He moved out of the chamber into the passageway and stood, crossbow ready. The door facing him slowly opened, and a figure crept in cowled and masked. Corbett spoke. 'Good evening, my friend.' The man turned. Corbett released the catch and watched the crossbow bolt shatter the man's forehead.

A set of shutters were pulled back, a fiery torch hurled through. Corbett, running at a crouch, snatched the burning brand and tossed it back through the opening. Ranulf and Chanson arrived fully harnessed and hurried to crouch beneath the open windows. At Corbett's signal, they rose and loosed bolts into the pools of light created by the attackers' torches. Corbett heard screams as the quarrels found their targets. The tables had now turned. Corbett and his two companions were protected by the walls of the guest house, whilst they had the windows through which to loose quarrel after quarrel at their attackers. The wolfsheads now realised their mistake in carrying torches, which only made them clearer targets. A group of assailants brought a log to smash down the front door. They made one paltry attempt, then dropped the ram and retreated. Corbett, peering into the dark, realised that the attackers were now worried about an enemy behind them.

The convent bells were ringing out the tocsin. Corbett glimpsed some of the sisters gathering in a doorway of one of the buildings. The fury and commotion abruptly died and a sinister calm descended, an eerie silence broken only by the cries and groans of the wounded outside; eventually even these ceased. Ranulf shouted at Corbett to remain where he was, whilst he, sword and dagger drawn, crept out of the guest house, moving swiftly into the inky darkness.

A short while later he returned, gesturing that the threat had disappeared. Corbett and Chanson joined him outside. Prioress Margaret and Sisters Marie and

Perpetua came hurrying across, each carrying a torch. Corbett was surprised at how the good sisters seemed so calm and composed, Prioress Margaret in particular. She informed him that the convent had been attacked by outlaws and wolfsheads in recent times. She also added that she had dispatched a courier to bring in Stigand and other labourers from the nearby village. She asked what they should do. Corbett declared that they should leave the fallen where they were; Ranulf would ensure the wounded were tended to. The good sisters said they'd entrust such matters to Sir Hugh and hurried off in a pool of torchlight, chattering vigorously amongst themselves.

'Were there any wounded?' Corbett asked as he and his companions shared a jug of freshly brewed morning ale from a small tun the buttery had sent across earlier in the day. They'd also fed on a platter of cold meats, cheese and bread left under a linen cloth on a side table. Corbett drank, feeling the excitement drain away. He allowed the warmth of the chamber, the richness of the ale and the close companionship of his comrades to relax him.

'There were none, master. We'll inspect the corpses at first light, but two of the dead had had their throats slashed.'

'The mercy cut?' Chanson asked.

'Yes, my friend. Those wounded were unable to retreat but could not be allowed to live long enough to be questioned by us.' Ranulf laughed grimly. 'And they would have been, hung over a roaring fire in the convent smithy!'

'Well, we know where our attackers came from,' Corbett declared. 'Undoubtedly emissaries from Mother Midnight. They were dispatched to deliver her murderous regards. Believe me, my friends, I will see that witch-queen burn.'

'But we have no proof,' Ranulf retorted, 'and when we go through the corpses tomorrow, we will find nothing. Not a scrap of parchment, nothing to link those murderous bastards to that wicked woman.'

'We expected the attack.' Corbett sipped from his tankard. 'We knew it would come. Mother Midnight rides high. She has got rid of two royal clerks; why not make it five? Our assailants were not blessed with intelligence. They came carrying torches, they were frightened. They hoped to burn us out rather than engage in dagger play. And did you notice something very interesting, during the dying moments of the attack?'

'Yes, yes, I did.'

'What?' Chanson demanded.

'Well,' Corbett replied, 'in a word, Chanson, some-body followed our attackers in, someone favourably disposed towards us. Whoever it was began to loose crossbow bolts from behind. I would say at least two of our attackers were killed by this benevolent stranger. Of course the gang responsible became frightened, panicked, and so they fled. I do wonder who our mys-terious ally was and why they should intervene now.

Anyway, Ranulf, Chanson, try to sleep. I'll take this watch. I'll guard the guest house and keep an eye on the corpses.'

At first light, Corbett and his two companions were joined by the abbess, the prioress and the other leading nuns of the convent. All of them confessed that they had slept little, for the attack had caused concern and excitement; what Prioress Margaret coolly termed 'a true flurry in the hen coop'.

'Well, the fox has gone.' Sister Marie spoke bluntly. 'And badly burnt he was.' She gestured at the seven corpses laid out in the yard, a puddle of blood drying around each of them.

Ranulf and Corbett had set them out, pulling back hoods, removing visors so that the faces could clearly be seen. As Ranulf had said, two of them had had their throats slashed, heads hanging back. The others had been killed by crossbow quarrels, and Corbett noticed how two of these lay slightly arched because the heavy quarrels had pierced them between the shoulder blades. The men looked like any group of rifflers from the city: shaggy haired, bearded, garbed in motley rags with cheap boots and battered war belts. Only one of them wore a sword sheath; the rest of the weapons were either small hand axes or daggers.

'I have searched them thoroughly,' Ranulf declared. 'I found nothing, not a scrap of parchment nor a piece of jewellery, that tells us anything about them.'

'Abbess Eleanor.' Corbett walked over and looked

pityingly into the abbess's worried white face. 'Mother Abbess, Prioress Margaret, my good ladies, did any of you come to our assistance last night? No, no, I did not expect any of you to become embroiled. But did anyone here loose an arbalest at our attackers?'

'No,' the abbess retorted firmly.

'Did that happen?' Prioress Margaret demanded.

'Oh it certainly did,' Corbett replied. 'These wolfs-heads were attacked from behind. For them it was the final straw; they broke and fled. Prioress Margaret, you have organised a search of the grounds?'

'Of course. Stigand and his labourers are under strict orders to search for anything or anyone connected with this attack. We must inform the sheriff and the city council, but that will do little good. From what I gather, everyone is caught up with the king's . . .' she hesitated, choosing her words, 'our gracious king's involvement with Lord Gaveston.' She paused. 'Sir Hugh, what should be done with the corpses?'

Corbett dug into his purse and, ignoring the prioress's protests, pushed a silver piece into her hand. 'You'll need this,' he declared. 'Ask Stigand and two of his comrades to load the corpses into the cart, cover them with a canvas sheet and take them to the Paradise, the city's mortuary hall. They should speak to the Harrower of the Dead. I will furnish Stigand with a brief letter in which I will ask the Harrower to bury these corpses in Poor Man's Lot. I'll also arrange to have a requiem sung for their souls; God knows they'll need it.'

The prioress looked as if she was about to refuse, but Sister Marie intervened.

'I'll go with Stigand,' she said. 'I know what you want, Sir Hugh: the removal of these corpses as swiftly as decency can allow.'

Corbett and his two companions left the nuns to their discussion and returned to their respective chambers, where they washed and changed. They attended the brief low mass celebrated by the visiting chaplain, then broke their fast in the buttery. Corbett instructed Ranulf and Chanson to go into the city and search out the young women on the list given to them by the abbess. Ranulf was reluctant to leave his master, as he put it, unguarded and undefended. Corbett laughingly reassured both his companions that they would find him hale, hearty and hungry on their return.

He watched them leave, then, lost in his own thoughts, wandered the convent grounds. He revisited the jetty stretching out into the freezing carp pond. Once again he studied the sluice gate and the two bum boats. 'I just wonder,' he whispered, 'what Sister Fidelis saw here. I really do.' He stayed for a while listening to the crows crying out against each other, then made his way to Devil's Tower. The door to the stairwell and the steps leading up still hung open. He climbed up slowly, examining every step. Once he'd pulled himself through the hatchway at the top, he stood leaning against the crenellations, staring out across the mist-hung countryside. 'You were here,' he murmured, 'weren't you, Fidelis? You had your little wine skin and your platter of food, your petty luxuries, something to comfort you after the long climb up, but then what? What sent you hurtling down those steps in such a hurry? Ah well.'

He returned to his own chamber and busied himself for a while. The day drew on, and he joined the nuns in the choir stalls to sing vespers. He would have loved to become involved in the chant, that melodious fall and rise as the verses to the psalm were sung out and answered. Nevertheless, he kept silent, realising that his voice would only shatter the harmony of this perfect prayer at the end of the day. Once vespers was over, he joined the good sisters in the refectory for a cup of wine and a light collation. He was deep in conversation with the sharp-eyed prioress, who was curious about his work in the city, when Ranulf and Chanson arrived. Corbett excused himself and followed his two companions out into the darkness.

'Sir Hugh, it's best if we go to your room.'

Corbett glanced over his shoulder. Sisters Marie and Agatha had followed him out and were watching him curiously. He smiled bleakly at them and led his two companions back across to his chamber. Ranulf closed the door behind them and leaned against it.

'Master, listen to this. We didn't complete the list, but we found nothing, which in itself is suspicious.'

'Ranulf, what on earth do you mean?'

'We found nothing. Let me give you an example.' Ranulf pulled the list out of his pocket and stabbed the first name with his finger. 'Read it, master. Imelda

Holbrook, daughter of a mercer whose dwelling was in Bridle Lane, next to the tavern the Golden Cockerel. Both the merchant and his wife died. Imelda became a foundling, an orphan of the parish, so when she came of age, the parish placed her in St Sulpice. They thought they were doing the best for the girl. According to the testimony of neighbours, Imelda was in full agreement. In other words, master, she had nothing to flee to in the city. No relatives, no house, no kin, nothing to support her. So why should she leave St Sulpice? Where did she go? What happened to her?'

'And you found the same with others?'

'Yes, I did,' Ranulf declared. 'Perhaps they fled because they didn't want to be here at St Sulpice, or maybe they didn't leave of their own volition but were forcibly abducted—' He broke off at a knock at the door. Chanson answered it and Sister Marie bustled into the chamber.

'Sir Hugh,' she declared, 'Abbess Eleanor and others of our council need to meet with you in our chapter house. They would like you to join them now.'

'Ranulf and I will be there shortly,' Corbett informed her.

Sister Marie left. Corbett pulled a face at the closing door, then glanced at Ranulf.

'I'm sure they wish to question us about the attack, so let us go and see the good sisters.'

Sister Marie was waiting for them outside the guest house, garbed in a thick fur-rimmed cloak and stamping her sandalled feet against the cold. She ushered them across into the chapter house and insisted on thrusting goblets of hot posset into their hands. Corbett sipped from his; the hot wine was delicious and laced with savoury herbs. Even after the first gulp, he could feel the warmth spreading through his body. He raised his cup in toast at the abbess and the other nuns sitting either side of her.

'My lady, this is appreciated. You wish to see us?'

'The attack last night . . .'

'The attack is nothing to do with the convent,' Corbett retorted.

'It is now.' Prioress Margaret spoke sharply. 'Our buildings were attacked and damaged, blood was spilled on consecrated ground and our God-fearing community placed in mortal danger.'

'I am not responsible for that,' Corbett replied. 'I am the king's justiciar, so the attack on me last night was treason, and all those involved deserve the full punishment: being hanged, drawn and quartered. I regret the damage and the fear caused, but I am entrusted with the king's law and it is my duty to enforce his peace come what may. If you have any objection to this, write to the Chancellor, or indeed His Grace the king, if you can discover where he is.

'Now, my ladies, I have questions for you. My good friend Ranulf here visited a number of houses in the city. They had one thing in common – a young woman from each of those houses entered St Sulpice as a novice. A number of these, however, left this convent and haven't been seen since. When we checked on the particulars given, we found that each of the young women who disappeared was a foundling or an orphan with no kith or kin to return to. So I ask myself two questions. Why did they leave the security of this place for virtually nothing: no family, no kin, no house, no dwelling? And where did they flee to?'

'Are you implying,' Prioress Margaret demanded, 'that these young ladies were abducted?'

'I have no proof of that.'

'And that is important.' Abbess Eleanor spoke up, fingering her Ave beads, eyes blinking furiously. 'Sir Hugh, listen. We take in orphans and foundlings who have no roots in the city and, to be truthful, they have none here either. Perhaps that's the reason they leave. They want to find a life for themselves, rather than moving from here to there like a piece on a chessboard. Go to any convent in the kingdom, you'll find the same: young ladies come, young ladies go. Sir Hugh, once a young woman leaves these precincts, I have no power over her whatsoever. If we try to bring her back by force, we render ourselves liable to the law. We could be accused of kidnapping or abduction. Wouldn't you agree?'

Corbett nodded slowly.

'And yet,' Ranulf spoke up, 'the nuns who left are a mystery except for one: Katherine Ingoldsby, much beloved by our now dead comrade Ralph Manning. Isn't it true that she was happy enough here? Manning left no indication to the contrary, so why should she flee? Forsaking not only comfortable lodgings here but a man who apparently loved her deeply.'

Corbett smiled to himself. He was pleased at what Ranulf had asked; he had not thought of that himself. According to all the evidence, Katherine Ingoldsby had been content at St Sulpice. Manning had made no attempt to withdraw her. So why had she disappeared?

'Tell me,' he asked, breaking the uncomfortable silence, 'who would know that a certain novice was an orphan or foundling?'

'I for one,' Prioress Margaret declared. 'But there again, Sir Hugh, as my good sisters will attest, the novices chatter amongst themselves. They hold nothing back. They talk about where they came from, who they know. In other words, it was common knowledge where any novice came from or what they intended.'

Corbett murmured his understanding and sat back in his chair, studying these nuns. Abbess Eleanor, Prioress Margaret, Sisters Perpetua, Marie, Agatha and Callista. Clever women who were probably relieved to escape from the world for the pleasant harmony of St Sulpice. He felt slightly guilty that he had played a part in the disruption of such peace, yet he was also deeply uneasy. He was growing increasingly aware of two strands of murderous mystery. The first strand was here at St Sulpice. Two nuns killed in the most gruesome way, with warnings apparently left before or after the murders were committed. The second strand was not so clear, but there seemed to be some form of connection, surprising though it might be, between this convent and its community and the murky politics and salacious life of the Queen of the Night. Manning had certainly sensed the latter, but why? What was his evidence? So far very little. The only real proof being those notes pinned to the abbess's door allegedly signed by Mother Midnight. But in itself, that was spurious.

Corbett rubbed his eyes, glancing swiftly at the abbess and her companions. It was time for the abrupt question.

'Turbeville!' he exclaimed. 'Thomas Turbeville. Does that name mean anything to you?'

'Of course,' Prioress Margaret replied. 'He was a local knight, yes? Found guilty of treason and executed. His wife, Mathilda, came here, sick and destitute. She died in our infirmary and now lies buried in God's Acre.'

'Did she come alone?' Corbett asked, recalling what he'd learnt from Mepham and Benstead the previous day.

'Why shouldn't she?' Sister Marie demanded, her face all pert and stubborn.

'Her two daughters, Edith and Emma – they didn't accompany her?'

'No, no,' the prioress replied. 'She came by herself. It must be, what, sixteen or seventeen years ago.'

'So she died alone, with no kith or kin?'

'Yes, God rest her.'

Corbett chewed the corner of his lip.

'Why do you ask about Turbeville?' Sister Marie demanded.

'Oh, Manning made reference to him in his notes. I just wonder. But tell me, Abbess Eleanor, was there any other reason why you wanted to see me?'

'Sir Hugh, another message has been left pinned to my door.' She opened the small casket beside her, took out a scrap of parchment between finger and thumb and disdainfully tossed it onto the table. Corbett stretched out, took it and read the stark message written in blood-red ink: *And so through fire in this life and beyond, judgement shall be awarded.*

'Mother Abbess, do you know what this means?'

'To me it is nonsense.'

'True, true,' Corbett murmured, getting to his feet. 'But it is also a clear, stark warning that another murder may be imminent.'

Corbett and Ranulf left the meeting. Chanson, waiting outside, was impatient to return to the stables, so Corbett let him go. The two clerks then wandered the convent grounds. Workmen had removed most of the signs of the recent attack. The corpses had been stripped and carted away, blood splashes cleaned, doors and shutters repaired. Ranulf excused himself, declaring he was exhausted and eager for bed. Corbett bade him well and continued his walk. He wondered what the most recent message pinned to the abbess's door really meant. What was the assassin plotting? Lost in thought, he found himself outside Devil's Tower. The door was open and he stepped into the dusty stairwell. He was thinking of Fidelis's fall when he abruptly felt cold and realised he was not alone. He reached for his dagger.

'Stay your hand, clerk,' a voice rasped behind him.

Corbett heard the click of a crossbow being primed.

He turned swiftly, going down into a crouch, dagger out. The shadowy figure holding the crossbow stepped away, lowering the weapon.

'Sir Hugh Corbett, Keeper of the Secret Seal, good day. I mean you well. I am Megotta.'

# PART FIVE

The said Thomas Turbeville was seized on the
Saturday before the Feast of St Michael Archangel.

Corbett rose to his feet. Megotta placed the crossbow down and pulled back her hood. A lovely strong face, beautifully formed, with deep expressive eyes and a determined mouth. He took an immediate liking to her. He grinned, pulled off his gloves and extended his hand, which she clasped with both of hers.

'Megotta, it is a pleasure to meet you. You know Manning is dead, Faldon too, both brutally murdered?'

'I heard the same,' she replied. 'From a street herald.' Her voice was surprisingly strong and sweet. 'The street swallows are full of such news. But only for a while. Matters in the city gain pace. They say the king will go to war with Lancaster over Gaveston.'

'That's not news,' Corbett declared. 'The confrontation's been coming for years.' He picked up the arbalest. 'I'll carry this; pull up your hood, hide your head and face.'

They left Devil's Tower and made their way through the gathering mist to the guest house. Corbett sighed with relief that no one saw them. Once inside, he made Megotta comfortable, sitting her on a stool with a cup of mulled wine from the jug placed on the top of a fiercely burning brazier. She sipped at this and nibbled at the usual daily platter of bread, ham and cheese sent from the buttery.

Corbett left and roused Ranulf. The Clerk of the Green Wax was all sleepy eyed as he slouched into Corbett's chamber. Once the introductions were made, however, he abruptly changed. Much taken with their visitor, he became charm incarnate, asking her if she was comfortable and did she want anything more to eat? Corbett watched intently. Megotta was courteous enough, yet there was a hard watchfulness in her, as if she was deeply wary of the world of men. He had encountered the same when he had talked to women who had been abused by soldiers during his time with the royal array. He let Ranulf chatter for a while, using the time to study his visitor more closely. Eventually he intervened.

'We have business to pursue,' he declared. 'I warn you, mistress, the city and the Queen of the Night pose a real danger to you, as does this place. But you know that already, don't you? The recent attack on us. You were there, weren't you? You helped us. You came up behind our attackers and used that crossbow, killing at least two of them. Am I correct?'

Megotta, eyes still wary, nodded her agreement.

'So.' He leaned forward. 'Tell us what happened, what you know.'

In a harsh, clipped voice, she described her rescue by Manning; how she'd been sentenced to hang and he'd secured a pardon. She paused as Corbett lifted a hand.

'Mistress, I deduced all that from his papers. He placed you here at St Sulpice, yes? How?'

'He secured the services of a goldsmith, a leading alderman, claiming that I was a foundling, an orphan of the parish. At Manning's urging, the goldsmith contacted Prioress Margaret, who interviewed and accepted me. Certain monies were handed over.' She smiled. 'And I became a novice at St Sulpice.'

'And?'

'Sir Hugh, I was happy. Life here was harmonious, secure, warm and blissful. I slept in a clean bed, I ate good food, I had companionship. It was no trial. Indeed, I was so comfortable, I began to believe Manning's wits were disordered. We used to meet close to Devil's Tower. I told him I had nothing to report, nothing untoward. But then things changed.' She paused, breathing in deeply.

'In what way?' Corbett asked.

'At one of our meetings, Manning told me that before Katherine's disappearance they had become betrothed to be married. In fact, she was expecting a second child.'

Corbett stared in amazement. 'Surely not?'

'That's what he said. And I, like you, cannot accept that a young woman betrothed to be married, possibly pregnant, would leave this convent and hide from her lover, her future husband. For what? In God's name, Sir Hugh, what could Katherine Ingoldsby obtain anywhere else? Manning was a rich clerk, a man of power, of influence. Why should she forsake such a lover?'

Corbett leaned back on his chair, staring at the ceiling. He had to accept the logic of what Megotta was saying. No doubt Katherine Ingoldsby had deeply loved Manning. So why should she flee from him?

He sat forward. 'Surely Manning informed you about other matters?'

'Yes and no.' Megotta smiled. 'He was like you, Sir Hugh. He would ask abrupt questions and sometimes not wait for an answer. Now and again he would refer to things I didn't know anything about.'

'Such as?'

'Well, he spoke about the Turbeville family. He claimed there was some connection between the Turbevilles and St Sulpice. I never discovered what it might be. One night when I met him, he questioned me closely as to whether I had discovered anything about the Turbevilles. I told him I didn't know what he was talking about. He then elliptically referred to something Katherine had seen. Something rather strange, but he didn't tell me what. All I can say is that Manning maintained that young women were being kidnapped from St Sulpice. For what reason I do not know. He truly believed Katherine was one of them. She had no reason to flee. More importantly, Sir Hugh, I can assure you that I certainly was abducted. Let me tell you what happened, for it is deeply cruel.'

She then gave a pithy description of everything that had happened to her. She spoke haltingly, eyes downcast, as she described being raped time and again in that cellar. She spat the words out as if she wished she could vomit the horrors inflicted upon her.

Ranulf sat silent, Corbett too. He could not meet this young woman's gaze. He could only imagine the hideous violation of her body and soul. When she paused in her account, he reached out and gently touched her arm. She smiled and continued speaking, telling how she had escaped and taken great joy in killing her abusers.

'You did right,' Corbett declared. 'They were lawful killings. I am the king's justiciar, and I rule, as any judge would, that you killed in defence of your life and your honour. The men responsible would have hanged. I am sorry, do continue.'

Megotta described her careful watch over *The Picardy* and the Queen of the Night. She became more fluent, especially as she talked about the cart she had seen going to and fro from the tavern, and what had happened along the riverbank.

'Undoubtedly the disposal of a corpse,' Ranulf declared. 'It must be. A corpse from the Queen of the Night. But whose, and why? You see, mistress, we have been to that place. We believe there are no prisoners there. It would be easy to suggest that women are being abducted from here or elsewhere and made to serve in a London brothel. But that's too simple, too easy an explanation. It also makes Mother Midnight, who guards that place, vulnerable. No, there is a twist to this that we have yet to discover.' He broke off as the bells of the convent began to ring out the tocsin.

Corbett rose and strapped on his war belt. 'Megotta, stay here. Do you understand me?'

She nodded in agreement.

'Whatever happens, do not open that door, only to me or Ranulf.'

The two clerks hurried out of the guest house. The mist had thickened, the daylight fast fading. They hastened across to the convent chapel, the usual place for the community to gather when the alarm was raised. Mother Abbess and her companions were already there, along with Stigand and another labourer. Torches glowed through the misty dark. Here and there doors opened and shut. Exclamations of surprise rose and fell. Corbett and Ranulf greeted the abbess. The bells ceased their tolling. A number of novices drew close, holding blazing torches that kissed the darkness and drove it back.

'Stigand has found a corpse, much decomposed,' Mother Abbess declared. 'Sir Hugh, would you and your henchman follow him. He will show you where.' She pointed at the bier lying on the ground behind her. 'We cannot go; we do not want to. We have experienced enough terrors of the night. So will you carry the torches? We shall meet you at the death house.'

Corbett could sense the mounting hysteria amongst the good sisters, so he quickly agreed. He and Ranulf followed the two labourers into the gathering night, the flames of their torches leaping up like tongues to lick the darkness.

'We were working,' Stigand declared over his shoulder, his broad burr sharpening his words. 'We were clearing ditches in preparation for the spring rain when we discovered the corpse. Definitely a nun; we glimpsed the brown habit, the cord around her waist, the glimmer of blonde hair. Wolfsan, I said, more trouble here.'

They trudged on. Devil's Tower loomed out of the dark, soaring up into the blackness, a lonely, desolate building, brooding and sinister. Stigand whispered something about ghosts playing like flames around the battlements. They turned left, following the curtain wall to a narrow postern gate built into the wall. They stopped as Stigand fumbled with bolts and a rope clasp. Corbett stared around. Despite the tocsin and the news they'd received, it seemed quite a serene evening; even the crows and ravens that constantly haunted the trees around St Sulpice had fallen silent. He recalled stories his grandfather used to tell him. How ghosts, sprites and demons that stayed fastened in trees and bushes during the day broke free to roam and cause all kinds of mischief once night had fallen. Stigand was certainly fractious, quietly cursing Sister Marie for going round the convent to ensure all ropes were properly tied.

At last he drew back the bolts and, using his dagger, cut through the knotted cord that held the postern fast from within. The door creaked open, and he led them out, keeping to the curtain wall. As they went along a coffin path, Stigand abruptly stopped and put down the bier, pointing to where the bushes, gorse and bramble had been ruthlessly pulled back. In the dancing light of the torches, Corbett glimpsed a deep ditch running alongside the wall. He pushed his way through, crouched down and stared at the corpse sprawled there, spattered with mud and tendrils of bramble grass.

He rose and stepped back as Ranulf and the two labourers pushed their way forward. They lifted the corpse and placed it on the bier. Ranulf moved the cadaver gently so it rolled over on its back. A truly gruesome sight. Wolfsan turned away to retch and gag. Corbett, pinching his nostrils, stared down, scrutinising the face. It was much decayed. The eyes deep in dark sockets, the cheeks hollow, the lips mere slits exposing the teeth. He sensed, despite the decay, that the corpse was that of a young woman, her hair strangely bright and soft. He gently tilted the head so he could fully see the slit across the young woman's throat, undoubtedly the cause of death. Woodland creatures had nibbled and torn at the soft parts of the body, the nose, ears, cheeks; the brown gown had been bitten and rent, the flesh beneath puckered and gouged.

Corbett rose to his feet and crossed himself. He dug into his purse and thrust a coin into Stigand's hand.

'My friend, thank you. Let's take her to the death house.'

The abbess and her council were waiting for them in the convent mortuary. Sister Agatha, all sweet faced and eager to help, had prepared a table. Stigand and Wolfsan gently eased the corpse onto the slab and left. Corbett beckoned Mother Abbess and the sisters to gather round. At first there was confusion. Sister Maria and Sister Perpetua had to withdraw to settle their stomachs. Sister Agatha opened a coffer and distributed sweet-smelling pomanders for them to hold against their nose and mouth. Corbett and Ranulf stood waiting either side of the mortuary table. Such death houses were now common to them; they were used to the reek of pinewood juice and the rich aroma emanating from braziers crammed with fiery coals and heavily laced with herbs of every sort.

'Who is it?' Ranulf demanded.

'Why, sir,' Prioress Margaret replied, 'correct me if I am wrong, but that is no other than Katherine Ingoldsby. Wouldn't you agree?' A murmur from her companions confirmed this.

'So here we have her,' Corbett declared, 'a novice nun garbed in the robes of this convent, found dead in a ditch weeks after her disappearance, her throat slit from ear to ear.'

Hand to his mouth, he turned and walked away, going to stand before a crucifix nailed to the far wall. 'I have entered a place of darkness,' he whispered as he stared at the tortured figure of Christ, 'and all hell has risen to greet me.' He crossed himself and quietly prayed for help. He truly believed that he was walking the rim of a pit of wickedness. He closed his eyes and recalled Manning roistering in a tavern. He had also noticed the bulge in the stomach of the corpse he'd retrieved; bellies did swell after death, but he believed two people had been killed when Katherine Ingoldsby had her throat slit: the innocent mother and the even more innocent child. 'I swear,' he whispered, 'I truly do, that I shall see those responsible hang.'

As he walked back to the table, he was aware of the torchlight leaping as though eager to leave this dark place, the abode of ghosts that must hover close. The silence of the death house was oppressive. Mother Abbess and her sisters clustered like chickens in a hen coop, fearful of the fox prowling outside. This was now a place of terror. Katherine Ingoldsby had been an innocent novice. People thought she had fled, but the truth was now starkly obvious. Katherine had been lured out of this convent and brutally murdered. Corbett stared down at the mangled corpse. The remains of this young woman were truly pathetic, face all shrivelled and twisted, her body reeking of corruption.

'We have seen enough,' he declared. 'We have found the body in the place where it was hidden. Let us make sure that we have missed nothing else. Mother Abbess, I ask for the corpse to be stripped.'

Sister Agatha, all anxious, drew a deep breath and began to undo the dead woman's robe. She paused as Corbett touched her arm. 'Search the pockets,' he urged. 'And the purse. Let us see if there's anything hidden.'

The infirmarian did so. The leather wallet hanging from the belt around Katherine's waist was empty, but when they pulled the brown robe away, a thin roll of vellum was discovered beneath the cuff on her right wrist. Corbett undid the small scroll, crossing to a candle to study it more closely. He made out the emblem inscribed there, a three-stemmed fleur-de-lis. It seemed that she had copied this, then hidden it away. He watched as the rest of her clothing was removed. At last they were down to her soiled shift. Corbett could sense that the abbess and her companions were deeply embarrassed at the presence of himself and Ranulf. He quickly checked that there was nothing else concealed on the body, then took a silver coin from his purse and placed it on the mortuary table. 'Mother Abbess, when your chaplain comes, have masses said for Katherine Ingoldsby and Ralph Manning. God have mercy on their souls.'

The two clerks returned to the guest house, where Megotta was patiently waiting. Chanson, who had stayed with their visitor, volunteered to sleep in the stables with his beloved horses so Megotta could have his chamber. Corbett gratefully accepted, though it was too early to retire. He sat for a while, face in his hands, whilst Ranulf and Megotta gossiped about life on the roads and the customs of the moon people. Eventually he sat back in his chair.

'Sir Hugh,' Ranulf asked, 'what are your conclusions? Another corpse, another murder. This is really no longer a convent, a house of prayer, but a temple to death. We have found three corpses. Surely it is only a matter of time before these matters are referred to the Bishop of London and Lord Reynolds, Archbishop of Canterbury. We have murder, abduction, not to mention assault on royal clerks in the dead of night.'

'Ranulf, my friend, you may have stated the obvious. It's been hidden away, but now it's growing more apparent.' He pointed at Megotta. 'Here is a young woman whose story would create deep anxiety amongst the clergy of London. A convent is supposed to be a place of solitude, serenity and prayer.'

'Sir Hugh?'

'Can't you see it, Ranulf? What if all these murders, these grisly happenings, were intended to create the impression you and I have just described?'

'Master?'

'In other words,' Megotta spoke up, 'these attacks are really part of an attempt to bring St Sulpice into grave disrepute.'

'Precisely,' Corbett replied. 'What if the deaths of Constantia and Fidelis were acts of revenge, but also intended to provoke speculation about the integrity of this convent? Perhaps we have two killers at St Sulpice. The first intent on waging a gruesome war against the convent, killing whomever they wish, whenever they want, and so creating a great fear, a terror that strikes at the very heart of this community. And then,' he continued, 'there is a second strand, this tenuous link between the convent and the whorehouse the Queen of the Night. No doubt there *is* a connection. Manning believed the same and was searching for evidence. Better still, our good friend Megotta is living proof of it.'

'Sir Hugh,' Ranulf declared, 'whilst you were brooding, I informed Megotta of what we've just discovered.' He turned to the young woman.

'Is it possible,' Megotta said, 'that Katherine Ingoldsby was murdered by her lover, Manning?'

'Do you really believe that?' Corbett asked.

'No, I don't.' She shook her head. 'Just a thought. But I tell you this, Sir Hugh, I have reflected on everything Manning told me, and one item hangs like a loose thread. I have mentioned this before, how Katherine Ingoldsby glimpsed something out of the ordinary at St Sulpice. She'd informed Manning of this, but he never told me what it was. In short, would you agree that Katherine Ingoldsby may have been murdered because of what she'd seen?'

Corbett said he did agree, but then pronounced himself tired. Ranulf offered to make sure that Megotta was lodged comfortably. Corbett insisted that the young woman remain hidden and keep well away from the community. 'Early tomorrow morning, Ranulf,' he declared, 'take her away. Climb over the wall, escort her back to the city. Megotta, stay in the Inglenook until I send for you again. You have money?'

'I have enough, clerk,' she replied heatedly.

Corbett smiled and gently stroked her on the shoulder. 'I am not your enemy, Megotta. You must remain safe. A plan is forming and you will play a great part in that. However, for the moment, you must stay hidden. I believe there are people in this convent, certainly in the city, who would rejoice to see you dead.'

Ranulf and Megotta left. Corbett said his prayers and retired to bed. For a while he lay staring up into the darkness. He was pleased with his analogy of two strands. He was certain of the first: Constantia floating in that boat, a dagger thrust through her heart; Fidelis tumbling down the steps, cracking her skull and breaking her neck. The notes pinned to the abbess's door. All this was the work of one killer, someone secretly at war with the community of St Sulpice. He scratched his cheek, not yet sleepy, trying to recall things he'd seen and heard, those small items out of place yet so important.

Then there was the second strand, linking the convent to that wicked brothel and the witch-queen, Mother Midnight. Manning had been certain of a connection. The dead clerk was fully convinced that young women were being abducted from St Sulpice. But taken where? Manning had also believed his beloved Katherine had been kidnapped but, in truth, she had been brutally murdered, her corpse hidden away.

Corbett's mind turned to Turbeville. Sir Thomas had been a great traitor who had done terrible damage to the English cause. He had been executed and his family turned out on the streets. Apparently Mathilda Turbeville had arrived at St Sulpice sick and tired. She had died in the infirmary and lay buried in God's Acre. She and her daughters had been branded with the fleur-de-lis, the public symbol of any French whore, a cruel punishment by the old king on a family whose lord had prostituted himself and the secrets of England for rewards from the French. So, Thomas Turbeville had died on the gallows, Mathilda Turbeville had spent her last days in this convent. But where were her daughters? And why had Katherine Ingoldsby carried that inscription, now in Corbett's purse, of the three-stemmed fleur-de-lis? Corbett abruptly sat up. Had Katherine seen that in this convent or elsewhere?

He lay back again and allowed his mind to drift. The day's business was done. He thought of Maeve and their two children. He plucked his Ave beads from the table next to the bed and began to thread them through his fingers. He prayed for all those he loved, then drifted into a deep sleep.

The next morning, he rose late. He shaved, washed and changed into fresh clothes. Then he sat on the edge of the bed as he wondered what to do next. He was delighted to have encountered Megotta and recalled what she'd told him. She had been abducted and abused, but, ever resourceful, she had turned on her captors and escaped. Yet there was something in her story he had missed, a loose thread. That mistake that often cost the murderer his or her life. Something very simple that Corbett was sure he had overlooked. If he could only find it and pull it loose, the tissue of lies he faced would crumble.

He did not attend the morning mass, so he went over to the chapel and sat before the lady altar quietly reciting the mercy psalm. 'Have mercy, O Lord, in your great kindness, in your infinite compassion blot out my offence.' As he murmured the words, he watched the tongue of candle flame light the darkness around the statue of the Virgin. A cloud of incense drifted by, and he wondered if that was God's grace travelling through the air, searching for its home.

Sister Marie came bustling into the church, informing

him breathlessly that Katherine Ingoldsby's corpse had been washed and dressed for burial and the requiem mass would be held the following day. Corbett heard her out and she left. He again reflected on the two murders that had occurred here, but then went back to Megotta's account of her abduction and the hideous abuse she had suffered.

'Something simple,' he murmured, 'there is something very simple and obvious I have missed, but what is it? Manning placed Megotta here. By her own admission the young woman was happy, and she saw and heard nothing amiss until she was abruptly abducted. In heaven's name, Hugh,' he spoke to himself, 'what have you missed? And what can be done?'

Corbett had the power to enter the city and seize Mother Midnight. Ranulf would brutally interrogate her, but that would upset Lancaster. Faucomburg was under strict orders to protect that witch-queen, and Corbett did not want this to end in dagger play along the streets of Cheapside. Moreover, the Queen of the Night was undoubtedly a powerful place, frequented by all the great and good of the city. So what could he do? Faucomburg was a mailed clerk. If he knew the truth, would he be so fervent in his support of a woman who brutalised and murdered young women?

Corbett again reflected on what Megotta had told him. There was no doubt that the Queen of the Night housed prostitutes, but all its young ladies came from France. They might have been abducted and told to remain silent or suffer the consequences. A few might object and try to break free. Were these the ones whose pretty faces were smashed, their corpses loaded onto a cart and taken by the master of *The Picardy* to be tossed into the river? Corpses unknown and unrecognisable. 'Yes, yes, possible,' he breathed. A crack to the back of the head, hammer blows to their faces so they could never be recognised. Some poor French girl plucked from her family, brought to England and savagely mutilated and killed for daring to protest. That would explain the delicacies found on those corpses, nails and skin carefully tended; it would also account for no one ever being able to identify them.

The tocsin began to sound again.

'Heaven help us,' Corbett prayed. He grabbed his war belt and hurried out.

As soon as he left the church, he could smell the sharp tang of burning and glimpse the smoke drifting up against the pale blue sky. The good sisters were now hurrying out, hastening towards the threatening plume rising about their convent. Ranulf appeared all sleepy eyed. He breathlessly informed Corbett how *The Picardy* was due to sail on the morrow at evening tide. Chanson also came running up, concerned about his beloved horses and the safety of the stables, declaring how horses feared fire most of all.

Corbett let him go, then he and Ranulf made their way across the convent grounds into the gardens on the far side of the church: a spacious, elegantly laid out tableau of grass, flower beds, herb and vegetable plots with a small orchard of pear, apple and plum trees. A fragrant place; even the harsh frost could not fully conceal how beautiful it would be in full summer. In the centre of the gardens stood a large fountain carved in the shape of a leaping porpoise, though no water spouted now. To the far right of this was a single-storey red-brick pavilion. A fire raged within, though the only signs were the trailing smoke seeping out through the firmly shuttered windows and doors. Just as Corbett and Ranulf arrived, however, the flames erupted like a storm through the black-tiled roof, causing a hideous crash of stone and wood. Now that the flames were free, they leapt up and spread like frenzied dancers.

Mother Abbess, her council and all the sisters had come rushing down, but they could only stand and gape at this raging inferno at the very heart of their convent.

'God help poor Perpetua,' Sister Marie cried, fingers to her face. She turned and ran across to Corbett. 'God help Perpetua!'

'She is in there?'

'Yes, she is,' Prioress Margaret declared. 'She always goes in there at the beginning of the day. She calls it her Manor of Eden.'

Corbett stared at the blazing fire, which had totally engulfed the garden pavilion.

'If Perpetua was in there,' Ranulf whispered, 'then she's surely gone to God. A dreadful accident?'

'No, Ranulf, remember that message pinned to the abbess's door about fire in this life and beyond? Rest assured this is murder, coldly carried out before a host of witnesses. God knows how it was done, but we must recognise the truth of the matter. Perpetua, for whatever reason, was marked down for death. And so we have it, Ranulf, another nun, a member of this community, has been foully murdered. However, this will have to wait. Now listen, and listen carefully. Let us for the moment ignore the murders committed here. On one matter we have proof positive.'

He paused under the shade of a tree, beckoning Ranulf closer. 'Thanks to Megotta, we know that the cog *The Picardy* plays a part in all this wickedness and, according to you, it's to sail on tomorrow's evening tide. So let us leave the issues of St Sulpice for a while. Go into the city, collect Megotta from the Inglenook and seek out Sir John Kyrie, King's Admiral from the mouth of the Thames to the north. You must hand him the instructions I will give you. You will find him in his chancery offices at Castle Baynard. He has at his disposal a formidable war cog, *The Royal Glory*. Kyrie is to prepare that ship for sea, but only after he and the Thames harbourmaster have carried out a survey of all crafts berthed in Queenhithe, Dowgate and other quaysides. You and Megotta are to lodge at Castle Baynard. Use the royal warrants you carry to secure whatever you need. And Ranulf,' he plucked his henchman by the sleeve, 'be gentle and very kind to Megotta. She acts as if nothing has really hurt her. In truth she is bleeding from within. She has suffered but she has the courage of a warrior. She would rather die than show her fear.'

\* \* \*

Later that day, Corbett returned to the scene of the conflagration. The flames had now died down, the pavilion nothing more than bleak scorched walls with tumbled masonry. Wisps of smoke still curled. Stigand and his labourers had, on the abbess's instructions, combed the ruins. Perpetua's corpse, or what was left of it, had been removed and lifted onto a canvas sheet stretched out on one of the grassy verges.

Corbett crouched beside the remains. Perpetua, he reasoned, had been turned into a living flame, a raging fire that had consumed flesh and bone, reducing everything to a hideous blackness. He nursed deep suspicions about what was happening at St Sulpice, but he had to make choices. The business of *The Picardy* was more pressing. He had evidence to suggest that that cog played a prominent part in the murderous mayhem he was investigating. He was determined not to let the ship sail off into the sunset to continue its wicked dealings. Nevertheless, he was also caught up by what was happening by the hour at the convent. So, not letting any opportunity slip, he attended a specially convened chapter meeting.

Abbess Eleanor was beside herself, hysterical and totally dependent on the plate of smelling salts Prioress Margaret placed into her hands.

'How?' she wailed. 'How could all this happen? The bishop will visit us! He will bring the inquisitors, and what can we say? Let us reflect, sisters! Constantia murdered on a boat. Fidelis tossed like a rag down the steps of Devil's Tower, and now poor Perpetua reduced to nothing more than a scorched tangle of bones.'

'Mother Abbess.' Corbett intervened. 'Can anyone here describe what Perpetua did in that pavilion?'

'Yes.' Sister Agatha spoke up. 'I can. The garden pavilion, the Manor of Eden as Perpetua called it, was her chancery chamber, where she tended pots and plants, not to mention the tools for her gardens. She loved to sit at her desk, just opposite the door, where she would cut stems and strands, studying them curiously so she could understand the roots and flowering of various herbs, spices and flowers.'

'Were there braziers, chafing dishes, anything that was fiery?'

'Of course, but these were small. Warming pans, candles, no real danger to anyone.' The prioress clutched her Ave beads, threading them through bony fingers. 'Sir Hugh, the fire seemed to leap out of nowhere. It's as if . . .' she lowered her voice, 'as if hell itself erupted in that little pavilion.'

'And you heard no screams?'

'Nothing, Sir Hugh.'

'The source of the blaze must have been close to where she sat.'

'What do you mean?'

'Well, the door and windows remained shuttered throughout the conflagration.'

'True,' the prioress agreed. 'They only burst open towards the end. The flames were so fierce, it was too dangerous to approach; you saw it yourself, Sir Hugh.

The convent well is some distance away, but no amount of water would have helped. We had no choice but to let it burn.'

'And Sister Perpetua apparently made no attempt to escape. Which means either that she was dead before the fire broke out, or she was close to the cause of the eruption. Fire moves, it leaps and dances, it can speed through the air like an arrow. Sister Perpetua must have been caught up in the first flames. Perhaps it was something she wore.' Corbett paused. 'I have seen the same at sieges, where flames leap out swift as a bird from a bush to engulf some siege man whose clothes are drenched in oil. Is that what happened here?'

He got to his feet, his mind teeming with a number of possibilities. Loose threads were appearing that he wanted to pluck at, but not now. He was in no doubt that Sister Perpetua had been brutally murdered, but he needed more time to reflect. Yet time was passing and pressing hard! *The Picardy* was soon to sail. At this moment in time, that cog presented the greatest challenge and one he would have to deal with. He bowed towards Mother Abbess, excused himself and left the chapter house.

He kept to his chamber for the rest of the day. He no longer trusted the grounds or buildings of St Sulpice. According to the meagre evidence he had collected, not to mention his own burgeoning suspicions, he was certain he was hunting at least two assassins. He grudgingly conceded that he had made mistakes during his stay at the convent, but so had his opponents, yet they could wait for a while. In the meantime, he busied himself, eager to leave early next morning.

His preparations, however, were interrupted by a surprise visit from Mepham and Benstead. The two clerks clattered into the bailey of the convent. Corbett was informed of their arrival and hurried down to greet them. He could tell from their furtive glances and wry expressions that they were reluctant to speak until they were alone.

Once their cloaks, hoods and war belts were heaped over a stool, Mepham toasted Corbett and Benstead with his goblet of mulled wine. 'Sir Hugh,' he drank deep and smacked his lips, 'we have been very busy on your behalf. We have searched the records both in the Chancery and the Exchequer for any trace of Mathilda Turbeville and her two daughters, Edith and Emma. In a word, after the execution of Sir Thomas some seventeen years ago, his daughters disappeared. Of course, no one really vanishes, it's just a matter of discovering where they are hiding. So we turned to the records of the various city wards. Again nothing spectacular or significant, though I shall return to this later.'

Corbett sat back in his chair and smiled at these two clerks who loved nothing better than to hunt through the records. 'You are like lurchers,' he murmured. 'And you have startled a hare.'

'Oh yes, Sir Hugh, and a very elusive one. We passed from one baptism and wedding record to another. We followed Sir Thomas Turbeville back to his parents.' Mepham waved a hand. 'We discovered very little, so we began a similar search on Mathilda Turbeville, born Mathilda Maltravers. We went two generations back until we came to the name Rohesia Poppleton.'

'What?'

'Yes, Rohesia Poppleton. I understand that Mother Midnight's real name is Edith Poppleton, so there we have a link. However,' Mepham held up a warning finger, 'we then went searching again. I admit the connections we tried to forge are fairly tenuous, but bear with us. Anyway, to cut to the chase, Turbeville's wife disappeared.'

'We know that,' Corbett replied 'She is buried here, in a pauper's grave. Never mind, continue.'

'In my view, and that of Master Benstead,' Mepham went on, 'Turbeville's daughters Edith and Emma assumed the name Poppleton because Turbeville was now cursed. We also found another very interesting pathway to follow. Edith and Emma Poppleton undoubtedly lived in the city. On the coroner's roll for Farringdon ward, we have a situation that occurred twelve years ago, the year of Our Lord 1300, the time of the Great Jubilee. According to the court record, Edith and Emma Poppleton, seamstresses, residing above a shop close to Cheapside, were charged with soliciting and lechery beyond the limits of Cock Lane. The charge was one of being a public nuisance and exposing themselves in an indecent way. To be fair, the allegations against both young women were totally untrue. They were maliciously brought by city beadles who, we suspect, wanted to lift these ladies' petticoats. Anyway,' Mepham spoke hurriedly, catching Corbett's impatience, 'the case was heard before Sir Oliver Ingham.'

'Oh dear.' Corbett smiled. 'Ingham was a born lecher with more than an eye for the ladies.'

'Precisely, Sir Hugh. I suspect our noble justice was much taken by these two pretty seamstresses. The case was dismissed and the beadles punished for bringing false allegations. Edith and Emma were honourably discharged and, again they disappeared, until a roll call was made of the ward. It will come as no surprise to you that Edith and Emma Poppleton were listed as members of the household of Sir Oliver Ingham. I went to the house and talked to old servants, those who had served Sir Oliver for many a year. They praised him to the skies but said he was a drunk and a lecher. Apparently he was sweet on both his seamstresses. They may well have served him together in bed. Sir Oliver certainly appreciated who they were and what they did. He left each a generous bequest, which his heirs had no choice but to honour.'

'And what then?' Corbett demanded.

'Why, nothing. The sisters seem to have separated and, if I understand correctly, Edith Poppleton is now no less a person than Mother Midnight.'

'But who is the other daughter?' Corbett wondered. 'Where does she live? What does she do?'

Mepham and Benstead just shook their heads. Corbett invited them to stay for the night, but both clerks were insistent on returning to Westminster. They explained how the tensions in the city were rising, and provided a pithy description of the way Westminster was divided. Royal troops camped in the abbey grounds and along the quayside near King's Steps, from where they could seek urgent assistance from troops garrisoned in the Tower. However, the retainers of the Lords Ordainers, those nobles in opposition to the king over Gaveston, now swaggered the streets of both Westminster and Cheapside, Faucomburg among them, with Catesby and others of their coven. The Lancastrians, so Benstead declared, were now permanently quartered at the Queen of the Night. Corbett half smiled at such news, for it showed that Mother Midnight was certainly intent on protecting herself.

'For the rest,' Mepham declared, getting to his feet, 'we shall just have to wait and see. Sir Hugh, are you safe here? We have heard about the murder of three nuns. I pray that you stay protected.'

'I will.'

Corbett clasped hands and shared the kiss of peace with his visitors. The two men left, and he continued his own preparations for the morrow. However, as the noises of the convent faded, and the chamber grew warmer and more comfortable, he returned to sit behind his chancery desk. For a while he tried to pull together the different strands of the mysteries, but he grudgingly conceded that he was distracted. He needed to deal with *The Picardy*. Once he had done that, he would have some peace of mind and be able to concentrate on other problems.

He was interrupted by Chanson, who came bustling in asking about what was to happen.

'At this moment in time, my friend, not very much. Would you like to go to sea?' Corbett laughed at Chanson's abrupt change of expression. The clerk looked so doleful and pathetic, he raised a hand and shook his head. 'Chanson, I tease you. You hate the sea and anything that floats. Now listen, I am bound for the city. As you know, Ranulf has been dispatched to Sir John Kyrie to prepare *The Royal Glory* for sailing. But keep that quiet. I want you to stay here and keep a sharp eye on proceedings. Yes?'

Chanson replied that he would be delighted. Clearly relieved at not being included in any journey along the Thames, he fair skipped from the chamber.

Corbett heard him go down the gallery, then pulled across a sheet of vellum and began to write his own conclusions. First Manning and Faldon. He now knew what Manning had been searching for: his beloved Katherine. He had believed she had been abducted. In a sense he was correct. The poor girl had been lured out from St Sulpice and brutally murdered, probably to silence her, to take care of what she had glimpsed in this convent, although what that was remained a mystery. Was it the brand of the fleur-de-lis, the mark of a French whore? But where had she seen that? Wherever it was, she regarded it as so important she even made a fair copy to take to Manning, though she had never had the chance to do this.

Manning, not knowing the truth, had continued his hunt. He had discovered the link between the Queen of the Night and the Turbevilles. Perhaps he had revealed his hand too early. Perhaps he had hinted at what he had discovered, and in doing so became a truly marked man. Mother Midnight and her minions had silenced him with the full help of Faldon, who had probably been seduced and suborned by the charms of the fair Janine. But what then? Did Faldon turn on his new friends? Did he feel guilty? Was he resentful? Did he threaten Mother Midnight with exposure? Did he hint that he might turn king's approver and seek a pardon through Sir Hugh Corbett? Faldon had been foolish; he had totally underestimated Mother Midnight, who had responded in the most cruel and ruthless way. She'd removed Faldon and silenced him, both as a punishment and as a possible warning to Corbett himself.

The Keeper of the Secret Seal sat back in his chair. The chamber had grown truly warm and he could feel the effects of the wine he had drunk. 'Have I made progress?' he murmured. 'And if I have, what have I done to resolve matters? Mother Midnight still squats at the centre of her filthy web like some fat malignant spider. Does she truly believe she can do what she likes and remain scot free?' He closed his eyes. Mother Midnight had murdered Manning and then turned on Faldon. Yet nothing had happened to her. She had threatened Corbett, and he could do little to respond to her menaces. Even if he rode down into London and arrested her with the help of troops from the Tower, Faucomburg would be waiting for them. And of course she must have very powerful friends in the city, men who had enjoyed the soft young bodies of those French girls. Men whose secrets she nursed. What chance would there be of a fair trial? Juries could be suborned, bribed or threatened, and the same for royal justices. She would stand in Westminster Hall and lie through her teeth, then skip away like a young bride, all innocent and pert, to continue her wickedness. 'No, no,' Corbett murmured to himself. 'That is something I must take care of, but again, not now.'

He sipped his wine and his thoughts turned back to St Sulpice. 'What has happened here, and what are the loose threads?' he asked himself. 'Megotta, surely.' He needed to question her more closely about her time here. Her meetings with Manning and what actually happened on the evening she was abducted. A thread he needed to pull along with several others. For example, that freezing mist-shrouded jetty. What had Fidelis glimpsed? And what had he himself seen, both there and at the top of Devil's Tower? He recalled what he had found in Fidelis's pockets as well as in her chamber, not forgetting what Stigand had said. He needed to reflect and to plot a way forward.

Now heavy eyed with tiredness, he solemnly swore to return to these various strands in the tapestry of murder confronting him. For the moment, however, tomorrow beckoned and he must be ready for that.

Edith Poppleton, born Edith Turbeville and baptised as such, smiled faintly to herself as she sat in her private accounting chamber at the Queen of the Night.

'So many names,' she whispered, 'so many titles.' She

glanced into the mirror of polished steel and studied her reflection, taking great pride in how she looked so much like a nun, with her starched wimple, unpainted face and dark blue veil. 'And I am Mother Midnight,' she murmured. 'I am what I am and I know the truth about myself.' She plucked at the pieces of parchment that littered her leather-covered chancery table. She had finished her accounts in the ledgers hidden away in her secret arca. Now she was waiting. She closed her eyes at the surge of anger she felt. She would love to destroy Corbett. She recognised him as a deadly adversary. He was clever, keen witted and swift. Like a hawk, he could turn on the wing, and she truly believed she had to destroy him before he struck her.

Corbett was a royal clerk, but times were changing. The kingdom was drifting towards civil war, and the power of the Crown had greatly diminished. Corbett might have the protection and patronage of Edward and his favourite, Gaveston, but she, Mother Midnight, had the constant support of Lancaster and the other great lords, not to mention powerful merchants in the city who had sampled and enjoyed the rich fruits of the Queen of the Night. Oh, everything had been flowing so smoothly until that interfering royal clerk had arrived. She had recognised the threat immediately. She had whispered her poison into that fool Faucomburg's ear. She had wheedled and teased, enticed and encouraged him to confront Corbett and deal with him. In the end, this had proved fruitless. Indeed, Faucomburg had walked away from the tiltyard with a profound respect for his opponent. Mother Midnight had reached a decision. She had made it known to the heralds of the night that she wished once again to meet the Solace. Now she was waiting for their arrival.

She heard a rap at the door, and the sinuous Janine slipped into the room.

'Mistress, you have visitors. They are in the stable yard, deep in the shadows. They said they will wait for you there.'

Mother Midnight rose, took her thick fur-rimmed cloak from a peg on the wall and wrapped it about her. She wore soft buskins on her feet and her cloak had a muffler to protect her hands against the cold. She followed Janine out of the chamber, snapping her fingers at one of her bodyguards to follow but whispering that he should keep a discreet distance. The tavern lay quiet. The festivities and revelry were over. The hour had passed and new beginnings had to be plotted. Mother Midnight reached the taproom, where most of the candles and lanterns had been doused. She left the tavern, going out into the yard, then paused at the sound of a flute. The sweet, reedy tune came from the shadows deep in the corner of the yard. A dark shed wedged between the smithy and the first of her stables. She walked slowly across, glancing over her shoulder. Janine and the bodyguard still stood in the doorway leading back into the tavern, two dark shapes against the light.

'Don't worry about them, mistress,' a voice whispered from the shadows. 'Just stand where you are and say what you want.'

'Sir Hugh Corbett. I want him dead. He has not yet arrived in the city, but his henchman has.'

'Oh, we know about that. We are the Solace. We live in the twilight world of London. We know what passes here, what occurs there. Corbett is not here, but his henchman Ranulf-atte-Newgate is, along with a young woman, Megotta, otherwise known as Sister Isabella, a girl you abducted from St Sulpice. A veritable Amazon, a war goddess, she killed three of her captors and escaped.'

'And you will deal with her?' Mother Midnight fought to keep her voice even.

'Oh, we shall deal with both of them and we will name our price. We shall decide on the how, the where and the when. We take orders from no one. But rest assured, Corbett will die and Megotta with him.'

'Can you take her alive to be shipped abroad?'

'We will do what we can,' the voice replied reassuringly. 'But we make no promises. Death can be simple, but it can also be a drama, more prolonged or convoluted than any mummers' masque. One more thing, mistress.'

'Yes.' Mother Midnight tried to keep her voice calm. She was deeply offended by the patronising tone of her visitor, and yet she needed them. The Solace were a guild of assassins well known for their success.

'One more thing,' the voice repeated. 'We are going to destroy a royal clerk, no less a person than the Keeper of the King's Secret Seal. This may well provoke royal wrath and retribution.'

'And?'

'Once we have done what we promise to do, we need to leave this kingdom, shelter abroad for a while. We will demand safe passage on the cog you use, *The Picardy*, to take us to whatever port we want. The full passage will be included in the price you pay us, but we want your assurance that this cog will be available after it has returned from its present crossing.'

'Available for you?'

'Oh yes, mistress. Corbett's murder will not only disturb the royal hive but tip it over. The bees will swarm angrily, so we will need a safe hiding place. *The Picardy* is the ideal choice. You will arrange and pay for that. Send word to Sherwin.'

'Of course.'

'Good. You know that we always succeed in what we do. We advised Faldon about the removal of Manning and, when that fool, driven by his lusts, turned against you, we certainly settled with him. We dealt out punishment and a warning. You pay us good silver and we deliver a service that cannot be faulted. Yes?'

'Yes,' Mother Midnight agreed.

'Do not worry about Corbett. We shall come,' the voice taunted, 'like thieves in the night, and Corbett does not know the day nor the hour. Ranulf his henchman shelters in Baynard's Castle. Corbett will undoubtedly join him there. Good, good.' The mysterious voice faded. 'We are done here, at least for the time being.'

Silence descended. Mother Midnight thought she

heard a sound, only to realise she was staring into the empty dark. She wiped sweaty hands on her gown and returned to her chancery office. She knew the dangers of delay, of probing questions about the Solace. They came, they went. They swept in like a river mist, then they were gone.

She glanced down at her table, at the scroll rolled out and kept straight under small silver weights. She leaned over and pulled the sheet of vellum closer. She knew it by heart. The official account of her father's execution. She picked it up and read, lips moving silently:

*The said Thomas Turbeville was arrested on the Saturday before the feast of St Michael the Archangel and taken to the Tower of London. On the following Saturday, after the feast of St Faith, Turbeville was put on trial. He was taken from the Tower, mounted on a poor hack in a coat of striped cloth and shod with white shoes. His head was covered with a white hood, his feet tied beneath the horse's belly and his hands fastened before him. On either side of him rode six torturers dressed like devils, one of whom held the reins of Turbeville's horse, the other the noose with which he was to be hanged. The traitor was led from the Tower, through London towards Westminster, and was brought before King's Bench in the Great Hall, where the Chief Justiciar pronounced the following judgement on him: that he should be drawn and hanged and he should hang so long until nothing was left of him. After sentence was pronounced, Turbeville was drawn on a fresh ox hide from Westminster to the Great Conduit in Cheapside and then to the gallows at the Elms in Smithfield. There he was hung by a chain of iron and left to rot until nothing remained of him.*

She drew a deep breath and pushed the document away. 'So many years ago,' she whispered into the darkness that fringed the pool of light cast by a host of beeswax candles burning fiercely on the great spigot on her desk. 'So many, my dearest father, but now everything is settled. All accounts are paid.'

She closed her eyes. Despite the passing of the years, she could not forget her father dancing and dangling from that great gibbet in Smithfield. Afterwards, she and her sister, fresh from France, had accompanied their mother to plead before the king in his private chamber at the Tower. Edward had sat enthroned in a chair like this one, the only others present three Brabantine mercenaries, mailed and armed, who stood close to a fiery brazier where irons were being heated. Her sister and herself, mere children, had knelt garbed only in their shifts. Their mother had begged for help and sustenance, but the old king had brought them before him not to help them, not to pardon them, but to condemn and punish them. He had screamed how Thomas Turbeville was a filthy traitor who had betrayed the Crown of England to the French, while his wife and daughters were no more than whores of King Philip of France and thus would be branded like the prostitutes who wandered the streets of Paris without permission. Mathilda Turbeville was then seized by the Brabantines and her shift pulled off. They had branded her, then Emma, and finally Edith herself.

Mother Midnight opened her eyes, tightly gripping the leather-covered arms of her great chair. She could recall it so clearly. The hideous pain, the sheer clammy shock, the harrowing screams and the pungent smell of burning flesh. She and her sister had fainted and were left to lie on the floor. One of the Brabantines forced them to drink from a wine skin, then they were dragged to their feet, crying and whimpering with pain, and thrust out of the Tower.

For a while they wandered the convents of the city, begging the nuns to take them in, including those hypocritical bitches at St Sulpice. They had been cruelly rejected but eventually saved by the Minoresses. The years had passed and Fortune's fickle wheel had slowly turned. Edith and her sister had sown a rich harvest and reaped plenty, be it revenge or wealth. She now loved to meddle in the politics of both court and city, suitable vengeance against the old king's son. She had won the support and patronage of Lancaster and others. She was protected in more ways than one. God knew what would happen, but Faucomburg and his bully boys now lodged within. Sure protection against Corbett, who, if the dice rolled right, would soon be removed from the game completely.

# PART SIX

And know that I am in great fear and dread.

Corbett, swathed in a heavy cloak, a beaver hat warming his head, sat with Sir John Kyrie in the small master's cabin beneath the stern of the great war cog *The Royal Glory*. Both men clasped goblets of mulled wine, quickly heated on the small portable stove kept under guard close to the mainmast of this great ship. Corbett sipped at his drink, then turned and peered through the narrow squint hole built into the cabin wall.

'It will soon be dawn, Sir Hugh.'

He murmured his assent. From the little he could see, darkness was fading, the light strengthening. *The Royal Glory* was sheltering in a small inlet along the Thames, hidden by trees and thick sprouting gorse. Kyrie had deliberately taken up station here. The inlet, as he said, even on a fine day was a haunt of dappled moving shadows. More importantly, it looked out across the river to the Gates of Hell, massive sandbanks that thrust up through the surging water of the Thames, creating an obstacle that every master mariner feared. A truly sinister part of the river, the sandbanks had taken a host of craft and the lives of many sailors. Consequently, all vessels, be it fishing smacks, herring boats or merchant cogs, slowed to a crawl as they carefully plotted their way through.

The Gates of Hell were not only a real threat to shipping, but also a grim gallows yard. On each of the sandbanks soared four-branched gibbets from which pirates were hanged, their bodies left to moulder and rot in baskets of rusty chains. Around each gibbet were pointed stakes driven deep into the mud on which other outlaws had been impaled. The place reeked like a slaughter yard and the rotting flesh brought in birds of every kind to feast. The banks seemed covered in black and grey feathers as buzzards, ravens and crows gathered for the gruesome banquet. Nevertheless, Kyrie had advised that the Gates of Hell was the ideal place to wait, as *The Picardy* would have to slow, reef its sails and glide its way through.

Corbett and Kyrie were both concerned, however. *The Picardy* had apparently left Dowgate the previous evening. Swift-riding couriers had brought the news. According to all calculations, the cog should have reached the Gates of Hell some hours ago. Corbett suspected what had happened but decided to keep his thoughts to himself. He forced himself to relax, leaning back against the bulwark to the side of the cabin door. The chamber was narrow, dark and musty. Kyrie was already dozing. Corbett closed his eyes and did likewise. He let his mind drift, his body relax as he recalled the events of the day.

He had left St Sulpice late that morning, riding directly to Castle Baynard, where he met Ranulf and Megotta. They were both impatient to join him on board ship, but Corbett insisted that they stay in the city.

'Should anything happen to me, Ranulf,' he had passed across a sealed scroll, 'open this and you will find the detailed conclusions I wrote out before leaving the convent.'

'So you intend to embark on *The Royal Glory*?'

'I certainly do.'

'You'll be in danger.' Megotta grasped Corbett's hand, a friendly, warm gesture. 'Sir Hugh, I would love to confront that evil cog armed with sword and hammer.'

Corbett shook his head. 'Stay here, assist Ranulf and wait. What I intend will take only a day or two at the very most. Do not wander the streets or bring attention to yourselves. God keep you safe.'

He had then journeyed down to Queenhithe. Kyrie and the harbourmaster were already on board *The Royal Glory*, a majestic, fat-bellied war cog fitted with all armaments and ready to sail. Corbett knew Kyrie of old, a veteran seaman completely loyal to both king and Crown. Kyrie had explained how, under the guise of an inspection of all craft berthed in Dowgate, they had carried out a rigorous search of *The Picardy*'s hold and its cargo.

'Nothing but wool,' he declared lugubriously, his

northern accent clipped and sharp. 'Nothing suspicious, nothing hidden, nothing to declare. The searchers were sure of this so they passed on to the next vessel. Sir Hugh,' Kyrie added warningly, 'are you sure about what we do, that we are not chasing after shadows? I already have sealed orders from the king to set sail and stand off Scarborough Head.'

'This is no will-o'-the-wisp hunt,' Corbett assured him. 'We must discover the true villainy at the root of all this – the murders, the disappearances – because I tell you, Sir John, we have only just begun. *The Picardy* could very well be the key to open other doors and the murderous secrets they protect.'

Now Corbett started awake as the cabin door opened and a freezing cold breeze swept through the cabin.

'Sir Hugh, Sir John,' Kyrie's henchman gasped. '*The Picardy* is approaching the Gates of Hell.'

'It surely is,' Corbett murmured. 'So let's pursue it and send it through.'

He strapped on his war belt and swung his heavy coat about him. Kyrie did the same and both men went out on deck. The light was strengthening. The sky was a greyish blue, windswept and distant. Gulls and other birds were beginning their dawn dance, wings extended as they swooped and turned over the river. The inlet was deep, yet Corbett could feel the strong pull of the Thames.

He glanced around. *The Royal Glory* was a cog ready for war. Sand and grit covered the deck to provide sure footing. Pots of lime stood ready to fling into the wind if the direction was right. Small braziers glowed, primed to torch the pitch-soaked fire arrows of the Tower archers, who sat cloaked and hooded against the taffrail. Two of the ship's boys had been sent up into the falcon's nest, fixed high on the great central mast. Sailors stood ready to adjust the coarse canvas sails. Heavily matted rigging was being prepared, a sure defence against enemy arrows and anyone wishing to board. Small catapults had also been brought up.

Corbett followed Kyrie up into the forecastle. The mist had thinned and they were able to get a clear view of *The Picardy* threading its way carefully through the Gates of Hell.

'Good, good,' Kyrie breathed. He turned and beckoned to his henchman. 'Once she is through,' he ordered, 'we set sail, deep into the mist.'

*The Royal Glory* now prepared for combat. Hatches were opened to bring up more armaments. Archers queued beside the hatchway to collect their weapons, deadly war bows and heavy quivers crammed with arrow shafts. Sails were unfurled to the clatter of winches, the screech of ropes and the harsh snapping of canvas. The war cog was a hive of activity. Sailors as sure footed as squirrels shoved the clumsy archers aside as they clambered about, and *The Royal Glory* began to move, abruptly swaying and pitching as it broke free of its moorings.

It cleared the inlet and carefully made its way through the Gates of Hell. At last it was free and, with its sails bulging under a strong north-westerly, it caught the full surging flow of the river, thrusting its way forward through the turbulent water. The wind was strong. Kyrie, standing with his henchman beneath the great mast, voiced his pleasure, declaring that the cog was like a greyhound loosed from the slips, swift and sure. They would soon catch *The Picardy*. He shouted at the boys in the falcon's nest to keep sharp and constant watch. A short while later, one of them sang out, 'Nothing to the north, nothing to the south, nothing to the west . . .'

'Boy, what's the matter? Why do you pause?' The admiral's voice carried across the ship.

'I see sails, all full, bearing east.'

'Look again, boy, look again,' Kyrie bellowed back.

'It's *The Picardy*, sir,' the boy sang out. 'I see *The Picardy*.'

All pretence and deception now ceased. *The Royal Glory* was a war cog in full pursuit of its quarry. Kyrie ordered the royal standard to be hoisted, along with the great black and red war banners, a stark warning that *The Royal Glory* intended to attack, board and sink *The Picardy* in what would be a fight to the death, with no mercy shown, no quarter given, no prisoners taken.

A lookout in the prow, together with the boys in the falcon's nest, kept *The Picardy* under close scrutiny. Abruptly both lookouts began to cry out in alarm. Kyrie, shouting at Corbett to join him, hurried along the deck. Corbett followed, slipping and slithering, before staggering into the taffrail as the ship surged up only to crash down then shudder violently sideways. His mouth full of salty sea spray, the bitter wind stinging his eyes, he hung on grimly until a sailor, grinning from ear to ear, helped him forward up the steps and into the narrow prow. The wind buffeted and shook him. The ship, now in full tack, echoed with sharp, strident sounds. Corbett prayed that he would not be sick or show his fear. At Kyrie's shouted insistence, he knotted a rope that would hold him fast on the narrow platform.

The lookout turned to shout at the admiral. 'Sir, they are throwing something overboard!'

'Lord have mercy!' Kyrie screamed. 'Lord have mercy, Corbett, they are throwing people overboard.'

Corbett leaned forward, straining his eyes; then he caught it, a glimpse that lasted only a few heartbeats, a figure, arms and legs thrashing, tumbling over the side of *The Picardy* to disappear immediately into the turbulent, fast-flowing river.

Kyrie turned and shouted. 'Archers, prepare to loose.' The bowmen massed on the deck below readied themselves. 'Archers!' he repeated, lifting his hand. 'On my signal.'

The archers swung back their war bows, arrows notched, a mass of small, razor-sharp blades.

'Loose!' Kyrie screamed, dropping his hand.

Corbett heard the twang of cord, followed by an ominous hum as a flock of black shafts rose against the sky then fell like some deadly rain onto the decks of *The Picardy*. Even from where he crouched, he heard the patter of shafts as they smacked down hard, followed by cries and screams carried faintly on the wind. *The Royal Glory* was now surging forward, sails bulging, cords, rope and timber creaking and screeching as the cog's massive bows thrust through the water. Corbett was pleased that he was tied to the prow rail. The ship was now moving so swiftly that anyone who fell overboard would be lost immediately. He glanced over his shoulder at the war banners floating like deadly warnings against the bluish-grey sky.

Kyrie undid his own straps and moved crab-like to free Corbett. He then grasped the clerk firmly by the arm and led him safely down onto the deck. Corbett's comrade Ap Ythel, Captain of Archers, was now organising a second hail of arrows, some of them flame tipped. Again orders were rapped out. The archers loosed and the shafts sped away, followed by a volley of fire arrows. Some of these missed their target, but others hit. A few started fires, though these were easily doused. *The Picardy*, however, was no longer able to control either its direction or its speed. *The Royal Glory* drew closer until it stood off the stern of its quarry, ready to pull out and go alongside. Corbett, glancing over the taffrail, could clearly see *The Picardy*'s deck, where blood swilled with water and the open places were littered with corpses. Most of the crew were now sheltering.

Ap Ythel was ordering his bowmen to notch for a third volley when a cry rang out.

'They surrender, they yield!' one of the lookouts called.

Corbett glanced over the side, then stood up. *The Picardy* was loosening its sails, whilst one of its crew was holding up a white sheet and a makeshift crucifix fashioned out of two sticks.

'Probably the only religious symbol that cog has ever owned,' he murmured as Kyrie came to stand next to him. 'So, my friend, let us see.'

*The Royal Glory* was now fully alongside, towering over its quarry as grappling irons were hurled across, to be securely fastened along *The Picardy*'s taffrail. Kyrie ordered the archers to mass along the war cog's starboard side, ready to release an arrow storm at the first sign of treachery. Catapults were also loaded, braziers pulled forward so the bundles of pitch and tar in the catapult cups could be quickly fired. Men-at-arms and crewmen from *The Royal Glory* swiftly clambered down a rope ladder, dropping onto the deck of *The Picardy*. Once they had control of the vessel, Corbett insisted on going across himself. He murmured a swift prayer as he made his way gingerly down the ladder, gratefully accepting the help of Kyrie's henchman, who was waiting for him on the blood-soaked deck. Kyrie and others followed.

For a while, Corbett just leaned against the taffrail to secure his bearings and become accustomed to the sway and pitch of the cog. He felt a little sick, unsteady, but eventually this passed. Kyrie asked if he was ready. Corbett nodded. The admiral's men had been busy arranging a makeshift court, a place where Corbett and Kyrie could investigate and carry out judgement. The best place was the broad sweeping deck between the mast and the stern. They had also gone down into the hold and brought up five bedraggled young women garbed in stained shifts and wrapped in coarse blankets; these now squatted at the foot of the mast. Corbett crouched beside them, speaking gently and reassuringly, but he could get little sense from them. They were terrified, hysterical and exhausted. They could only gabble at him, eyes beseeching, faces pleading. They could not understand why their world had collapsed, and he sensed they had no trust in any man. Nevertheless, he kept talking quietly, and at last the young women fell silent, staring at him hollow eyed.

Corbett raised his hand in oath. 'I swear,' he murmured, 'by Our Lady the most fragrant Virgin of Walsingham, I mean you no harm. You are safe. No one will hurt you, no one will snatch you from us. We will take you home. We will reunite you with those you love.' He smiled. 'You are safe, but it's best if you leave this devil's barge. Sir John!' He shouted across at the admiral. 'Have these poor girls taken over to your cabin. Let them be given food and good rich wine so they sleep, at least for a while. They must not see what might well happen here for, I assure you, it will be one horror piled upon another.'

Kyrie hastened to comply, and a group of sailors gently shepherded all five girls up the rope ladder, going behind them, coaxing and pushing them over onto the deck of the royal cog. Corbett then busied himself with the matters in hand. He was determined to dispense justice and do so as swiftly as possible.

The surviving members of *The Picardy*'s crew – including its captain, Sherwin, a rough-faced, coarse-haired individual, and his sly-looking henchman, Brasby – were dragged, hands tied behind their backs, to kneel before Corbett and Kyrie. There were eight survivors in all from a crew of fifteen. The others had been killed in the arrow storm. Corbett ordered their corpses to be tossed overboard.

'They can meet God there,' he declared. 'In the same waters as their hapless victims.' He leaned forward and glared at Sherwin and Brasby. Both men had an archer standing alongside them. 'You are what you look like,' he jibed. 'Killers to the very marrow! Scum of the earth! All fit and bound for hell, and I am here to send you there.'

'We are honest seamen,' Sherwin retorted. 'We have a cargo of wool in the hold.'

'Captain Ap Ythel!' Corbett shouted, beckoning the archer closer. 'Take one of the prisoners and hang him over the side. Do so now.'

Ap Ythel summoned two of his company, who seized a prisoner and pushed him across to the exposed side of the ship. Fastening a noose around his neck, they tied the other end to the taffrail, then tossed the man over. An eerie silence descended; even the clatter of the turbulent river seemed to subside. The only noise to shatter this chilling calm was the horrid gurgling of the hanged man as he strangled to death, his quivering body beating against the bulwark as he twisted in his death throes.

An archer from *The Royal Glory* came clambering down the rope ladder. He whispered to Kyrie, who leaned across.

'Sir Hugh, according to one of the girls, there were nine of them, abducted and held here. Apparently four of their company were tossed overboard. We saw that: these hounds of hell were desperate to remove any evidence.'

Corbett nodded his agreement. He placed both hands on the hilt of his war sword, its point driven into the water-soaked deck.

'This,' he proclaimed, 'is a symbol of royal authority, and Sir John is my witness. I carry warrants and licences declaring that their bearer enjoys the full confidence of the king. That what I do must be accepted for what it is: the king's justice, the king's peace. So let me, Sir Hugh Corbett, Keeper of the Secret Seal, begin again. You,' he pointed at the line of prisoners, 'will truthfully answer any questions I pose or face summary justice. Do you understand, yes or no?' The prisoners mumbled their agreement. 'Sherwin, do you understand?' The terrified man nodded. 'Good, so what is this cog?'

'*The Picardy.*'

'And where are you bound?'

'Boulogne-sur-Mer.'

'Your cargo?'

'Wool.'

'Anything else?' Corbett asked warningly.

'We had nine young women. They were passengers . . .'

Sherwin paused and gulped noisily as Corbett pointed to one of the prisoners.

'Hang him,' he ordered.

The archers hastened to obey. The man was noosed, fastened and tossed over the side of the cog. Corbett waited until the death struggles ebbed away. Kyrie glanced at him, eyebrows raised, but Corbett just shrugged. He had no qualms, no guilt, no remorse. He was the king's own justiciar. This was a court, a military tribunal, but still a court. All these prisoners had been caught red handed, actually committing their crimes, and these crimes were truly heinous. Each and every one of these wretched prisoners had been party to abducting innocent young women, the king's own subjects, and using them horribly, murdering some of them. They had shattered innocent lives, be it those of the girls themselves or their families. God knew what foulness had been perpetrated against them, or how long their agony would have lasted. In addition, when justice came calling, when vengeance beckoned, Sherwin and his accomplices had tried to escape. They had callously tossed four young women into the surging river: a cold, hard death to end their agony.

'Sir Hugh?'

'Sir John.' Corbett nodded towards his fellow justiciar, then turned back to Sherwin. 'We shall continue. Answer me truthfully: you had nine young women abducted to be sold abroad. Yes or no?'

'Yes.'

'And where did they come from?'

'Villages, hamlets, farms in south Essex and north Kent.'

'And they were to be sold to brothels. Where?'

'Normandy and elsewhere.'

'They were not brought aboard at Dowgate?'

'No, we never do that.'

'So how many of these voyages have you made before?'

Sherwin glanced away.

'More than we can count,' Brasby gabbled hastily. Sherwin's henchman could hardly keep still, trembling so much that one of the archers had to clasp him firmly on the shoulder to prevent him staggering.

'And what would happen at Boulogne?'

'The women disembark at a desolate place; they are then handed over to others who take them away.'

'Where to?'

'Paris or Rouen, Dijon, even further south.' Sherwin's voice trailed away.

'And then you take French girls, young women, abducted from heaven knows where, back to London.'

'Yes. We leave Boulogne and follow the coast to a prearranged inlet where an ancient beacon tower stands; there are similar places along the Thames.'

'And the money paid?' Corbett demanded.

'There isn't any. The profits for each batch are collected by the owners of . . .' Sherwin stuttered into silence.

'The brothels?' Corbett demanded. 'The whorehouses, those places of sin that corrupt the soul as well as the body?'

Sherwin just nodded, so frightened he could hardly speak.

'And the root of all this murderous mischief is mine hostess at the Queen of the Night. Edith Poppleton, otherwise known as Mother Midnight. Yes or no?'

'Yes.'

'Of course, these poor girls have little choice but to cooperate. They are simple young women plucked from small villages or sheltered nunneries. They would find it hard to escape. Almost impossible to trudge the roads of a foreign country and face the many challenges and dangers that would confront them. Can you imagine some poor wench from a place like Walton buried deep in the Normandy countryside? What could she do? How could she escape? And the same is true of French girls brought to London. However, I am sure some tried to flee, though I doubt very much if any succeeded. Yes or no?'

'Yes.'

'I am sure that some of the ladies brought from France, though given little choice, would embrace their new life. The Queen of the Night is truly luxurious, the alternative most bleak. Except of course you cannot subdue the human spirit. Some of those French girls did object. They tried to break free, they protested, they voiced their objections. And so they were dealt with. Yes or no?'

'Yes.'

'Just like those unfortunates you tossed overboard. Did you cut their throats?'

'You must have done,' Kyrie interjected. 'They sank so swiftly beneath the water.' His voice faltered. 'There was nothing we could do; they just disappeared.'

'And those girls at the Queen of the Night, the few who dared to protest? We have a witness.' Corbett pressed on, oblivious to the salt-soaked breeze and the shuddering movement of *The Picardy* as it swayed against the side of *The Royal Glory*. He glanced up. The day suited his mood: the grey sky bereft of any real sunlight, the swollen river, the bitter cold, the creak and rasp of the ships. Nevertheless, these shadows were nothing compared to the horrors he was investigating. He found it hard to control his anger. What confronted him was sheer wickedness; pure evil. Innocence shattered, abused, so someone else could make a filthy profit. He pointed at Sherwin. 'You murdered those who caused trouble at the Queen of the Night. You slit their throats or cracked their skulls, then you took their corpses to a lonely spot along the river. You stripped their bodies and smashed their faces with a mallet so no one could ever recognise your victims. As I have said, we have a witness who will swear . . .'

He broke off at the murmured curses from the archers who stood listening intently to this heinous litany of crimes. 'Our witness,' he continued, 'will swear to what she saw on a certain evening when you took a cart to the Queen of the Night. You collected a corpse and carried it for further degradation to the riverside. Once done, you hurled that corpse into the Thames, where, like other such cadavers, it could float until collected by the Harrower of the Dead.' He paused. 'Yes or no?'

'Yes.'

'Very well.' Corbett rose to his feet. He pulled his sword out of the deck and held it up, fingers clenched around the crosspiece. 'I am Sir Hugh Corbett, king's justiciar in these parts. I carry the king's power and authority. Members of the crew of the English cog *The Picardy*, you have been charged and found guilty of numerous hideous and disgusting crimes: abduction, rape and murder of the king's most loyal subjects, innocent victims slaughtered more brutally than cattle in the field. You have perpetrated heinous crimes against the king and mortal sins against God. You are all deserving of death. However, is there anything any of you would like to state in your defence?'

The cog fell silent. An ominous stillness broken only by the constant creaking of the timbers, the snap of cords and the flap of canvas. Gulls flew overhead, dark, sinister shapes against the sky, almost like demons gathering to witness the awful crimes of men.

'Is there anything,' Corbett repeated, 'anything you have to say?'

'Mercy,' one of the prisoners wailed.

'Mercy indeed,' Kyrie retorted. 'Like that you showed your victims.'

'I will turn king's approver,' Sherwin yelled. 'I will plead for a royal pardon. I will tell you everything.'

'But you have,' Corbett retorted. 'And you have done so in the presence of witnesses, no less a person than

Sir John Kyrie, King's Admiral. Not to mention these yeoman archers, loyal subjects of the Crown. You have nothing to plead.' He held up his sword. 'And so to sentence.'

'Wait!' Sherwin shrilled.

'What is it?' Corbett lowered his sword and went and stood over Sherwin. 'What is it, man?'

'Just before we sailed, Mother Midnight sent a messenger. She urged me to make swift voyage, so that I could return immediately to collect the Solace.'

'The Solace?'

'In heaven's name,' Kyrie whispered hoarsely. 'I've heard of them.'

'Who, what is the Solace? Tell me now and I will spare your life.'

'Assassins! Mother Midnight has used them before. More than one, they are,' Sherwin gasped. 'They are a guild, a society, a brotherhood of professional killers. She must have asked for their help against you. Once done, whatever it was, I was to be ready to spirit them abroad.'

'That's logical.' Kyrie stepped closer, whispering into Corbett's ear. 'If assassins need to leave the kingdom so swiftly, they must have perpetrated a hideous crime.'

'Treason,' Corbett declared. 'The malicious slaying of the king's own clerk. I believe Mother Midnight has already tried to kill me: those ruffians who stormed the guest house at St Sulpice. She used the cudgel; now she is wielding a dagger.' He turned back to Sherwin. 'Do you have anything to add? Do you know who the Solace are? And if you did collect them, would they show themselves to the likes of you?'

'No, no,' Sherwin replied. 'We have done the same before. Such passengers come on board hooded and masked. They keep to themselves and we are under strict instruction to stay well away from them. Sir Hugh, that's all I can tell you. You promised me my life.'

'So I did. Sentence has been pronounced, punishment to be carried out.' Corbett called Ap Ythel across and pointed at Sherwin. 'Throw him overboard. Hang the rest and burn the ship.'

Corbett, cloaked and cowled, stood clutching the rail high on the stern of *The Royal Glory*. He watched impassively as flames leapt up from the deck of *The Picardy* as if hungry to catch the drooping sails and rigging. Brasby had been hanged from the bowsprit of the doomed ship. The rest of the crew dangled by the neck along the crosspiece of the soaring mainmast, macabre black figures twisting against the strengthening light.

'You did not want to take them back for trial?' Kyrie came up alongside him.

'No, Sir John. You know that I have the authority and power to do what I have done here. To take *The Picardy* and its crew back to Queenhithe would have been a grave mistake. Those pirates were minions of Mother Midnight. Only God knows what would have happened. Remember that witch-queen has powerful friends in the city. Prisoners could be freed, and they'd

soon flee. Or the trial would be delayed and delayed.'
Corbett waved a hand. 'You know how such things go.
No, Sherwin and his coven were cruel killers, ruthless
slayers, but not now! Now they are God's problem, not
the king's!'

Corbett sat in the bleak, stark council chamber of Castle
Baynard, a place of grim grey stone both within and
without. A place of refuge and defence with little to
delight or comfort the heart. The council chamber was
no different from the rest of the fortress, a long,
cavernous chamber of dark stone. Cresset torches blazed
along the wall, for the windows were lancets and
allowed in only narrow slivers of light. Corbett was at
the head of the table. Down either side ranged those
he'd invited: Ranulf, Megotta, Kyrie, Mepham and
Benstead. He had urgently summoned the two clerks
with the information he had asked for.

The Royal Glory had berthed at Queenhithe the
previous day. The destruction of The Picardy was now
well known throughout the city, its annihilation a grim
and gruesome reminder that royal justice was still active
and vigorous. Corbett had in the main kept to himself,
reflecting on all the evidence he had collected at St
Sulpice. Certain matters eluded him, and a number of
questions needed to be answered. For the rest, he took
very seriously what he had learned from Sherwin.
Mother Midnight was a truly dangerous opponent, and
professional assassins such as the Solace were a very
real threat.

'My friends.' He tapped the tabletop. 'You have all heard what we did on board *The Picardy*?'

'All of London knows!' Mepham exclaimed. 'But what do we do now?'

'We wait and watch. You have brought the information I requested?'

'Sir Hugh, Benstead and I have thoroughly searched the records of King's Bench and the city coroner's rolls. We have carefully been through the index of indictments.'

'And?'

'We searched for any references to the Solace.' Benstead rubbed his brow. 'We found what can only be called allusions. A great deal of hearsay. The Solace are mentioned, but it's a question of much suspected, nothing really proved. They are more than one. The little we've gleaned is that they could be a family of four. Father, mother, son and daughter. They are of Welsh stock and may also be warlocks, members of a secret coven, but this is all conjecture. You know how it goes, Sir Hugh: people acquire a name, a reputation, be it for good or evil, and so it grows, like a ball of snow rolling down a hill. The Solace crawl like spiders out of the dark; they are glimpsed, but by then it's too late and they scuttle back into hiding.'

'They are very clever, subtle.' Mepham took up the story. 'They insinuate themselves into their victims' homes under a number of guises, wearing a variety of masks.'

'Give me an example.'

'Edmund Pettifell, a merchant who lived in Ironmongers Lane, a leading guildsman, a fairly rich merchant with a number of enemies and rivals. Pettifell had a viper's tongue. He loved nothing more than to ridicule his opponents both within the Guildhall and without. All such nonsense was brought to an end when he was discovered floating face down in his own cesspit. To all appearances he had slipped, fallen in, been unable to clamber out and so drowned.'

'Sweet heaven,' Ranulf breathed.

'No other mark of violence was found on his body. However, a very sharp street bailiff decided to make strict enquiry. He knew Pettifell well, and I suspect Sir Edmund used to give him a coin or two for his troubles. Anyway, this bailiff investigated Pettifell's death and sent a report to the coroner. Apparently on the day of his death, he received a delivery of wine. The cart stayed outside the house, the reins held by two women. The cargo, small tuns, was rolled in by the two carters, one of whom seemed to be a man of mature years, the other much younger.'

'And why are those carters suspects?'

'Sir Hugh, the street bailiff ordered a thorough search. However, despite the arrival of that cart, those wine tuns were never found in Pettifell's house.'

'And why did the bailiff suspect that the carters were in truth the Solace?'

'They had the impudence, the arrogance to announce themselves as such.'

'What?'

'Evidently the carters arrived just as the servants were leaving for their Angelus meal. Of course they were hooded and visored against the cold, as such individuals usually are, though it was easy enough to distinguish between male and female. Anyway, one of them told a servant they would not be long as they'd simply come to bring solace to Sir Edmund Pettifell. An innocent enough remark; most people would regard a tun of wine as a comfort, a solace. The servants thought no more about it. Only afterwards did a royal coroner notice a similar use of the word "solace" in other unexplained deaths across the city.'

'Very well. If the Solace do exist,' Corbett pulled a face, 'and I accept that they probably do, how are they hired?'

'We don't know. Taverns like the Queen of the Night prove to be a most suitable listening post. I suppose the Solace fasten on the murderous rivalries and furious feuds amongst the lords of the city. Wealthy men with a determination to settle a grudge or a grievance.' Mepham shrugged. 'And so it goes.'

Corbett sat back, staring down the table. After he had informed everyone about what had happened to *The Picardy*, there had been questions and some argument, but now that matter was finished. Kyrie gave witness to Corbett's account, adding that he and *The Royal Glory* would stay in London for as long as possible. Corbett was relieved at this. The admiral and his great war cog were desperately needed. If the coming confrontation with Mother Midnight turned violent, if Faucomburg and his bully boys intervened, if certain powerful city merchants were also drawn in, Corbett might have to confront a hideous violence that might escalate into street fighting across the city. Ranulf had advised moving to the Tower, but Corbett did not want to be trapped inside. If he sheltered there and later tried to break out, he would need to get to the nearest quayside, find a suitable vessel, then navigate a perilous journey under London Bridge, and only God knew who would control that vital thoroughfare across the Thames. No, he had decided to stay where he was. Castle Baynard was a formidable fortress.

'Sir Hugh?' Kyrie pushed back his chair. 'I and my vessel are at your disposal. I lodge here with my henchman, but if for the moment we are finished . . .?'

'Yes, yes,' Corbett replied absent-mindedly. 'And you, my friends.' He gestured at Mepham and Benstead. 'Is there anything else?' Both clerks shook their heads. 'In which case,' Corbett rose, 'I thank you. I shall never forget my debt to you.' He clasped hands with the clerks and the admiral, who then left.

Corbett sat down. Ranulf and Megotta rose and crossed to the buttery table, where a steward had left a light collation. He thought of the Solace, those secret assassins. They could strike anywhere and at any time. 'Don't touch, don't touch!' he shouted. Ranulf and Megotta turned round. 'Don't touch,' he repeated. 'And where is Chánson?'

'Master, you know where he is. Gossiping to the other grooms about bloody horses. He's safe enough. Are we?'

'Sit down, sit down,' Corbett urged. He pointed to the buffet table. 'Be careful about what you eat and drink. Let's deal directly with the kitchens. I want to see what they pour and serve. For the moment, our bellies must wait.' He waved a hand. 'I apologise for the inconvenience caused to you, but let's reflect.' He smiled thinly. 'Let us pray for divine help, for we the hunters have now become the hunted.'

'But you're safe,' Megotta declared, 'as long as you stay here.'

Corbett smiled at this young woman. The more he learnt about her, the greater he liked her; she was strong and resolute and, despite the horrors inflicted upon her, she had a genuine caring nature with a keen sense of humour. A woman who regarded Ranulf and Chanson as natural prey for her sardonic wit and sharp tongue.

'Are we safe, though?' Ranulf murmured. 'Really?'

'Explain yourself.'

He shrugged and scratched his head. 'The murder of Pettifell is significant in three aspects. First, Solace attacked when their victim was alone. Second, in their arrogance they announced themselves and, finally, the murder was carried out in such a way that it could easily be dismissed as a nasty accident.'

'In other words,' Corbett declared, 'they will do the same here.'

'If that's true,' Megotta declared, 'will they attack outside, along a reeking runnel or from the shadows of some doorway?'

'No, no,' Ranulf replied. 'That would be too

dangerous for the likes of the Solace. If they launched a street attack, they could be seen, trapped and apprehended. Sir Hugh, Mistress Megotta,' he rapped the table, 'my deepening suspicion is that the assassins are already in Castle Baynard. First, Mother Midnight knows our movements. We've been here since you set sail on *The Royal Glory*. Second, the news about the destruction of *The Picardy* has given her and the Solace time to act, to plan and to implement. Third, Castle Baynard is an open fortress: merchants, suppliers, purveyors, tinkers, chapmen all flock into the great bailey below. Then of course there are the hosts of servants and retainers, guards and sentries, household officials and others who wander its corridors and passageways. Sir Hugh, you must be aware that in such a place, the Solace would merge like the shadows.'

Corbett stared down at the tabletop as he fought off a spasm of panic. This was his nightmare. Not the violence, the battle fury or the sharp dagger play in the streets and alleyways of the city. Such terrors were part of his life. No, his real fear was the silent assassin, slipping swift as a shadow across a glass, a dark malevolence hiding from the light and waiting for its moment.

'You are correct,' he declared. 'So let us reflect on Pettifell's murder. He was by himself, and that is interesting. In most assassinations the killer makes sure that any guard is either withdrawn or being withdrawn. Once that happens, they strike swiftly before fresh defence can be assembled. Pettifell was in his chamber.

I am in the Candle Tower of Castle Baynard. As far as I recollect, there is only one staircase. Yes?'

'Yes, Sir Hugh,' Ranulf replied. 'You've lodged here since you arrived. There are no secret passageways, tunnels or hidden entrances. The Candle Tower is a stoutly built edifice, with narrow door and lancet windows.'

Corbett got to his feet and began to pace up and down. Megotta glanced at Ranulf, who lifted his eyes and simply shook his head, a warning to remain calm and patient. He knew Old Master Longface. He could sit or pace here all the hours of the night until he reached a conclusion. Ranulf just prayed that this time it would not take so long.

Corbett abruptly paused. 'We know,' he declared, 'that the Solace are not interested in some street attack. Ranulf, you are correct. They are already inside Castle Baynard. It would be nigh impossible to hunt them down. We must lure them into a trap, and my chamber in the Candle Tower provides the best way forward. Once they believe I am there by myself, they will undoubtedly strike.'

'Sir Hugh,' Megotta spoke up, 'we must not forget their one weakness.'

'I haven't.' Corbett grinned. 'They are arrogant.'

'So much so,' she replied, 'that when they killed Pettifell, they actually announced themselves. Somehow I suspect they will do the same here. Indeed, I am sure of it.'

'I believe you're correct,' Corbett murmured. He

continued his pacing. 'Castle Baynard is their hunting ground. They are safely within. God knows who they are or where they lurk, but they will be watching the castle and its daily routine. They will also be waiting for us. So we must encourage them out into the light, and kill them. Ranulf, you, Megotta and Chanson must leave immediately for the city. You must depart with as much ostentation and fanfare as possible. I want the Solace to believe that I am here alone by myself, that I fear no danger here in this fortress. They want me lulled, quiet and unprepared. I'll have words with the constable of the castle, as well as Admiral Kyrie. You must be gone within the hour.' He paused. 'And once darkness has descended, creep back unobserved by anyone. Trust me, what I propose is our best line of defence. Anything else is too dangerous.'

Megotta sat, as she had for the previous two days, in the watchman's lodge of the Candle Tower at Castle Baynard. The lodge was situated at ground level, close to the narrow entrance. Corbett's chamber was on the floor above, the only access being a narrow, twisting staircase. No one else occupied any of the other chambers in the tower. Corbett had quietly arranged this, as he had the guard who had taken up night duty from dusk till dawn. Once the sentry had gone and day had begun to break, Megotta had left Corbett's chamber garbed in a ragged hood and cloak, a bucket in one hand, a box of brushes in the other, and made her way carefully down to the watchman's lodge. Once inside, she'd fired the brazier to fend off the chill and resumed her vigil, sitting patiently on a high stool so she could peer through the arrow-slit window at the approaches to the tower.

The light was strengthening. The noise of the castle increasing. Torches and lanterns flared. A river mist swirled in, twisted, thinned, then disappeared. Castle folk wandered across the bailey, chattering and laughing as they prepared for a day's work. Trumpets sounded, horns wailed, dogs barked, bells rang, all competing against the rising noise of the livestock being pushed out of the castle to graze. Megotta closed her eyes and murmured a prayer. She had suffered, yet she had fallen into the hands of men like Corbett and Ranulf. She liked both clerks; they were men of integrity. She was confident that they would bring those responsible for the abuse inflicted upon her to justice. Corbett's annihilation of *The Picardy* was, in her view, God's judgement. Now she was bound to him in seeking retribution against Mother Midnight, the root cause of all this murderous mischief.

Corbett had made one request of her. Before she'd left, he had taken her aside, clutching her by the arm, standing very close. 'Megotta,' he murmured, 'I beg you, I urge you, reflect very carefully on your last day at St Sulpice. Try to recall the events of that day, above all the hour you went out to Devil's Tower. Who knew you were going there? Who gave you permission? Did anyone ever accompany you there? How often did you meet Manning, and what did you do in preparation for such meetings? I don't want you to be hasty. I want you to establish a pattern that might explain your abduction. Will you do that for me?'

She had promised she would. She still wasn't sure about what exactly had happened on that traumatic evening, though she sensed that in time her memory would sharpen.

She picked up her satchel and took out some bread and cheese as well as a small wine skin Corbett had prepared for her. She ate and drank, listening to the various sounds outside, remembering what he had asked her. Sometimes she wished she had a quill and parchment. As she peered through the lancet window, she stiffened, and her heart gave a skip. The guard had gone. Four people, hooded and masked against the cold, were approaching the tower. She climbed down off the stool and stood by the door, opening it just as they entered the stairwell. Two of them were women; they carried between them a basket heaped with blankets and bolsters. The men were carrying a chest.

'Where are you going?' Megotta demanded. She was confident of her disguise, the dirt on her face, her ragged clothing. Her voice reflected the slang of the streets, the patois of the London alleyways. 'Where are you going?' she repeated. 'Because I've got to clean this place later. I'm off now, I'm hungry, my belly's empty.'

The women put down the basket. One of the men quietly laughed and pulled at the visor across his face.

'Mistress, all we do is bring fresh blankets for the great Lord Hugh and some food and drink for the day.

As I said to the porter, we bring solace for those who need it.'

Megotta felt the hot sweat on her body cool. She tried to hide the sharp shiver that shook her. 'Well if you're coming in,' she declared boldly, 'I'm going out and I'm taking my bucket with me, so stand aside.' She climbed the steps and grasped the great water pail she'd left there. She pretended to stumble and let the bucket bounce down the steps. 'Clumsy me, clumsy me,' she murmured. 'I'm too weak to hold it. I'm hungry, I need my food. You take care now, goodbye.' She fled through the tower door.

Corbett heard the bucket clanging down the steps, a clear warning of the danger creeping up to destroy him. He urged Ranulf and Chanson to overturn the chancery desk and pull alongside it the two great chamber coffers, so creating a line of defence. He lifted the latch and pulled the door slightly open. He then retreated behind the desk, gripping an arbalest, primed and ready, with another lying beside him. Ranulf and Chanson were armed the same way. They crouched, trying to compose themselves, as they heard the clattering steps and pretended chatter of the assassins sweeping in for the kill. A rap on the door.

'Sir Hugh?' a voice wheedled. 'We bring supplies: clean blankets, fresh purveyance.'

'Oh come in.' Corbett tried to sound as languid as possible. 'Come in, come in, the latch is off. Be quick now.' The door opened. Three figures garbed in black, cloaks swirling, burst in. They looked like giant bats swooping into the room. One assassin peeled off to the left, another to the right. The killer in the centre was the first to realise their mistake. He turned, but the doorway was narrow, his companion slightly in the way.

Corbett screamed, 'Loose!' He and his companions released the catches on their powerful crossbows. Two of the assassins were immediately brought down, flung back against the wall. The third lunged towards Corbett, but Ranulf was swifter. He darted forward with all the skill of a born street fighter. Dancing in front of the assassin, he shifted backwards and forwards, distracting his opponent, then slashed with his long Welsh dagger, opening his opponent's throat, creating what looked like a second mouth, the blood gushing out as the assassin crumpled to the floor.

Corbett tried to push the table back, eager to close with the fourth assassin, a woman by her black dress, but the table stuck and he stumbled. The assassin turned to flee back down the steps. She flung open the door and almost walked onto the quarrel loosed at close quarters by Megotta, the feathered barb shattering the woman's face in a heartbeat.

'Well done, Megotta! Well done!'

Corbett, breathing heavily, came hurrying down, followed a short while later by Ranulf and Chanson, dragging the corpses of the dead attackers by their feet; they threw all three onto the broad entrance steps next to the assassin Megotta had killed.

'All dead,' Ranulf declared. 'I searched each one; none

of them needed a mercy cut, more's the pity. Sir Hugh, that was cleverly done.'

'I suspected they would come once the guard was removed. It was only a matter of hours. They thought you, Chanson and Megotta had left for the city; they never dreamed that you'd stolen back under the cover of dark.' Corbett grinned. 'I know it was hard, difficult for all of us to share one chamber, but it was the only way. Megotta, you fooled them. They really thought I was alone, sitting at my desk. Ah well, search their pockets and purses again, though I doubt you will find much.'

Ranulf and Chanson did so. Megotta sat down on the steps and put her face in her hands. Corbett stretched out and softly caressed her shoulder.

'It always happens,' he murmured, 'after every fight, a feeling of deep weariness.'

She glanced up and smiled. 'At first I was terrified, but I knew that at least one would try to escape. She died before she even knew it.'

'Nothing, master.' Ranulf got to his feet. 'Nothing at all to show who they are or where they came from, though that's to be expected.'

'Then let's see their faces; remove the masks.'

Once done, Corbett carefully scrutinised each corpse. The older man was grey haired and bearded; he had a warrior's face, lined, weather beaten and scarred. The older woman was plump, once beautiful, though her fairness had now faded. He felt a slight pang of regret for the younger man and woman. The latter had raven-black hair, and her face before it had been destroyed by Megotta's bolt must have been as smooth and dark as an olive. Corbett stared hard and realised he had seen similar-looking people amongst the many Welsh he had met, particularly those living along the March.

'We did what we had to,' he declared, gesturing at Ranulf. 'Raise the alarm.'

Ranulf took up the hunting horn hanging on the war belt beneath his cloak. He cleared his throat and spat, then blew three long blasts, which echoed across the seemingly deserted bailey. Corbett, however, had prepared well; a short while later, Sir John Kyrie, the constable of the castle and Captain Ap Ythel joined him and his companions outside Candle Tower. All three expressed their surprise as they inspected the corpses.

'Well, well, well,' Kyrie declared. 'Sir Hugh, for what it's worth, these four came into the castle dressed like servants; they assured a porter that they were here to bring solace to you, food and supplies you badly needed. No one gave them a second thought or glance.' He breathed noisily. 'It could have gone the other way. You should have had better protection'

'No, no.' Corbett shook his head. 'I could have asked Captain Ap Ythel for a cohort of Tower archers, but to what good? The Solace would have withdrawn and waited for a fresh opportunity. These were professional assassins; they had a name and reputation to maintain. They planned to strike when they believed circumstances were in their favour. They truly thought I was closeted alone with no guard, no companion. They did not know that we knew so much about them, especially the way they proclaimed themselves. Strange, isn't it?' he mused. 'All killers are arrogant and the Solace were no different. They made that dreadful mistake, creeping out of the shadows to boast, to mock, to ridicule. In the end, it was easy: their plot was based on pretence, secrecy and swiftness. They never dreamt they would be opposed so resolutely.'

'What would you like done with their corpses, Sir Hugh?' Ap Ythel asked in his sing-song voice. 'Shall we put all four in a cage and sling it over the castle walls?'

'No, no.' Corbett shook his head. 'Have them taken to the gallows close by the river. Gibbet them there and let them hang till they rot. Once your men have done that, let them spread the news. By the time Mother Midnight sits down for her evening meal tonight, the assassins she dispatched against us will be dining in hell, and in a few days she will join them at table. Make sure that message goes out.'

'Will you confront Mother Midnight?' Kyrie demanded.

'Yes, yes, I will, perhaps tomorrow. In the meantime, Captain Ap Ythel, I want a guard put upon my chamber and those of my three companions here. They are to keep close watch lest Mother Midnight instigates another assault. In the meantime, gentlemen, let me think.'

Corbett returned to his chamber. Ranulf, Chanson and Megotta insisted on putting everything right and removing all signs of disturbance. Once this was done,

Corbett invited his three companions to join him for morning ales and fresh food in the castle refectory. He sat with them, letting their chatter about the attack soothe his mind and quieten his humours. After they had finished, he made his farewells to Chanson and Megotta, but asked Ranulf to accompany him back to his room. Once there, he slumped in his chair, staring at the floor.

'Master?' Ranulf, sitting on a stool, warming his hands over a brazier, stared questioningly at him. 'Sir Hugh, what is the matter?'

'I'll tell you what the matter is, Ranulf: towers, spiral staircases and guide ropes.'

'Sir Hugh?'

'Come with me, Ranulf, come!'

Corbett left the chamber. He grasped the guide rope nailed into the wall and began slowly to descend. Ranulf followed gingerly. 'You see, Ranulf, when I tried to pursue that assassin down these steps, I was frightened, I was angry, my humours all disturbed. I was of course in fear of death. Any man would have been. Now I could have killed myself if I had missed my step and stumbled. However, I then clutched this rope as I do now and safely reached the bottom.'

He turned abruptly, tapping his henchman on the chest. 'Now let us go back to Devil's Tower at St Sulpice. Sister Fidelis left the top of that tower in a hurry. She must have grasped the guide rope and hastened down. Now first, she knew those steps, she'd gone up and down them many, many times. So why did she stumble?

Second, we later examined that staircase. We found nothing that might account for her fall, no oil, no grease. Third, here in Candle Tower, I tried to pursue someone intent on killing me; that would explain my haste, perhaps even my carelessness. My desire to close with a deadly opponent drove me on.'

'But Sister Fidelis was different.'

'Of course she was, Ranulf. Why was she hurrying down those steps? There was no danger. She wasn't in fear of her life, so why the haste, and above all, why did she fall?'

'Master?'

'Ranulf, tell me, why would you leave a chamber and run down the steps so swiftly?'

'Well, either something had forced me to flee, or I was compelled to go down to address some urgent matter.'

'Very good, but, as far as we know, there was nothing at the top of that tower to disturb Fidelis, and again, from what we have learnt, nothing at the base to warrant her attention. So I ask you once more: why the hurry, why the haste?'

Ranulf simply shook his head.

'Let us remember poor Fidelis. When we discovered her corpse, we found she had vomited. We put that down to the effects of the accident, the shock of such a brutal fall. But what if she was actually doing something very simple, very natural: answering a call of nature?'

'Of course,' Ranulf breathed. 'And the jakes closet was at the bottom of those steps.'

'Good, good, Ranulf. Remember, Fidelis was a nun, dainty, graceful, clean and tidy. Can you imagine her suddenly feeling a stomach gripe, a spasm? She wants to vomit but not there, not on the tower top where the beacon is kept, where other sisters might join her and see what she has done. Oh no, Fidelis, like any of us, wants to keep her dignity. She has an urgent disturbance of the stomach and is desperate for the jakes closet. So she hurries down, but then stumbles and falls to her death, and the key she holds in her hand drops to the floor beside her.' Corbett paused. 'So simple,' he murmured. 'Though two questions remain, or possibly three. First, what caused this upset of the belly? Was it natural or induced? Ranulf, I truly suspect the latter. Second, *why* did she stumble? Again, was it an accident or had someone placed a cord across those steps that caught her and sent her tumbling down?'

'But we found nothing.'

'That doesn't mean there wasn't something there. All it signifies is that somebody removed it. So I must ask myself who else went up that tower immediately after Fidelis's death. What was the proper sequence of events?'

'You said there was a third question.'

'Yes, yes, I did. What if somebody visited Fidelis at the top of Devil's Tower? What if they tainted her wine or food with an emetic to cause a flux in either bowel or belly? What if the assassin then went down the steps and prepared the trap, a piece of cord or twine stretching from one wall to the other? What if, once they'd reached the bottom, they locked the door and pushed the key beneath? To all intents and purposes, it would look as if Fidelis had come hurrying down those steps, and accidentally fell and died of her injuries, but not before she'd let the key to the tower slip from her grasp.' Corbett breathed in deeply. 'Let us leave that for the moment, Ranulf. We must prepare for Mother Midnight.' He paused at a strident creaking below.

'They've brought carts,' Ranulf declared. 'They are removing the corpses, taking them down to the scaffolds to be gibbeted.' He turned from looking through the lancet window. 'So tomorrow we confront Mother Midnight?'

'No, Ranulf, I said that in order to mislead any spy the witch-queen may have here; I suspect a few of the castle folk are in her pay. No, no, we do not go tomorrow. As the Bible says, "sufficient unto the day is the evil thereof". We go tonight. So look, let us prepare. Let us gather for a confrontation that will bring this murderous nonsense to a close. I need to see Ap Ythel urgently. Inform Chanson and Megotta that once the vespers bell sounds and the beacons flare in the city belfries, we shall dance with the devil and dine with Mother Midnight.'

# PART SEVEN

Sir Roger Brabazun pronounced judgement on
Turbeville.

L ater that day, Corbett met Ap Ythel and his cohort of archers close to the watergate of Castle Baynard. The bowmen, fifteen master archers, were harnessed and helmeted, and carried stabbing swords and long kite shields as well as their bows and quivers. Another company were ordered to stay close to the quayside should Corbett decide to retreat. Nevertheless, as he led the archers up into the city, he felt confident. Kyrie, Ranulf, Chanson and Megotta accompanied him, swathed in cloaks, swords and daggers at the ready. Corbett had also asked the Harrower of the Dead to join his comitatus; he was to wait for them outside the Queen of the Night with the gruesome evidence Corbett had asked for.

The evening was bleakly cold. The day's trading had ended. Merchants and apprentices put away stalls and secured cases and coffers. The fiery beacons placed in the belfries of all the city churches were now being answered by the lanterns hanging on door posts and windowsills. The Brotherhood of the Flame were busy, their task to provide as much light and warmth as they could during the night hours. Some lit great candles before the crossroad shrines, whilst others of the fraternity were dragging all available rubbish into a pile. Once ready, this would be soaked in oil and fired to produce warmth for the dispossessed as well as a means for the hapless poor to toast the food they'd filched, begged or grabbed from some stall. The notorious legion of the beggars was also busy, while London's underworld was waking, the counterfeit men emerging together with the whores and the pimps, the dark-dwellers gathering for whatever mischief the night might provide.

The appearance of Corbett's phalanx of mailed men, however, created an abrupt eerie silence along the streets and alleyways. They did not stop, but walked purposefully until they reached the Queen of the Night. The tavern was lit in all its splendour. Lanternhorns glowed either side of the majestic doorway, whilst candles burned at every window. Corbett was pleased. They'd apparently caught Mother Midnight unprepared, and he swiftly exploited this. The tavern watchmen were summarily dismissed under the threat of arrest and imprisonment. The taproom swiftly emptied, and the archers, led by Ap Ythel, scoured the galleries above. Corbett heard girls scream and customers shout. However, once the clientele realised what was happening, they swiftly fled, many of the men carrying their clothes, belts and boots in a makeshift bundle. The kitchens and buttery were closed down. The clatter of doors being flung open and slammed shut began to fade.

At Corbett's insistence, the well-furnished taproom became a courtroom. A table and three chairs were set along the dais, with the large shuttered window behind them. Below the dais, facing the court table, was a high-backed chair, and beyond this a row of benches. Chanson and two of Ap Ythel's bowmen hurried off to the stables to ensure all was well. Other archers guarded the doors leading into the taproom. Corbett waited, staring around at the warmth and comfort of this chamber: the fruit of other people's lives, the profits of abduction, rape and murder. He steeled himself. He truly believed Mother Midnight was evil, but she was well protected. He just prayed that what he had prepared would work.

He broke from his reverie at the shouts and cries echoing along the passageway. A cohort of young ladies were escorted in. More clamour, and Mother Midnight swept like a queen into the taproom, her strong, pale face contorted in anger. She advanced on Corbett, hand outstretched, but abruptly halted as Ranulf drew his dagger and came to stand beside him.

'What is this?' she shrieked. 'Why are you here? What allegations do you bring against me or my ladies?' She glanced over her shoulder at the gaggle of young women now clustered close on the benches, their sweet faces coiffed like any nun, head and hair hidden beneath closely pinned veils.

'You,' Corbett pointed at the young women, 'will stay

there. Megotta and one of my bowmen will guard you and keep good order. You, madam,' he turned back to Mother Midnight, 'will sit there.' He pointed at the high-backed chair, then stepped onto the dais and took the centre seat facing it, Kyrie to his right, Ranulf to his left. Ap Ythel guarded the door.

Corbett took a deep breath and crossed himself, then rose and glared down at Mother Midnight. 'Now let me explain. Let me make things very clear. I am Sir Hugh Corbett, king's justiciar in these parts. I carry the king's commission to determine all cases brought before me. I have the power to appoint fellow justiciars and I have done so. They sit to my left and my right. Sir John Kyrie, Admiral of the King's Fleet from the mouth of the Thames to the north, as well as Ranulf-atte-Newgate, Principal Clerk in the Chancery of the Green Wax. I carry all the letters, mandates and warrants to prove this. Above all, I have a letter, which I am sure your lawyers will look at, stating that its bearer has the full confidence of His Grace the king, and that what he does is for the good of the Crown. Now, mistress, I know you have a similar letter, but that is signed by Thomas of Lancaster, who has no authority here. Mine, however, enjoys the full power of the Crown.'

He paused at a crashing sound from outside. Faucomburg and at least ten of his mailed clerks swaggered through the door, swords and daggers drawn. Mother Midnight turned in her chair, and would have leapt to her feet, but the archers guarding her pressed her back. Ap Ythel, speaking swiftly in Welsh, ordered his other bowmen to notch and raise. Corbett himself was surprised at how swiftly the war bows appeared. Faucomburg stopped, his hand going to his face to scratch a bead of sweat.

'What are you doing here?' he mumbled. 'You have no right—'

'I have every right,' Corbett retorted. 'Faucomburg, listen and watch and you might become a wiser man.'

He rose to his feet, came round the table and stepped off the dais. He kicked the leg of the chair on which Mother Midnight sat.

'This witch-queen,' he declared, 'is responsible for the deaths of two royal clerks, Manning and Faldon. Shut up!' He gestured at Mother Midnight. 'You'll have your time and your say.' He glanced at Lancaster's henchman. 'You either believe what I say or you don't. I have the Crown's authority for what I do.'

'The king is in the north. Indeed, we may no longer have a king.'

'That's nonsense. The king is active and well and expects all loyal subjects to maintain his peace. This bitch hasn't. She has murdered two royal clerks. She is the daughter of a traitor, Sir Thomas Turbeville. She is full of vengeance and has created a fortune trading the lives of innocents. She was in alliance with the pirate Sherwin. They took young women from England to the brothels of French cities and forced similar innocents back to work in places like this.'

'Nonsense, nonsense,' Faucomburg replied. 'What you are saying, Corbett, is that Mother Midnight exported girls to France and brought young women back to serve here. Yet they seem happy enough.'

'In truth, they are terrified.'

Faucomburg, fingers tapping the pommel of his dagger, stepped forward.

'Can I remind you,' Corbett declared, 'that I am the king's justiciar and this is a court.'

'If it's a court,' Faucomburg declared, 'we need proof.'

'Yes, ask him that!' Mother Midnight shrilled. 'He swaggers in here and creates mayhem without any evidence.'

'If you want proof . . .' Corbett gestured at Ranulf. 'Tell the Harrower of the Dead to bring in his casket. Let them see the proof.'

Ranulf hurried out, and a short while later came back into the taproom accompanied by the Harrower of the Dead. They were carrying a coffin casket between them and, even from where he stood, Corbett could smell the sickly-sweet odour of putrefaction. The casket was placed on the ground, the lid lifted. Corbett sat silently listening to the cries and exclamations. Mother Midnight hardly spared the coffin a glance, but her young women, despite the smell and the horrible sight within, gathered around.

'Do you recognise her?' Corbett declared.

'I think it's Brigitte,' one of the ladies replied. 'I am sure of it; I knew her well. She was homesick. She wanted to return to Bayeux. She often whispered about it, be it in the dead of night or when we gathered in the buttery.'

Corbett summoned Faucomburg forward. 'Look,' he hissed. 'Look at this poor girl who objected to the way she was treated. She was killed, murdered, her throat slit, her face mashed with a mallet, her body taken to the riverside then tossed into the Thames. Is that what you want to defend? Would you want that inflicted on your wife, your betrothed, your mother, your sister – on any of your womenfolk? Believe me, Faucomburg, if you intervene here, more innocent blood will be shed. Look beyond this. The present storms will pass. Peace will be restored. The king and his council will demand an explanation for what happens here tonight.'

'Faucomburg!' Mother Midnight shrieked.

The Lancastrian ignored her as he gestured at Corbett. 'You have proof of all this?'

'Stay and see.'

He nodded, and he and his escort sheathed their weapons, though they stayed clustered near the door.

'So . . .' Corbett exclaimed. 'What do we have here, truth or fiction?' He went and stood in front of the gaggle of young women now back on the benches. He glanced at Megotta, who stood to one side, then turned back, staring at this row of pretty faces. He steeled himself. He would have to terrify these women so he could gain the truth and dig up the root of all this evil. The taproom had fallen silent. Faucomburg and his cohort watched from the doorway. Kyrie sat behind the judgement bench, fascinated by what he was seeing and hearing. Ranulf was leaning forward, ready to spring. Corbett knew he must hold his nerve so that justice might be done. He drew a deep breath as he jabbed a finger at the young women.

'Must I,' he declared, 'hang one of you to make the others talk? Because as God is my witness, the wickedness perpetrated here must be resolved. Very well,' he continued. 'Janine, stand up.'

The woman rose, nervously clutching a set of Ave beads.

'Captain Ap Ythel.' Corbett beckoned the captain across, then winked as he pointed to one of the rafter beams. 'Take down the hams and the cheeses, the nets of food and anything else that gets in the way. Once that is done,' he indicated Janine, 'hang her.'

His declaration provoked screams and protests. Faucomburg took a step forward, but Corbett, holding his gaze, shook his head. The Lancastrian paused and stepped back. Ap Ythel and his henchman cleared the food nets from their hooks on the beams and fashioned a rope with a slip-knot noose. Then they seized Janine, so terrified all she could do was stand and quiver, and pushed her up onto a stool.

Corbett watched intently, steeling himself. The women gathered here were terrified of Mother Midnight, so he had to present them with an even greater threat, a fear that would make them break free. Janine was now sobbing. Ap Ythel, staring anxiously at Corbett, had tightened the noose around the girl's soft, tender neck. Abruptly one of the other women lunged forward, screaming in Norman French, the patois of the countryside, though Corbett understood the gist.

Janine shouted back, eyes all fearful. 'It is true.' Her hands still unbound, she pointed at the desecrated corpse. 'I recognise Brigitte, silenced as a warning to the rest of us, as others have been. Cruelly slaughtered.'

Corbett sighed in relief. Progress was being made. Harmony and order would be restored.

He paid the Harrower and thanked him. Ap Ythel and his archers helped to fasten the coffin lid tight before taking the casket out to the waiting cart. The air still reeked with the stench of corruption, so Corbett ordered the shutters across the windows to be opened, whilst handfuls of herbs were taken from their pots and sprinkled over the braziers standing close by. He returned to his chair behind the judgement bench and watched as Ranulf imposed order, coaxing the young women to comfort and compose the trembling Janine, who had rejoined them on the benches.

He sat for a while in silence, listening to the various sounds trailing in from outside. He looked at Mother Midnight sitting on the chair before him. The witch-queen had lost her arrogant assurance; she slumped, shoulders down, glancing constantly to left and right. Now and again she would lift a hand to wipe her mouth as she stared down at the floor, lost in her own thoughts. Corbett suspected she knew exactly how this would end and her best way of escape. Faucomburg still waited, whilst there were other very powerful men in the city who would intervene on her behalf. He had to assert himself. He wanted Faucomburg to withdraw and he wanted to take this hideous woman out of the city's jurisdiction to a place where judgement could be imposed.

Mother Midnight abruptly sat up, head going back.

'I'm waiting, clerk,' she snapped. 'What is this all about?'

'What is this all about?' Corbett retorted. 'You abducted women from London and the surrounding shires. You and your minions imprisoned them in some cellar, then took them down to desolate, isolated places along the Thames. They were herded like cattle, like beasts of the field, onto *The Picardy*. They were shoved down into that cog's stinking, filthy hold and carried across the seas to a location near Boulogne, a small inlet overlooked by an ancient watchtower. The English girls were herded off and taken God knows where. French girls were then pushed aboard and brought across, taken into London, subdued until they were cooperative, then garbed as if they were novices in a nunnery and brought here.'

'Proof, proof,' Mother Midnight snarled. 'Where is the proof for all of this?'

'They sit behind you!' Corbett yelled. 'Look around at the benches, stare at their faces.'

'Nonsense!' Mother Midnight screamed back. 'They are terrified, you terrified them. They confessed under duress.'

Corbett glimpsed Faucomburg nodding in agreement.

'Oh, enough of this nonsense.' He rubbed his face. 'Let us go for the truth, Mother Midnight – though that's not your real name, is it? You are in fact Edith

Poppleton, daughter of an attainted traitor, Sir Thomas Turbeville, who was executed some seventeen years ago for high treason. You were disgraced and, I concede, you were abused, branded.'

'What is this?' she demanded, though, for the first time, she looked frightened.

'You know full well what I mean,' Corbett replied. 'Captain Ap Ythel, take your dagger and slit the gown over the prisoner's right shoulder.'

'Sir Hugh?' Faucomburg spoke.

'If I am wrong,' Corbett replied, 'I will let her go, but this is important.'

At first there was confusion. Mother Midnight leaned forward, screaming abuse at Corbett. She tried to rise from her chair, only to be gripped firmly by two burly archers. Ap Ythel drew his dagger and slashed at her gown, pulling the cloth down.

'It is true,' he declared, his voice ringing through the taproom.

'What is true?' Corbett retorted.

'What you told me earlier, Sir Hugh, when we prepared for this.' Ap Ythel tightened his grip on Mother Midnight's shoulder as she squirmed to break free. 'She has a brand mark on her right shoulder, a fleur-de-lis; we all know what that means.'

'Very well,' Corbett replied, 'and so we have it. You are Edith Poppleton, the daughter of a traitor, and I suspect you are full of hate. You hate both God and the king. You resent any authority; you have never forgotten the disgrace and indignity inflicted on your father, your mother, your sister and yourself.' He stared at Mother Midnight, who, strangely enough, now sat serenely on her chair, all calm and composed. 'We are not finished here,' he continued. 'I have business with your sister at St Sulpice.'

'What do you mean?' Mother Midnight's head jerked back.

'What I said. You have an accomplice at the convent.'

'Who?'

'In truth, I am not too sure.'

'In God's name, Corbett! What proof do you have for all of this?'

'Oh, I will come to that now. You know *The Picardy* has been taken and burnt, its crew hanged?'

'I don't know what you are talking about. I am not interested in shipping or the crew of some cog.'

'That's very strange,' Corbett retorted, 'and I say this in the presence of Sir John Kyrie, King's Admiral, as well as yeoman archers sworn to protect the king, who all heard what I heard.'

'Which is what?'

'Sherwin's confession. The master of *The Picardy* confessed everything.' Corbett smiled as Mother Midnight put her face in her hands. 'We pursued the vessel, we saw the crew throw innocent women overboard. We closed with that devil ship, we freed five other girls. Sherwin confessed all, and begged to turn king's approver. He named you, Mother Midnight, and I have the witnesses here to prove that. So let us proceed.'

Corbett moved the manuscripts on the desk before

him. 'We now turn to poor Manning, a loyal royal clerk who became infatuated with a young woman, Katherine Ingoldsby. You know the story. Katherine became pregnant. She lost the baby and her aged aunt moved her to St Sulpice. Manning, however, continued his relationship with her. He was honourable. He wanted to marry her. They made love and she became pregnant again. At the same time, Katherine began to tell him about strange happenings at St Sulpice. I don't know precisely what, but certainly something to pique his interest. Matters turned more serious when Katherine abruptly disappeared. Manning believed she had been abducted. In truth, he didn't know that the love of his life had been murdered at St Sulpice, her throat cut and her body buried in a ditch close to the curtain wall.

'Manning became all busy. Katherine had been abducted and he believed the convent was responsible. He also had a unique piece of evidence: she had seen something of great interest. Of course we can only speculate about that, though I suspect it's a reference to the fleur-de-lis, that brand mark. Katherine made a copy of it, I don't know why or how, but she had it on her when she met her killer. Manning persisted in his searches. Eventually he visited this tavern, the Queen of the Night. He questioned you, Mother Midnight. More significantly, he brought his henchman Faldon with him. Now Faldon, I believe, was susceptible to perfumed flesh. He caught the eye of Janine. He became intrigued with her and eventually infatuated. Get to your feet, Janine,' Corbett urged, 'and answer my question: yes or no?'

The young woman rose and pointed at Mother Midnight. 'She told me not to bestow my favours on Faldon without her permission. I was told to give him a message.'

'Come on, child, what was it?'

'That if he did what Mother Midnight wanted, he would have my favours free but, if he refused, there would be nothing. He eventually agreed. God knows what she asked him to do; I suspect it was *mauvais*, something bad. I am sorry, but all I did was inform her that he would fully cooperate.'

'What happened then?' Kyrie demanded.

'Janine!' Corbett's voice cracked like a whip across the taproom. 'What happened?'

'Faldon became infatuated with me. Truly infatuated. He begged me to flee with him. I know he threatened Mother. They had a confrontation. He bitterly regretted what he had done.'

'And what had he done, Janine?'

She just stared back glassy eyed.

'Who advised him how to poison his master, how to silence Manning? Was it you, Janine? Was it this witch-queen here? Or did she ask for the help of the Solace, souls steeped in slaying? We don't know do we? Except for the end. Tell me,' Corbett insisted, 'tell me what the end was.'

'I believe Faldon threatened Mother.' Janine drew a deep breath. 'One night, at her insistence, I served Faldon

wine and pleasured him. I added some powders to the
wine. He fell into a deep sleep. Shortly afterwards, four
figures garbed in black swept into my chamber. A hand
was pressed against my mouth, I glimpsed eyes glinting
behind a mask, then they took Faldon. They picked him
up. He could not resist; he was sottish in drink, deep
in his cups. They took him away.'

'They?' Corbett gestured at Mother Midnight. 'We
know who *they* were, don't we? The Solace. Four professional assassins whom you summon up for one
murderous act after another. You sent your bully boys
against me and that failed. So you hired the Solace to
steal into Baynard's Castle and murder me in my
chamber.'

'I don't know what you're talking about,' she blus-
tered. 'True, I've heard of the Solace.'

'They are assassins and you know them. They took
Faldon away to interrogate him, to discover what I
might know about Manning's murder. They didn't learn
much. You must have been pleased that I was making
so little progress about how a royal clerk could be
poisoned in his own chamber, locked and bolted from
the inside, with no trace of poison. Well we know now,
don't we? But to return to Faldon. He made the most
dreadful mistake. He allowed himself to be suborned
by Janine. Of course, sin is always hungry. Faldon
wanted more, he threatened. So he was abducted,
tortured, mutilated and left as a warning to me. God
give him good rest.' Corbett crossed himself. 'He made
a dreadful mistake and paid for it most grievously.

Nevertheless, I tell you this, witch-queen, he named you as the cause of his downfall, of his abduction and torture. He named you before witnesses; a royal clerk on the verge of death in the presence of people whose sworn testimony would be accepted without question.'

'How could he?' Immediately Mother Midnight realised the mistake she had made.

'And how could you know about his injuries?' Corbett retorted. 'That Faldon's tongue was removed, his fingers chopped off so that he could not say or write the truth, yet he did. He seized an hour candle and kept jabbing at the midnight circle. I asked if he was referring to you, and he nodded his agreement. You could hang for that alone.'

He paused and wetted his lips. There was no wine or ale available, no water; he wanted it that way. He was in the camp of his enemy, and anything and everything in this godforsaken place could be noxious and tainted.

'We killed the Solace,' he continued. 'We set a trap and they blundered into it.' He decided to bluff his way forward. 'One of them, the young woman, not so used to pain as she was to inflicting it, was grievously wounded. She confessed that you had sent them.'

'They never do—' Mother Midnight blurted out, then lifted her hand to her mouth as she sank into the chair. 'Such people,' she murmured, 'would never confess.'

'Well there's always an exception, and this is it. Finally,' Corbett smiled coldly at the accused, 'we have a living witness. Someone who experienced your malice, your sinfulness and survived.' He pointed to where Megotta stood half hidden in the shadows, close to the benches where the French women sat. At his signal, she stepped forward.

Mother Midnight twisted in the chair and glared up. 'I have never seen her before,' she declared. 'I don't know who you are or why you're here.'

Megotta leaned down. 'But I have heard of you, witch-queen. How I have longed for this hour. You are the cause and root of so much hurt to me and others. When Sir Hugh told me about Sherwin's death, I could have danced with joy. You killed poor Manning. All he wanted was his beloved Katherine. You are the moving spirit behind the abduction of so many young women, both here and beyond the Narrow Seas.'

'I don't know you,' Mother Midnight repeated. 'I have never met you.'

'I was abducted from St Sulpice.' Megotta's voice rose. 'I was taken and raped by men who by their own admission worked for you. I was kept in a filthy cellar where I was abused for days. I escaped, oh yes, I am the girl who killed three of your monsters. I fought back. I brought your hellish tavern under scrutiny. One night I saw that devil incarnate Sherwin and his henchman bring in a cart and carry away the corpse of that young woman we have just seen.' She leaned closer.

For a moment, Mother Midnight glared at her, lifting her hands as if beating the air, then she drew the knife concealed in the folds of her gown and lunged. A killing cut that would have opened Megotta's face if she had not swiftly leaned back. Mother Midnight rose, throwing the dagger at the archer closing to seize her. It slammed hard against his mail jerkin and fell to the floor. The woman, however, was swift as any whippet, and fled towards Faucomburg standing in the doorway. The Lancastrian clutched her in his embrace, then spun her round, shoving her violently back towards Ap Ythel and his archers.

'Corbett,' he yelled, 'the bitch is all yours. Hang her high for all I care. We are done here.' Snapping his fingers for his escort to join him, he turned and left.

Mother Midnight, screaming and writhing as the archers held her fast, was forced back onto the chair before the dais. Cords were brought and she was tied fast.

'Edith Poppleton,' Corbett intoned, 'you have been accused of heinous crimes against God, the king and the king's peace. You have grievously harmed His Grace's loyal subjects. Your crimes are manifold: treason, murder, abduction as well as gross interference in the jurisdiction of the Crown and its officers.'

'I demand the presence of my lawyers,' she yelled. 'My good friends from the guilds will stand surety for me.'

'You will demand nothing and you'll get nothing,' Corbett retorted. 'And if you interrupt me again, I'll have you gagged. Sir John, I would be grateful if you would take our young French ladies to the house of the Minoresses near Aldgate. Ask Mother Superior in my name to give you and them every assistance. Ranulf, once you have cleared everyone, and I mean everyone, from this tavern, you must seal each casket, coffer, chest, drawer, door and window shutter. Captain Ap Ythel, you will place a dozen Tower bowmen around the building. They will be under orders to loose at any intruder or trespasser. You,' he pointed to a now subdued Mother Midnight, 'will be accused of treason. You will be forced to plead. Do you understand, woman?'

She lifted her head, and Corbett flinched at the hatred blazing in her eyes.

'God damn you, clerk,' she hissed.

'God save me he will. In the meantime, within days you will be taken to the press yard at Newgate, and laid down on the sharpened cobbles. The executioners will place death's door over you as they urge you to plead. If you refuse, you will have one weight placed on and then another, until you confess, then you will be judged. I have no pity or compassion for you. I have the greatest pity, however, for those young women flung over the side of *The Picardy*. How many more made that sorrowful passage? How many families grieve for the loss of a loved one? How many young women had no choice but to accept the life of depravity forced upon them? When they were young, they probably dreamed of meeting their beloved at the church door to exchange vows in holy matrimony, of being someone's wife, someone's mother. You shattered such dreams, and now you will answer to God for it. Until then, you will not be imprisoned in some city jail. Oh no. You will not be allowed to influence certain lords at the Guildhall.

No, you will come with me to confront the ghosts. You will be taken to the hell pit in Devil's Tower at St Sulpice, where you can reflect on your murders and, perhaps, prepare yourself for death.'

Corbett rose. 'So we have finished here. Let us go.'

Corbett sat, Ranulf next to him, in the chapter house of St Sulpice. They occupied chairs facing the stalls where Mother Abbess and her leading officials now waited. Corbett simply stared at them. He wanted the silence to deepen whilst he prepared to present his indictment.

He had returned late the previous evening and, using his authority, deployed a cohort of Ap Ythel's archers around the nunnery as well as to patrol its grounds. Mother Midnight, her face hidden by a hood, was taken to the hell pit in Devil's Tower. She was given blankets, a small wine skin and a fresh loaf of bread, then lowered into the darkness, the only light being the flaring torches fixed on sconces in the tower stairwell. Chanson and two of the archers were left to guard her. Megotta had walked across and, according to Chanson, the young woman had stood for a long time just staring down into the pit before, hooded and visored, going back to the guest house. Corbett had instructed her to keep well hidden and not reveal herself. She had obeyed and now sat protected by Ap Ythel in the small waiting chamber just inside the chapter house.

Corbett drew a deep breath, then smiled at Abbess Eleanor, who sat enthroned flanked by Prioress Margaret,

Sister Agatha and Sister Marie. He caught a look of profound sadness in Agatha's eyes and, for a brief moment, he felt as if he was staring into the face of his beloved comrade Manning. A little embarrassed, he glanced away. Marie, Lady of the Halls, looked as pert and pretty as always. She was leaning slightly forward, staring at Corbett, lips parted, as if ready to smile yet again. Abbess Eleanor and Prioress Margaret, however, looked distinctly uncomfortable, angry and ill at ease at the abrupt intrusion into their lives by these king's men. Corbett chose to ignore their displeasure. He'd enjoyed the most refreshing of sleeps and prepared himself well. He would sit and wait until one of these nuns broke the silence and provided him with the way in. He played with the chancery ring on his left hand, then glanced at the hour candle burning in the corner before staring up at the ceiling.

'Sir Hugh,' Abbess Eleanor flustered, 'St Sulpice is now a fortress. Yeomen archers wander our cloisters and passageways. They speak gruffly, they swear and they look at our young nuns in a way . . .' she paused, 'well, you know, in a way that is not acceptable. I also understand that you have a prisoner lodged here without my permission.'

'Mother Abbess, my apologies,' Corbett replied. 'But time presses on and time wasted can never be retrieved. So let me move to the chase. I have summoned you here to hear the truth. Prioress Margaret, you are Emma Poppleton, the elder daughter of the traitor Thomas Turbeville, sister of Edith Poppleton, best known as

Mother Midnight. You are her close and fervent accomplice in the perpetration of a litany of evil acts, mortal sins and heinous crimes. I will arrest you in the name of the king, and I must warn you that your clerical habit will not save you. As for the rest, if you wish to hear my indictment . . .'

His words were drowned by screaming and yelling. Mother Abbess became hysterical, sobbing loudly as she leaned back in her throne-like chair and stared at the ceiling, as if expecting salvation or deliverance from above. Sisters Marie and Agatha jumped to their feet, shaking their heads and yelling. Prioress Margaret, however, just sat, her lean, pale face tense, hands gripping the arms of her chair as she glared at Corbett.

'You didn't know, did you? You never realised the prisoner we brought here was your sister.' He stared at the prioress. 'Oh yes,' he breathed, 'I see the likeness now, once the mask has slipped. You're a killer, just like your sister. You have no heart, not really, no compassion, no conscience. The old king branded you. I admit it was a dreadful act; he not only burnt your body, he burnt your soul. We humans are like farmers. We sow seed and do not realise what the harvest will be.'

He stared around. The agitation of the other nuns hadn't diminished. 'Ranulf,' he ordered. 'Let's have silence.'

Corbett's henchman drew his sword and beat the flat of the blade against the tabletop until all four nuns sat silent in their ornately carved stalls.

'So let me resume.' Corbett pointed at the prioress. 'You are the sister of Mother Midnight, Edith Poppleton.

You are the daughter of the traitor Thomas Turbeville. You fear neither God nor man. You are at war with heaven, the Church and the Crown. You were branded as children and so you sought revenge on the world of men. You would probably dance to see it all burn. Branded and humiliated, you were sent on your way. Your mother could not cope and wandered here to die and be buried. You and your sister, however, are of hardier stock. Edith used her wealth and expertise to establish a tavern, the Queen of the Night, as a pleasure house second to none. You took a different road, a life of quiet harmony and comfort here at St Sulpice.

'Of course, you and your sister recognised one important feature of men. How they love soft, pampered, perfumed flesh. It was only a matter of time before you realised that there was no better place for such a luxury than a nunnery housing novices under your care. Young women from good families, of delicate sensitivity and innocence. Why should such ladies, such a source of joy for others, be locked and sealed off from the rest of the world? What a marvellous source of income if they were sold abroad. Prioress Margaret, you are novice mistress. Your task is to manage and supervise these young ladies. Oh, young women entered the convent then left, and can still be found in the city. You were too clever to be trapped. You were selective. You chose those who were orphans, foundlings, girls without any family or protection; these were your natural prey. You would arrange for your victims to be in a certain place at a certain time, and your sister's ruffians would be waiting to abduct them and carry them away. These girls were given little comfort, little hope. They'd be herded to some lonely place along the Thames and put aboard *The Picardy* for export to France. In return, French girls were brought here. A very lucrative business, and who would know? What could some poor English girl do, stranded in the depths of Normandy, Gascony or even further south?'

'Surely this is nonsense!' Sister Agatha exclaimed, though her voice faltered.

'Is it?' Corbett retorted. 'Is it really? Let us move on and produce evidence so we can clearly establish the truth. Mother Abbess, allow two of my archers to escort Prioress Margaret to a nearby chamber. You can go with them. Let the prioress remove her gown and shift so she can demonstrate her innocence.' He dug into his wallet and brought out the small roll of parchment found on Katherine Ingoldsby's corpse. He unrolled this and held it up. 'However, let us see if the fleur-de-lis, as drawn on this scrap of parchment, can be found on the prioress's right shoulder. A brand mark that declares to the world at large that the person who wears it is a whore. I assure you,' he held up a hand, 'that the search will be dignified. I solemnly promise that if the mark is not found, I will end this, and leave, but in the meantime . . .'

The prioress sprang to her feet. Ranulf moved to seize her, but Corbett ordered him to stay. She stepped forward and removed her veil to reveal her shorn head, then loosened her gown.

'You,' she pointed at Sister Agatha, 'when I turn, pull down my gown and my shift. I will have no man touch me.'

She turned her back with all the dignity she could muster, loosening the gown even further. Sister Agatha hesitantly pulled down both gown and shift. Even from where he stood, Corbett could clearly see the purple-red mark of the three-stemmed fleur-de-lis. Sister Agatha and Sister Marie peered fearfully at this, then back at Corbett. Mother Eleanor stood up and stared at her prioress, then slumped down on her chair, put her face in her hands and began to sob. The prioress, however, did not lose her composure. She simply pulled up her clothing, kicked away the veil lying on the floor and sat down on her stall. Ranulf ordered the others to follow suit.

'So,' Corbett declared, 'you carry the brand mark; you are Turbeville's daughter. You are Edith Poppleton's sister and, above all, you are her accomplice, responsible for a litany of heinous crimes.'

'If that can be proved,' the prioress replied tartly.

'Oh, there's proof enough. First, you are novice mistress, as I have said; you know which of your flock is vulnerable – orphans, foundlings, women with no family, kith or kin. Once they leave the convent, what is that to you or St Sulpice?' Corbett paused as the abbess's loud sobbing rose to a sharp keening. He waited for it to subside. 'Evil prospered until Katherine Ingoldsby entered St Sulpice. She was loved by a royal clerk, Ralph Manning. In turn, Katherine was no ordinary novice.

Probably a young woman of enquiring mind. She must have mentioned to Manning about certain young women disappearing. Of course, he became intrigued. More importantly, Katherine noticed something about you, Prioress Margaret. You have a bath house here, yes?' His tone turned more aggressive. 'Yes or no?'

'Yes,' the abbess shrilled.

'A place of communal bathing and washing,' Corbett continued. 'Katherine was there with you, Prioress Margaret, and somehow glimpsed the fleur-de-lis brand on your shoulder. She informed Manning about this; like all royal clerks, he would have known what it signified, and would have been intrigued. He probably asked Katherine to make a fair copy. She did, but of course she was murdered before she could meet her beloved and give it to him.' He pointed at the prioress. 'Did you realise the ghastly mistake you'd made allowing Katherine to glimpse that brand mark? Something you'd kept hidden for years? Well, did you?'

The prioress gazed coolly back.

'Ah well,' Corbett continued. 'Manning then began his search for Katherine. He collected all the information he had gleaned, including the reference to the fleur-de-lis. He searched the records, talked to other clerks and realised the link between Turbeville's treachery and present events. So we have it. Katherine's curiosity about what was happening at St Sulpice was becoming highly dangerous. So you, Prioress Margaret, lured her to a secret place and cut her throat. Manning, of course, believed she had been abducted. He did not realise that her corpse lay deep in a ditch along the convent wall. You, on the other hand, thought you were safe.'

Corbett leaned back in his chair, staring up at the carved boss on a wall pillar just behind the prioress. 'Do you know something?' he murmured. 'Mother Midnight is a killer to her very marrow, and so are you, Prioress. You murdered Katherine Ingoldsby. You tried to murder me when I first arrived here, remember? Knocking on doors, rousing me, enticing me to leave my room. You were waiting, armed with a crossbow and garbed in a way so as to move easily and swiftly. You lurked in that chamber at the end of the gallery. You hoped I would stand in the doorway, a dark figure clear against the light, an easy target. You failed, of course. You dared not try again. You would leave my murder to your sister at the Queen of the Night.'

'Sir Hugh.' Sister Agatha got to her feet. 'I knew my brother Ralph better than anyone. He was of the same mettle as you. Like a dog with a bone, he would never rest until he had resolved some nagging problem.'

'Your question, mistress? You do have a question?'

'Yes, I do. Why should Ralph link St Sulpice to that den of iniquity the Queen of the Night?'

'Fair enough,' Corbett retorted. 'I don't know everything. He may have had information or evidence we do not possess. However, ask yourself this: who had the means and resources to kidnap young women from a convent, hide them away and eventually make them disappear? If you asked such a question of the lords of London's underworld, they would give you the same

reply – Mother Midnight. How else does she acquire
her young ladies? How else does she make a profit?
Mother Midnight is steeped in sin. She traded in flesh.
If a young woman was abducted and others made
enquiry, they would soon find themselves at the Queen
of the Night.'

Sister Agatha sat down. Corbett glanced swiftly at
Sister Marie. She was sitting at a half-crouch, listening
intently. Corbett believed that she could corroborate
what he'd said, but that was another matter, one that
would have to wait.

'Prioress Margaret,' Mother Abbess demanded, 'what
defence do you have to all this?'

'All I have heard is nothing more than straws in the
wind,' the prioress scoffed. 'What real evidence is there?'

'Your sister doesn't agree with you,' Corbett replied,
deciding to bluff. 'She's prepared to turn king's evidence,
to sue for a royal pardon, in return for which she will
name you as the *fons et origo*, the fount and origin of
all this murderous mischief. More importantly, and a
great source of joy to me, we actually have a living
witness to your wickedness.'

The prioress just gaped, all her arrogance drained
away.

'Bring in Megotta.' Corbett spoke over his shoulder to
Ap Ythel. 'Tell her to pull back her hood and come in.'

Megotta's arrival in the chapter chamber created a
deep watchful silence, followed by exclamations of
surprise. Prioress Margaret stared in horror, the abbess
half rose, whilst Sisters Agatha and Marie left their seats

and hurried forward. Ranulf moved to block their way. Megotta came to stand by Corbett's chair. He could sense how stiff and tense she was. He glanced up at her, but she only had eyes for the prioress.

'You know who I am,' she grated.

'Why, Sister Isabella Seymour,' the abbess flustered. 'We thought—'

'My name is Megotta. I am a moon girl. I was reprieved from hanging by the clerk Ralph Manning, a good man, kind and dedicated. He took me from prison, where I had been lodged for killing men in self-defence. He arranged a pardon and, as you know, he placed me here using the good offices of a leading London citizen. Ralph thought my keen observation and sharp wits would help him discover what secrets St Sulpice nursed. He was wrong. In truth, Mother Abbess, I found St Sulpice to be a place of calm harmony, until one horrid evening. I had walked to Devil's Tower, as I was accustomed to at a certain hour on a certain day, to meet Ralph Manning. On that evening, as on several previous ones, Manning did not appear.' Megotta shrugged. 'Of course I did not know he had been murdered in his chamber at Westminster. Anyway, on that evening . . .' She paused, fighting to control herself, and her hand fell to Corbett's shoulder; he stroked it gently and she pulled it away. 'On that evening, I was abducted. Men were waiting for me, a sack was thrown over my head. I was seized and taken away.'

'Oh sweet Lord,' Mother Abbess whispered hoarsely. 'What in God's name is all this?'

'You.' Megotta pointed at the Prioress. 'You are a cruel, heartless bitch. Those men were waiting for me at a time and a place known only to three people: Manning, myself and you. I confess I had totally ignored this until Sir Hugh asked me to reflect on each event of that particular evening and scrutinise everything that had happened to me. I was accustomed to ask your permission, as novice mistress, to take my hour of rest by walking across the convent grounds to Devil's Tower. You knew that, you used it. You sent me into the very pit of hell while you sat here washing your hands of any guilt, of any involvement. You then used your authority to clear my chamber so it would look as if I had fled. Prioress Margaret, you're the devil's own kind. You should hang for what you did to me and to others.' Her voice rose. Corbett could sense her deepening agitation.

'Enough.' He rose, gesturing at Ap Ythel. 'Captain, take Prioress Margaret to the hell pit in Devil's Tower. She and her sister can rage at each other till judgement is decided. They must not leave St Sulpice. They must not flee to the city to invoke the help of those who should really know better. Chanson and two of your archers will stand guard. Leave other bowmen here, one within, the rest outside. Take Megotta back to her chamber.'

He patted the moon girl on the shoulder, forcing her hateful gaze from Prioress Margaret. 'Megotta,' he whispered, leaning closer, 'you will be vindicated, you will have justice, but stay safe.' He raised his voice. 'Ap Ythel, one of your men will guard this young lady's chamber.' He gestured at the door. 'God save us all.'

Prioress Margaret did not resist as two of the archers seized her, bound her wrists and pushed her from the chapter house. Corbett waited until the rest had left, then he and Ranulf sat down at the table, staring across at Mother Abbess and the two sisters. Both younger women looked as frightened as their superior. Marie had sat listening keenly to Corbett's indictment against the prioress. Sometimes she would move abruptly, only to continue her silent reverie. Now she glanced up, staring fearfully at the royal clerk, who gazed back, allowing the silence to deepen. He waited until all the sounds outside had faded, then tapped the table.

'Sister Marie,' he began quietly. 'What is your surname?'

'Abingdon,' she stammered. 'I've already told you that.'

'And your maiden name?'

'Carfax.'

'Marie Carfax.' His fingers tapping the tabletop fell silent. He had prepared his indictment as soon as he had returned the previous evening. He had reviewed all the possibilities, then moved to the probabilities. He had reflected on each of the murders at St Sulpice and had conceded that they were almost the perfect crime. The assassin had been very clever, astute in her plotting, leaving very little evidence of her sinful crimes, so he knew he had to be careful. He had rehearsed his arguments time and again. He had carefully chosen the ground to begin, asking Ranulf to scrutinise yet again the names of those novices who had left St Sulpice.

'So your maiden name is Carfax?'

'I've told you that.' Despite her defiant tone, Corbett caught the woman's nervousness.

'Are you . . .' He studied the list Ranulf handed him, nodding as his henchman tapped it halfway down. 'Were you related to Hawisa Carfax?'

'Hawisa Carfax!' the abbess declared, now recovering from her hysteria. 'I remember her well, a lovely girl, very pretty.' She peered at Marie. 'Yes, yes, I can see the likeness.'

Corbett closed his eyes and quietly thanked God for this unexpected help. Sister Marie could not deny any knowledge of this namesake.

'Is this true?' he demanded. 'Is Mother Abbess correct? Was Hawisa Carfax related to you, Sister Marie?' He caught the woman's stubborn look. 'I am not here to play games,' he said quietly. 'Sister Marie, I can lodge you at Newgate whilst I wait for an answer to my questions from other sources. Sooner or later we will establish a link between you and this Hawisa. Once we do, we will then bring charges against you regarding your guilt. I asked you a simple question. Hawisa Carfax, what relation was that girl to you?'

'She was my niece.'

'I see. Now to go back to my original question, you were born Carfax and married a man called Abingdon?'

'Yes.'

'He was a seaman, yes? A master of a cog, a man of wealth?'

'I would say that was now fairly obvious.'

'Remind me, out of what port did your late husband sail?'

'The Cinque Ports, though we lived a good distance away. We owned a house overlooking Southampton Water. Why? What is this?'

'Your husband was a master mariner?'

'Yes.'

'And like the good seaman he was, he would describe to you his cog, his voyages and the various skills a mariner would need?'

'Yes.'

'And this included how to tie certain knots, such as the figure eight? Yes or no, Sister Marie? I repeat, he taught you how to tie that intricate knot, the figure eight. You in turn used that skill here at St Sulpice.'

'That's true,' Sister Agatha intervened, whilst the abbess, now fearful of even more revelations about what had happened in her convent, nodded in agreement. 'It's true,' Agatha repeated. 'Sister Marie is the Lady of the Halls, responsible for tying this and that. The figure-of-eight knot is a common sight throughout this convent, though,' she added slowly, 'not of late.'

'No, of course not,' Corbett murmured, staring hard at Sister Marie. 'Anyway, your niece Hawisa, how did she come to be here?'

'Her parents died swiftly of the sweating sickness. I was her only relative.'

'So you placed her here?'

'Well, yes, at my insistence, my late husband did. He supplied the gift to the convent.'

'A most generous donation, if I remember correctly,' the abbess declared.

'And what happened to Hawisa?'

'She left St Sulpice.'

'Of her own volition?'

'I . . . I don't know.'

'I think you do. Did you make enquiries?'

'My late husband did.'

'And?'

'Nothing! Like the moon girl Megotta,' Sister Marie rasped, 'she just disappeared.'

Corbett noticed how this pert and pretty nun had changed, her face and voice betraying a deep rancour.

'Sister Marie, why should a young woman, loved by you, flee this convent and then disappear? I could understand her leaving St Sulpice. I could understand her not going to London, where she now had no home. However, surely she would use whatever money she had to reach you at Southampton. Wouldn't you agree?'

'But she didn't flee St Sulpice, as you've demonstrated, clerk. She was one of those abducted from this place.'

'No, no.' Corbett shook his head. 'What I revealed today I believe you already knew. That was why you came here, wasn't it? Your husband died and you decided, God knows why or how, that the disappearance of your beloved niece was a matter that had to be resolved. Indeed, I will go further. I suspect that you knew what had truly happened to your niece and you came here to wreak revenge.' He rose and leaned against the table separating him from the nuns. 'This indictment is against you, Sister Marie. You came here to inflict terror, and so you did.'

'But why now?' Agatha asked.

'Why not?' Corbett retorted. 'The involvement of a royal clerk with one of the novices here, her later disappearance and that clerk's sudden brutal death created an ideal opportunity to inflict terror on a community already under a cloud of mystery and murder. Rest assured, Mother Abbess, when I am finished here, the Bishop of London will be informed and you will certainly have a visitation.'

He ignored the abbess's deep dramatic sigh and smiled at Agatha. 'Your brother was very proud of you. Ralph's soul and that of his beloved Katherine must hover close to witness the truth unfold and justice be done.' He turned back to Marie, now sitting rigid in her chair. 'Mistress,' he began, 'I salute you, I really do, for you have committed what I would call almost the perfect crime. You began your terror through murder, and each of the killings was carried out so cleverly. It is, I admit, difficult to discover the truth and produce evidence for what I am saying. Nevertheless, you will listen and, I assure you, His Grace's judges at King's Bench in Westminster will also listen. So hear me now.'

He paused and walked over to the buttery table, where he poured himself a stoup of morning ale, and one for Ranulf. He returned to his seat. For a while he just sipped, staring at Marie, who sat lost in her own thoughts, a slight smile on her lips. Corbett guessed that she was thinking about Hawisa, as well as the revenge she had so carefully inflicted. She abruptly leaned forward, eyes half closed, head tilted back.

'Clerk, I am waiting. This isn't a court and I have duties here.'

'Shut up and stay still,' Ranulf snarled. 'You are in the presence of the king's justiciar. He can sit here all day if he wants, and command you to sit with him.'

'And yet we shall not be long,' Corbett declared, putting his tankard down on the table. 'Sister Marie, you came here as a wealthy widow. You bought yourself in. You secured high office in this convent, you settled down. You enjoyed your life here whilst you waited for your moment, which eventually presented itself with Ralph Manning and Katherine Ingoldsby. You decided to act.

'Your first victim was Constantia, a rather eccentric nun who liked nothing better than to row across that small lake, her carp pond. She did that the morning she was murdered. You either followed her down, or even accompanied her there. She clambered into the boat; you joined her, then struck swift as a viper, a dagger thrust straight to the heart. Once done, you clambered out. You had no fear of being seen on such a dark, mist-strewn morning. After all, who would want to come down in that cruel weather to such a place? You loosened the rope; the boat drifted forwards slightly. You then moved to the sluice gate and lifted that to increase the force of the current, which would take the boat out to the middle of the pond. You were also armed with a long fishing pole. You used that to give the boat a vigorous push to send it on its way. You then threw the pole back in with the other fishing tackle.

'So it's done. You have killed a nun. You have created terror and mystery. How can anyone explain how a nun seated in a boat in the centre of an icy carp pond could be stabbed to death? Nonetheless, you made the most dreadful mistake. Once the boat carrying Constantia's corpse was close to the centre of the carp pond, you closed the sluice gate, tying it fast with a special knot in the figure-of-eight fashion. You are used to that. An ingrained habit, you did it without thinking. Sister Fidelis, however, glimpsed that knot. At the time, she couldn't recall what it was she'd seen, but she knew it was something amiss. She proclaimed as much to the members of the community. Nevertheless, it was only a matter of time before she remembered. Fidelis was sharp, keen witted. She would ask herself why Sister Marie had opened the sluice gate then fastened it shut with her special knot. For all her business and chatter, she was a real threat to you. Not only because of what she might have seen, but what she had with her at the top of Devil's Tower. However, we will come to that . . .'

'Knots, ropes, cords,' Marie shrilled. 'What proof is this, what evidence?'

'Oh, I agree,' Corbett retorted. 'You worked very hard to remove such evidence. Now, never mind what Fidelis had seen. I had noticed the rope on the sluice gate when I first went to the jetty, and it was tied in a figure-eight fashion. But when I went back later that same day, lo and behold the knot had been changed!

You did the same throughout this convent. Sister Agatha has already commented on the disappearance of this singular knot. Stigand, your master labourer, complained about how you had tied and untied ropes and cords across the convent.'

'He said so in the presence of witnesses. I was one of them,' Ranulf declared, 'on the occasion poor Katherine Ingoldsby's corpse was found. Last night, on our return, Sir Hugh asked me to raise the matter with Stigand. I went down to the stables, where he was cleaning mattocks and spades, and asked him what he had been referring to. He was very blunt. He told me how you, Sister Marie, the Lady of the Halls, for reasons best known to yourself, had tied and retied ropes, cords here, there and everywhere.'

'Shall we bring him in, Sister?'

The accused, her pretty face now pallid and tense, simply glared back.

'Very well,' Corbett continued, 'then tell us why you went around this convent refashioning knots. I concede,' he tapped the manuscript on the table before him, 'that what you plotted was in truth almost the perfect crime. Except for that dreadful mistake.'

'I await proof.'

'And I await your answer to my question. You asked for proof, so let us move forward. Fidelis posed a real danger to you. She was loudly proclaiming that she had seen something amiss, and then she began to remember what it was, didn't she, Sister? I found pieces of knotted string in Fidelis's gown pocket as well as in her chamber.

She was trying to re-create what she had seen without betraying her suspicions.' Corbett cleared his throat. 'One other matter that made Fidelis a threat to you. Didn't she claim she had met you before you joined this community?'

'She was stupid!'

'Oh no,' Corbett retorted. 'She had glimpsed Hawisa's likeness in you. Yes?' Sister Marie just glanced away. 'I am sure,' Corbett continued, 'that Fidelis also returned to the jetty, only to find that the sluice gate was tied in the normal way rather than the figure of eight. By then of course you had changed it. As I said, in many ways Constantia's murder was almost an unsolvable mystery. You must have been furious with yourself and Fidelis. You decided to silence her and take care of that box of heavy tallow candles at the top of Devil's Tower. Was it Stigand who brought it up all tied with the telltale knot? You had to get there, you had to undo that knot, one amongst many.

'You were with Fidelis at the top of that tower, weren't you? Oh, you would have acted all friendly. You chatted, shared gossip, but you were wondering how much she really knew. You made sure that knot on the wicker basket holding the candles was loosened, then you turned to the destruction of Fidelis. We all know she liked a sip of wine; she had her goblet and her wine skin. I think you poured an emetic, a tasteless substance, into that wine, something to purge the stomach, the bowel or both. You plotted well. You left the top of the tower, taking the key with you to unlock the door at the bottom. You told Fidelis not to worry, you wanted to save her a journey.

'On your way down that steep spiral staircase, you plotted her murder. You had already prepared a strong thin piece of cord; when this was stretched, it would be tight and taut, almost invisible to the eye, especially on a dimly lit staircase. At each end of that piece of cord was a sharply pointed nail, which you drove into the plaster between the bricks. You probably had a small mallet or hammer concealed in your robe. It wouldn't take long, a brisk rap and it was done. Fidelis would hardly hear it; if she did, she would think it was your footsteps as you clattered down the tower.'

Corbett paused to sip at his tankard. The silence in the chapter house now weighed heavy, oppressive. 'The ghosts gather,' he murmured. 'They come to watch judgement being reached. Yes, Sister Marie? Do you realise what I am accusing you of? You deliberately plotted Fidelis's death. You'd taken care of that knot on the wicker basket, you'd slipped the emetic into her wine and you stretched the killer cord across one of those steep sharp steps. You then continued down. You let yourself out, locked the door as you'd promised and slid the key underneath it. Meanwhile, at the top of the tower, Fidelis was drinking her death.

'In a short while, the emetic began to work. Fidelis was a lady, a nun, very aware of her dignity. She wanted to reach the jakes cupboard at the bottom of those steps, in the entrance stairwell to the tower. She hastened down; perhaps the gripes got worse. She clutched the guide rope, but when she reached that cord, nothing could save her. She tripped and toppled down, head and body battered and bruised by those razor-sharp steps. By the time she reached the bottom, she was dead.'

'And the cord was just left there for you to find?'

'No, no, Sister Marie, you know full well what you did. Let us go back to the events of that day. People were looking for Sister Fidelis. They couldn't find her. The door to the tower was forced and her corpse was discovered. I went in immediately and up the steps. Ranulf followed. We were both hoping to find some clue to her death at the top of that tower. After all, that was where she had been working. The cord you used had either snapped or been pulled loose by Fidelis rushing down. The light was dim, and the remnants of that cord would easily blend with the colour of the step. More importantly, we were not looking for it, not yet. The climb was steep and hard. We were desperate to reach the top. We did, but we found nothing amiss. You followed us up. So easy to collect the pieces of snapped cord, pull it out from the plaster if it was still held fast, roll it up and slip it into your pocket. And there you have it. I later went down those steps. I scrutinised each and every one, but of course there was no trace of what you'd done. Nevertheless, when I began to reflect on how such a murder could have been committed, I was left with one possibility, which must have been a fact. Fidelis had fallen not because she'd slipped; she'd fallen because she was in a most dreadful hurry and blundered into a carefully laid trap.'

'And poor Perpetua?' Sister Agatha spoke up. 'Consumed in that inferno?'

'Tell me, Mother Abbess, who is responsible for allocating candles around the convent?' Corbett asked.

'Why, Sister Marie, the Lady of the Halls.'

'And isn't it true,' he continued, 'that oil and other combustibles were kept in what Perpetua called her "Manor of Eden"?'

'Oh yes,' the abbess agreed. 'Of course. Perpetua was in charge of the gardens.'

'From the little I can gather about the start of the fire, Perpetua was neither seen nor heard. I think she was sitting at her desk. She took a tinder to light a candle placed close by to provide more light. This candle, however, was unique, although I've seen the same deadly trick done in London. Most of the wax is dug out and the space filled with oil. The candle is then resealed. Once it's lit, the flame will burn away the wax and everything will be safe until it reaches the oil. Once it does, that creates a small firestorm. The flames would have leapt across the desk and caught Perpetua's clothing. I am sure Perpetua also liked a glass of wine. Perhaps she was asleep when that fire erupted. Perhaps a water jug or a wine cup had been laced with a sleeping powder. Tired, she had slipped into a serene sleep from which she never awoke.'

Sister Marie leaned back, staring up at the ceiling as if lost in her own thoughts.

'We will do a careful search of your chamber,' Corbett warned. 'We'll find something. I admit, the murders you plotted were very clever. Three of the most intriguing; a true challenge. But now we have the truth. Sister Marie, you will be taken to Newgate and the press yard there. You will be interrogated in a most cruel fashion. They will pose the same questions as I do now. I now ask you this, innocent enough. Why did you enter a convent from which your own beloved niece was abducted?'

Marie kept staring up. She rubbed a hand across her stomach, then sat forward, smiling slightly, blinking as if recovering from sleep. 'I am not well,' she murmured. 'I am not well at all. But at least I did what I wanted to.'

'Which was?'

'Vengeance! So why should I care now? Hawisa has been avenged.'

'How?' Corbett asked gently.

'We thought she would be happy and contented here.' Again she tapped her stomach. 'I am unwell. I have a pain, a slight flux, but never mind that. Hawisa was my beloved niece. She came to St Sulpice, then she disappeared.' She pointed at the abbess. 'At your convent, you lazy fat bitch.' She spat the words out. 'Your only concern is your belly and your power. You are a false shepherdess. You did not exercise the due care of a mother. You are lost in your own stupid dreams. You think this convent is a haven of peace. Under a better superior it would be, but you didn't give a fig for what was going on under your very nose. You could have made the same enquiries as these clerks.'

She took a deep breath. 'From the very start, my late husband and I knew Hawisa had not left here of her own volition. We had received letters from her saying she was happy and contented at St Sulpice, so why should she leave? Then the letters stopped. There was no sign or trace of her and we knew something dreadful had happened, but I could do little at the time. My husband had a sickness; he fell very ill, then he died. I was left to tidy up his affairs. I was wondering what I should do with my life when, a month later, what I thought was a beggar girl came knocking on the postern gate of my house. At first I didn't recognise her. She was aged, diseased. Eventually I realised that it was Hawisa.

'After I had bathed and fed her, given her a deep bowl of red wine, I glimpsed something of her old self, but she had certainly been through the valley of death, a place of great darkness. She told me what had happened here at St Sulpice, a story very similar to that of Megotta the moon girl. How she was accustomed to taking walks, especially in the lonely part of the convent gardens. One afternoon, she was seized, hooded, tied and bundled over the wall into a waiting cart. She experienced all the horrors a young woman in that situation would face. I do not want to dwell on it, but she was taken across the Narrow Seas into Normandy. She was finally housed in a brothel at Provins, a small town on the Paris road. She became determined to escape, and so she did. She told me in great detail the filthy, obscene acts she had to endure both in the brothel at Provins and during her escape. She bought every scrap of help with her body. Her terrible experience had aged her. There were times when she looked like an old woman. She was sorely diseased in both body and mind. At night, ghastly nightmares ravaged her sleep. She knew no peace. All she wanted was revenge on those who had inflicted horror upon horror upon her.'

'Why didn't you petition the Crown? A letter to the King's Bench or even the Secret Chancery?'

'Who would believe her?' Marie retorted. 'What real proof did we have? The story would be peddled that she had chosen to leave St Sulpice, and they would say that what happened to her afterwards was her concern.'

'And?' Corbett asked.

'One morning, I could not rouse her. We forced the door. Hawisa had hanged herself during the night. For weeks I mourned. I reflected upon my life. My husband was dead. My beloved niece was dead. I was not in the best of health, but I did have wealth. I decided to use that to discover what had really happened here at St Sulpice. On the day of her burial, I took a solemn vow that I would avenge her death. In the months following, I worked to make that vow a reality. I sold all my property and possessions, turning everything into good silver and gold coin. I applied to join this community, and I was accepted. I paid my bequest and was given one responsibility after another. I certainly played the part of the pious nun, the dutiful religious, and all the time I watched.'

She shook her head. 'I do concede it was very difficult to see anything wrong except for those girls leaving. Of course that only deepened my suspicions. And then Katherine Ingoldsby arrived, and, of course, her lover, the royal clerk Ralph Manning. Oh, I thanked God for such a favour. For the first time, the authorities outside the convent were beginning to take an interest in this place. Manning often visited St Sulpice. Katherine once referred to these visits. She said something elliptical, that she and Ralph did not believe that everything in the convent garden was peace and harmony. But more than that, she wouldn't say.'

'And then she disappeared.'

'Oh yes and, once she had, I knew Manning would not rest. I prayed he would resolve the mysteries, but of course we all know what happened. And then you arrived, Sir Hugh. By then I had already decided to act. I wanted to exploit the deep unease caused by Katherine Ingoldsby's disappearance. I did think of starting a fire in the church but, deep in my heart, I knew that building had done no wrong. The nuns who so piously sang hymns through their noses were the ones responsible. I couldn't specify which nun was guilty, who was innocent, so I decided to punish as many as I could.'

She paused, dabbing at her mouth with a rag pulled from her cuff. She stared at it and Corbett wondered if it was bloodstained.

'I really did reflect. I watched each nun. I felt like a wolf studying a herd. Constantia came first, so easy on that mist-hung morning. A quick thrust to the heart, out of the boat and then open the sluice gate. I thought I was sharp, Corbett, but your wits are even keener. I admit I made a mistake. You seized on it. Fidelis certainly did. I knew all about her love of wine. How she enjoyed a secret sip at the top of the tower. The rest is as you describe it, though I didn't carry a mallet. I found small holes in the cement between the bricks on either side of a particular step. I knew what would happen, and it did. As for Perpetua, again there was nothing she liked better than locking herself in that paradise and indulging in a cup of the best Bordeaux. Now and again I would visit her there. I would see the great fat tallow candle burning against the dark. I noticed the small oilskins nearby.' She smiled to herself. 'And there you have it.'

'I feel dreadfully sorry for you and for your niece,' Corbett declared. 'But you murdered three innocent women for no other reason except vengeance against this convent. These slayings were not in self-defence, nor were they justified. You viewed it as a game, a means to instil and spread terror in this community, hence the taunting messages you pinned to the abbess's door. You signed them "Mother Midnight" because you had your own deep suspicion about that malignant lady. In truth, it was no joke. Death came for those three nuns, swift and cruel and, if I hadn't intervened, God knows how many more would have been dispatched into the dark.'

'As many as I could kill.' Marie pointed at the abbess. 'Including that fat bitch.'

331

Corbett sensed that her agitation was deepening, and he wondered if she had a knife hidden away in the folds of her gown. He asked Sister Agatha, helped by one of the archers, to search her, but nothing was found. He ordered Marie to be taken away.

'Let her join the others in the hell pit,' he declared. 'A meeting of murderous minds. Three killers in a cage, and I couldn't give a damn if they turn on each other.'

Once Marie had been removed, only Mother Abbess and Sister Agatha remained with the two royal clerks. Corbett stared down at the floor, tapping his booted foot.

'Sir Hugh.' He glanced up. Sister Agatha stood beside the white-faced abbess, gently stroking her arm. 'Sir Hugh, what will happen now? Remember I am Ralph Manning's sister. He talked to me about the world he lived in. Those two nuns, Prioress Margaret and Sister Marie, will plead benefit of clergy. They will argue that they cannot be tried by a secular court but only by their order. We have no real punishments except banishment on a diet of bread and water.'

'True, true,' Corbett declared. 'And I fear that Mother Midnight could also escape. She has very powerful friends in both the court and the city. She will use every favour owing to her. She will hint at blackmail, at revealing what she knows about the marital affairs of many leading men. I'm not sure how long I will be able to hold her before some writ is issued moving her to more comfortable quarters.' He leaned back in the chair and closed his eyes. He was tempted to leave, to go across to Devil's Tower and stare at those three murderesses locked in their cage.

'What you say is the truth,' Ranulf whispered, leaning closer. 'Faucomburg may have withdrawn, but there are others. We do not know what has happened to the king or Gaveston; we wait for news on that. Master, why not take all three women to the Tower of London?'

'That's where it might begin,' Corbett declared, shaking his head. 'Powerful royal household retainers lodge at the Tower. They will use their influence to move the witch-queen to more comfortable quarters. Or some physician will say that she's suddenly fallen sick . . .' He paused as he heard shouts echo from outside, then fade.

'Sir Hugh.' Sister Agatha leaned forward. 'What provoked your suspicions about Prioress Margaret?'

'One simple question Megotta had never asked herself: who knew where she was going on that fateful evening? And as for Sister Marie, her murders were perfectly planned. Isn't it ironic that a simple knot betrayed her?'

Corbett turned in his chair at the sound of running feet outside, followed by pounding on the door. He nodded at Ranulf, who sprang to his feet and opened it. Chanson and the two archers burst into the room.

'Sir Hugh, we are here, what is the matter?'

'Have you taken leave of your senses?' Ranulf snarled. 'There's nothing wrong except those three murdering bitches now kept secure in the hell pit. Why aren't you guarding them?'

'Oh Lord, no,' Corbett whispered. 'Megotta?'

'Megotta,' Chanson agreed. 'She came hurrying across. She claimed she carried orders directly from you, Sir Hugh, that I and these two archers were to join you here without delay.'

Corbett sprang to his feet. 'Mother Abbess and Sister Agatha, you had best join us.' He strapped on his war belt. 'And may the good Lord preserve us.'

They were no sooner out of the chapter house than he realised something was very wrong. Nuns and servants were streaming out from the various chambers and buildings. He glimpsed Stigand and his fellow labourers. The morning air was clear but, even as he hurried on, he caught the stench of burning. A small crowd had gathered outside Devil's Tower; its entrance was now a blazing inferno, flames leaping up creating an impenetrable barrier. The screams had now faded, leaving just the flames, the acrid smoke and the sickening stench of burning flesh. Stigand, holding a wet cloth to his face, went as close as he could, but came back shaking his head.

'Sir Hugh,' he declared, 'there's nothing anyone can do. You can smell the oil now.'

'Where's Megotta?' Ranulf demanded.

'Leave it.' Corbett plucked at his henchman's sleeve and led him away from the rest. 'Shall I tell you what happened, Ranulf?' he whispered. 'Megotta was determined on her own vengeance. She knew where the prisoners were kept. A pit in the ground, its entrance sealed with an iron grate. I suspect she went to the kitchens, found an oilskin, maybe two, came over here and hid them away. She then told Chanson and the two yeoman archers that I needed to see them urgently in the chapter house. They of course came hurrying across. She slit the oilskins, pouring the oil down into the pit, followed by a lighted candle or a piece of burning parchment. Can you imagine, Ranulf, in such an enclosed space, those prisoners drenched in oil, the flames leaping up like the devil's own dancers. She killed all three of them. She saw justice done for herself.'

'Sir Hugh, shall I organise a pursuit? She cannot have gone far.'

Corbett crossed himself. 'We have demonstrated the king's justice. What happened to those three prisoners was not our responsibility. I believe Megotta enacted God's justice. Think, Ranulf, Sister Marie slaughtering three innocents. As for the other two, the lives they blighted, the worlds they shattered! Even so, there was a very good chance that the two evil sisters might wipe their lips and skip away. But not now. Let them all dance in hell. Let Megotta the moon girl go back to her family, her tribe. Perhaps one day on the roads our paths will cross, and all I will do, Ranulf, is lift my hand in salute.'

# AUTHOR'S NOTE

*Mother Midnight* is of course a work of fiction. Nevertheless, the novel is strongly embedded in the history of the fourteenth century. Edward II did move into violent confrontation with Thomas, Earl of Lancaster over his favourite, Peter Gaveston. Lancaster eventually seized the Gascon, whom he described as 'the king's catamite', and had him summarily decapitated. Edward II was so distraught over the dramatic execution of his favourite that for years he refused to have his lover's body buried, until he was ordered to do so by the Church. He never forgot or forgave Lancaster's crimes and, in 1321, civil war erupted. Edward II was victorious; Lancaster was executed, but this was only the beginning of fresh troubles for the king.

Sir Thomas Turbeville was captured by the French, who persuaded and bribed him to spy for them at the English court. Turbeville was eventually caught and executed as described in the novel. His family as I have depicted them are a work of fiction; nevertheless, brothels such as the Queen of the Night did exist, and women such as Mother Midnight can be found in the coroners' rolls of medieval London. Human trafficking of course blights every age and era, and the fourteenth century was no different. Abductions such as I describe in the novel did occur, a violent and nasty trade, despite the best efforts of both Crown and Church.

Finally, the summary justice meted out by Corbett against the crew of *The Picardy* also reflects the real horror of war at sea, where no quarter was given or prisoners taken. If you read Chaucer's *Canterbury Tales*, you will find the likes of Sherwin in the great poet's depiction of 'The Shipman': happy sailing was not a feature of the fourteenth century!

For further information about Paul Doherty's books, visit: www.paulcdoherty.com.

We hope you enjoyed reading
*Mother Midnight*.


Don't miss the other gripping novels
in Paul Doherty's much-loved
Hugh Corbett series . . .

Sir Hugh Corbett confronts
macabre mysteries and a bitter enemy

# HYMN TO MURDER
## PAUL DOHERTY

**As evil spreads to the depths of Dartmoor, Sir Hugh Corbett enters a maze of murder . . .**

Spring, 1312. At Malmaison Manor, Lord Simon is the secret perpetrator of a hideous crime – yet he arrogantly assumes his evil deeds will never catch up with him. But someone has found a way to make him pay. When Lord Simon is found mysteriously slain, other deaths soon follow. Meanwhile, ships on the Devonshire cost are being deliberately wrecked, their crews slaughtered, their cargoes plundered.

Sir Hugh Corbett and Lord Simon are united by the Secret Chancery and their search for the most precious ruby – the Lacrima Christi. When Corbett learns of Lord Simon's death, he is drawn into a complex web of lies and intrigued and it's not long before his own secrets start to surface. As the hymn to murder reaches its crescendo, can Corbett confront an enemy from his past and live to see another day?

**Available now from**

**HEADLINE**

# PAUL DOHERTY

## THE MASTER HISTORIAN HAS CAST HIS MAGICAL SPELL OVER ALL PERIODS OF HISTORY IN OVER 100 NOVELS

**They are all now available in ebook, from his fabulous series**

Hugh Corbett Medieval Mysteries
Sorrowful Mysteries of Brother Athelstan
Sir Roger Shallot Tudor Mysteries
Kathryn Swinbrooke Series
Nicholas Segalla Series
Mysteries of Alexander the Great
The Templar Mysteries
Matthew Jankyn Series
Canterbury Tales of Murder and Mystery
The Egyptian Mysteries
Mahu (The Akhenaten-Trilogy)
Mathilde of Westminster Series
Political Intrigue in Ancient Rome Series

**to the standalones and trilogies that have made his name**

The Death of a King
Prince Drakulya
The Lord Count Drakulya
The Fate of Princes
Dove Amongst the Hawks
The Masked Man
The Rose Demon

The Haunting
The Soul Slayer
The Plague Laws
The Love Knot
Of Love and War
The Loving Cup
The Last of Days

LIVE HISTORY
VISIT WWW.HEADLINE.CO.UK OR
WWW.PAULCDOHERTY.COM TO FIND OUT MORE

HEADLINE